I'LL TELL YOU

YOU

EVERYTHING

OTHER TITLES BY REBECCA KELLEY

No One Knows Us Here

Broken Homes & Gardens

I'LL TELL YOU EVERYTHING

A novel

REBECCA KELLEY

LAKE UNION
PUBLISHING

Published by Lake Union Publishing, Seattle

www.apub.com

Amazon, the Amazon logo, and Lake Union Publishing are trademarks of Amazon.com, Inc., or its affiliates.

ISBN-13: 9781662517952 (paperback)
ISBN-13: 9781662517969 (digital)

Cover design by Caroline Teagle Johnson
Cover image: © trentonmichael, © Chris Clor, © Javier Zayas Photography / Getty

Printed in the United States of America

THIS IS HOW IT ENDS

It ends right where it began, on the shores of the secret lake they called Shangri-La. To get to it you have to hitchhike to a certain mile-marker sign on the side of the road and then follow a goat trail up the mountain until you approach a dense tangle of brush. It's like that old camp song "Going on a Bear Hunt." You can't go under it, you can't go over it—gotta go through it. So you bushwhack your way through those gnarled branches, twigs snapping underfoot, thorns ripping the skin from your arms. You start to wonder what you've gotten yourself into. Will you ever emerge from this, or will you die in here like some tragic little kid in a fairy tale, lost in the dark, dark wood, trying to follow a trail of breadcrumbs on his way back home?

The first time I ever went looking for Shangri-La, he was right there with me. We had written down the directions, handed down from another employee at the lodge kitchen. Passed along from employee to employee over the years. We promised—as all the others promised before us—to never tell anyone who wasn't also one of us, a seasonal worker at the lodge or one of the other hotels in the park. It was a difficult journey, up to this secret lake, but it was worth it. That's what they told us, and so we went.

We hardly knew each other, that first time. Our first date. We were dumb, back then. Twenty years old. I was scared but acting like I wasn't, like I was one of those wild and carefree girls always up for danger and excitement and adventure.

Once you get to the top, you finally see it: Shangri-La. A perfect little lake shimmering down in the valley. Visible only if you take this route, go to this much trouble. Unspoiled by the throngs of tourists who swarm all over the rest of the park.

That was when we fell in love, right then, looking down at the lake from above. We were silent, standing there, the earth spread out before us. We had never seen anything so beautiful in our lives, something so magnificent and grand, snow-dusted mountains stretching out for hundreds of miles, the green valley dotted with wildflowers, the shimmering mirror surface of the lake, so still you could watch the reflection of the clouds in the sky move across it like ghosts. He took my hand and we ran.

~

A year and three months later, I went back there, on my own. Nothing felt the same. The season was coming to a close. Only September, but it felt like the edge of winter. He knew the condition I was in and asked me to meet him there anyway. Anything could have happened. I could have been kidnapped, hitchhiking alone. I could have been tangled up in that brush. Slipped off the ledge. Everyone knows what they say about your center of balance, how pregnancy throws you off-kilter. Still I did it. I loved him. I really did.

And so I waited at the shores of Shangri-La, where we had agreed to meet. We were going to start over, start this whole new phase of our lives. The three of us. We were young but we were in love—we could make this work. I waited on the shores of that lake for hours, until the sun dipped behind the horizon and I knew I had to leave or I would be spending the night in the wilderness, left to die of exposure or get torn apart limb by limb by a grizzly bear looking for his last meal before hibernation.

He left me there to die, I used to think in my more dramatic moments, feeling sorry for myself. At the very least, he left me. When I finally made it back to civilization, I went looking for him. His room was empty. He had vanished.

CHAPTER 1

—

AMY

I blinked once and my gaze sharpened and that's when I saw her, sitting at a table right in the middle of the hotel dining room. She couldn't have been there the entire night—I would have seen her. I blinked again, rapidly, in an attempt to clear my vision. She was still there. My husband was looking at me expectantly, and I realized I had missed my line. I couldn't remember what it was—just stood there, eyes wide and scared, mouth open and silent.

A brief look of concern passed over his face, and then it was time for both of us to sing the closing lines of "Summer Nights" together. He sang the line, alone. He opened his eyes wider while he sang and nodded a bit, as if to remind me. I nodded back. Yes. Yes—okay. I pulled it together, and then both of us belted out the words in unison. I flashed a smile to the crowd—right to her, sitting there. She was looking back at me. I had only met her once before, but of course I would recognize her anywhere. That dark-brown hair, shoulder length and messy in that cool, effortless way. Those serious gray eyes that managed to appear wise despite her youth, like she was looking right through me and that ridiculous Sandra Dee costume, like she was wondering what on earth I was doing up there, singing my heart out to a crowd of tourists. Like she was wondering who I really was.

It was the last cabaret performance of the season. The cabaret was a treasured relic from the past, a Seven Glacier Hotel mainstay from 1953 to the early 2000s. I remembered it fondly from my days as a seasonal worker in the late 1990s. When my husband and I took over the hotel five years ago, I brought it back. Staff members dressed up in pedal pushers and tight jeans and leather jackets and crooned all those midcentury oldies for the audience: "Blue Moon," "Fever," "A Teenager in Love," "Silhouettes."

The cast members put on a show two nights a week, ten weeks in a row. Only on the very last show—this show—did my husband, Jonathan, our eight-year-old son, Gabe, and I join the cast onstage as a "special treat" for the audience. It was all a bit over the top, I would admit. No one in the audience ever dressed up. No one even combed their hair. They would come in to dinner hungry from their days of hiking, still in their fleece vests and those pants that zipped off above the knee and turned into shorts, their hiking boots tracking dirt onto the dining room floor.

Now the song was over. Jonathan and I clasped hands and raised them. Usually at that point I would make some further announcements, thank all the cabaret members for another wonderful season, remind people to come back next year, but I couldn't spend another second up there. I whispered to my husband to take over for me and then raised an arm to the crowd, a brisk goodbye. Then I slipped behind the curtain.

I couldn't catch my breath. I leaned over, resting my hands on my knees, and screwed my eyes shut. Breathe in, breathe out, I told myself. Get a grip.

"Great show," I heard her say, and I stood up to find her there. Through the curtain, I could hear my husband wrapping up the announcements. There was still time before everyone else filed in backstage. It was the last night, so they'd linger taking their bows. Maybe do an encore, if I was lucky.

The way she said "great show" was hard to decipher. Very deadpan. Either she was genuinely impressed by it or thought it was terrible. I really couldn't tell.

I tried to smile at her. Despite everything, I was happy to see her. I felt my throat constrict, and I raised a hand to touch her cheek. I thought better of it before my fingers actually made contact with her skin.

"Surprise." She offered me an apologetic smile, as if she knew it was strange, showing up here like this.

No one came here by chance. It wasn't as if she could say she was just in the neighborhood. It took effort to get here, to be here. It was a historic mountain lodge tucked away deep in a glacial valley of a million-acre wildlife reserve in Montana, miles and miles away from civilization.

Still, I took in a breath, slowly, and tried to smile back. The easy, glamorous smile of a successful hotelier—somewhat undercut by the poodle skirt, the goofy blond wig. Instinctively, I raised my hand and touched the fake hair, teased and stiff with hair spray. I was tempted to pull it off, to create one of those movie-style transformations in which the wig comes off and the real hair cascades down, sleek and perfect, revealing my true and natural beauty, but of course I knew it wouldn't work out that way. My real hair was plastered onto my head with bobby pins and elastic bands. "Ramona." I kept my voice neutral. Pleasant. "What are you doing here?"

Her face fell for a second—just a second, but I saw it, that flicker of disappointment—and then she seemed to pluck up some courage, looking me straight in the eye. "I wanted to talk to you," she said. "You *told* me to come here."

We had met only once before, in Seattle, in the lobby of our best downtown hotel. I had told her about Seven Glacier Park, about spending the summer here, but I am sure I wouldn't have told her to come here.

"You said I was *from* here. You said—"

"You should have called. It's such a busy time of year and—"

"I didn't think you'd talk to me," she said. When I opened my mouth to protest, she rushed to speak over me: "I didn't think you'd tell me the truth." She angled her head toward the stage. "In the Still of the Night" was playing. An encore. Thank god. "So that's your husband out there? Your son? He's really cute."

"Listen, Ramona. I can explain. Let me just change out of this getup first."

"You didn't tell me you were married. You didn't tell me you had a kid." Ramona looked much younger then, and in that moment I could imagine her as a child, Gabe's age. "*Another* kid," she added, her voice flat.

"I'm sorry. I should have told you. I thought it would be better this way." It sounded stupid even to me now, but it was true.

"Let me guess: they don't know about me, either."

"I'll tell them," I said.

Ramona gave me another one of her inscrutable looks. Maybe it was pity. "Listen, Amy, I'm not here to turn your life upside down. I just wanted some answers, that's all."

"No, you're right. You're right. I'm going to tell them. I'll tell them tonight."

"I just want to know who I am. Where I'm from," she said again.

"Where you're from isn't who you are," I said.

She gaped at me. "That's not what you said before." Her voice rose.

On the other side of the curtain, the closing notes of "In the Still of the Night" rang out, and for a second all I could hear was applause. I closed my eyes, trying to concentrate. We had a second before they all came filing back here, and then they would want to celebrate. Pizza and beers in the staff kitchen, everyone drinking too much and yelling all the cabaret hits at the top of their lungs, recounting the highlights of the season. The time Damien flicked off his sunglasses during "Hit the Road Jack" and hit Marissa in the face, requiring her to wear a bandage on her eye for a week, like a pirate. The time Nicholas had laryngitis and shy, unassuming Luis had to fill in on the solo in "Sherry," wowing everyone—maybe even himself—with his pitch-perfect falsetto.

The clapping died down. The curtain rustled. Footsteps. I had only a second before everything dissolved around me. Her eyes were pleading with me now. "You said I was from here," she said. "You said this place made you who you are. You said it all started here. Here, at this very lodge! You said without this place, I wouldn't even *exist*."

I wanted to help her, I did. Had I said that to her, last spring? I said a lot of things that day. We both did. I told her about this place, yes. I told her I would be here. But inviting her to come? Why would I? I had too much to lose.

Ramona was looking beyond me, though, distracted by the cabaret members rushing in, their chatter and laughter. "Room 12," Ramona said, and then she was gone.

"Hey, what happened out there?" My husband placed a gentle hand on my arm.

I looked up at him and then around me, as if emerging from some sort of dream. Ramona had slipped away without anyone noticing. The entire evening took on an unreal quality, and for a minute I wondered if I had imagined her there—a product of my guilty conscience, perhaps. Listen, Jonathan, I could have told him, right at the beginning. I have to tell you something, something about my past. But it wasn't exactly something to bring up on a first date, was it? We were already in our thirties when we met. We both had histories. It wasn't like I asked him for a complete and thorough account of every single woman he had ever crossed paths with, a list of his mistakes and regrets over the years.

So I never did tell him about Ramona, the baby I had put up for adoption years ago, when I was young. It was a secret and I was good at keeping secrets, and if it wasn't something to bring up on a first date, it wasn't something to bring up on a second date, either, and then it started getting serious and that would have probably been the time to say something, but I didn't, and once we were engaged it seemed like it was too late. He would have just wondered why I had refrained from divulging the information. Was I ashamed of it? No, of course not. I did it so she could have a better life. There was nothing wrong with that. In fact, it was (according to the "Consider Adoption" pamphlet they gave me at the agency) the most selfless act a mother could *do* for her child—

"Amy?" My husband was shaking my arm now. His expression had mutated from slightly concerned to alarmed.

I gave him a weak little smile. "I'm sorry." I pressed the palm of my hand into my forehead. "Migraine. I think I'd better go lie down. You'll take Gabe to the party?"

"You look pale. We'll come with you—"

"Don't be silly. We promised Gabe he could go. It's the last night." I put on a brave face. "I want to hear all about it in the morning."

"Mom, Mom!" Gabe was yanking on my poodle skirt and I winced slightly, as if the sudden movement had sent another shock wave through my head.

A bit more back-and-forth with Jonathan, a kiss on Gabe's hot little cheek, and I finally managed to get out of there.

CHAPTER 2

RAMONA

She wasn't what I had expected, and I thought I had prepared for every possible scenario: She had been a teenager. She had been having an affair with a married man. She was mentally ill, strung out on drugs. Living in a mental institution, or in a tent on the streets. She could even be dead. I could handle any of those, I decided. I just needed to know. It was the not knowing that got to me.

Once I found her, my birth mother, the image narrowed. Her name was Amy Linden. All those years looking without so much as a clue, and then, there she was on one of the ancestry sites I'd joined. A match.

I had always known I was adopted—that part was never a secret. They used to believe it was best not to tell children they were adopted. They would fit into their new families more seamlessly, perhaps, especially if the adopted child matched the adoptive parents physically.

They would have more of a sense of belonging that way, was the thinking. What could go wrong? It turned out, quite a bit. Maybe a lifelong sense that the story of your life didn't exactly add up. Why were there no pregnancy pictures, no story of the birth? Adoptees would go around with this ever-present sense that something just wasn't right, never understanding what it was. Only to discover, years later, that they had been lied to their entire life. That who they thought they were wasn't who they were at all.

So now they tell you. People have open adoptions. They're up front about it, right from the start. But the thing is, if you are adopted, you always know it's for some sad reason. Best-case scenario, your parents were loving and perfect and wanted you desperately but just didn't feel like they could give you a good life. Maybe their country was being torn apart by war or their parents wouldn't allow them to be together or—something. Like a character in a children's book. Or maybe the parents died tragically and no relatives were available to take over. More likely, though, the sad story was one about poverty or addiction or abuse, or all those things put together.

If it's a closed adoption, you spend your whole life wondering. Inventing. Coming up with your own version of events, good and bad. It would be better to know, you think. Rip it off like a Band-Aid, fast.

When I was eighteen, I left for college, and that was when I started looking for my birth parents in earnest. The agency that had handled my adoption no longer existed, the records were sealed. I signed up for various registries, DNA testing services, but nothing came of any of it. I tried to accept the idea that I might spend the rest of my life never knowing who I really was.

I didn't love college the way everyone said I would. It was hard to connect with people, hard to find friends. My sophomore year started out more promising than my freshman year. I fell in love with my roommate, assigned randomly to me, a transfer student. I was still in the dorms when a lot of others had moved into apartments with friends. Kate and I hit it off and before I knew it, we were a thing. In love, even. But then on winter break she broke up with me over text, offering me no reason whatsoever. She was moving out of the dorms, she said. I was crying my eyes out over that, and then my mom announced that she had something to tell me: she had breast cancer.

I went back the next semester, but I couldn't focus on my classes. I was still obsessed with Kate, and I was consumed with worry for my mom. I was constantly crying. I kept spoons in the dorm's mini fridge to hold over my puffy eyes. And in the midst of all that, I finally found her, my biological mother. Amy. I was sitting up one night, refreshing everything, looking for updates on all those sites I'd signed up for. And there she was.

I waited until my twentieth birthday, February 5, 2019, to contact her. Twenty years ago today, you gave birth to me in New York City, I wrote. I've had a good life. I don't want anything from you. I just want to meet you. Out for coffee sometime? And I signed my name.

We arranged to meet in a hotel in Seattle, where she lived. I was going to Seattle for spring break to meet up with some friends, I told her. Maybe we could catch up then? It wasn't true. I had no friends there. She might have even flown to meet me—she seemed to be rich, from what I could tell from the information I found online. I wasn't sure why I pretended I was already planning on visiting Seattle. I think I wanted to see her in her element. She ran hotels. She was young and beautiful and glamorous, or so it seemed. And she was thrilled to hear from me! That was what she said. She couldn't wait to meet me.

The hotel was beautiful, grander than even the photographs had suggested, with high ceilings and arched floor-to-ceiling windows; giant modern chandeliers, twenty feet wide at least; marble tabletops; and banquet seating upholstered in teal. Already I felt underdressed. I had layered two sweaters over each other, unused to the damp chill of the Pacific Northwest, and neither sweater was particularly nice. My hair, too, rebelled in this weather, the misty rain transforming my dark curls into unmanageable frizz.

It occurred to me, when I locked eyes with the woman at the back of the room, the woman standing up and raising a bare arm to greet me, that I had spent way too much time imagining that my birth mother would be destitute and no time imagining that she would be . . . whatever Amy was. I recognized her from the pictures I had seen online. She was wearing a floor-length gown in blue velvet with a deep V neckline. I walked toward her as she beckoned, sneaking a look at the other patrons as I made my way to the back of the room. A couple men and one woman in business suits. A group of tourists in Seattle sweatshirts. A young couple in brand name outdoor gear, fleece jackets and jeans. Definitely no one else was wearing a gown. It was two in the afternoon.

Then we were face-to-face, unsure what to do. Both of us smiling. Her eyes darted over me and we both laughed awkwardly and then we hugged, my hands pressing into the luxurious fabric of her dress. I was trying to take her in, this vision of her, her long dark hair falling in sleek waves, her big brown eyes, her narrow chin, her creamy pale skin. We looked nothing alike. I felt as though I loomed over her, like I took up twice as much space as she did, with my frizzy hair and the layers of sweaters.

"Should I . . . change?" I asked, though that was a ridiculous thought. I had watched movies where some uptight maître d' offered an underdressed gentleman a tie or even a jacket, but I had never seen the equivalent for a woman. Some backup gown, a pair of sparkly heels.

Amy waved her hand. "Oh no, no, no. I just like to dress up. For special occasions." I thought she might explain, then, that she had a ball to attend, or an appointment with the Queen of England, but she didn't elaborate. And then I felt flattered. She had dressed up for me. That was the only explanation. I was a special occasion. I smiled back at her, a real smile this time. I was so happy to see her at last.

She ordered us both drinks. I wasn't of age yet, but she seemed to be running the place, and no one bothered us. I told her about growing up in Saint Louis, about college in Ohio, even about Kate, my broken heart. She trained her eyes on me and leaned in as I talked, as if she were focusing very carefully on my every word.

Outside, the sky grew dark. Patrons streamed in and out. Several drinks in and we were clasping hands across the table and she was telling me she thought about me every day, every single day of my life, and that she was glad everything had worked out for me, that I had had such a wonderful life. She held on to my hands for what seemed like a solid minute, and we sat there, maintaining eye contact, squeezing each other's hands, like we were at a séance together, trying to summon a spirit. I felt like I could confide in her. She was looking straight at me, her eyes intense, her lips pressed together, nodding a little, as if to say, Go on. Ask me. Ask me anything.

"What about my dad?" I blurted out.

She dropped my hands. "What about him?"

Well, who was he? What was his name, where did they meet? Did she meet him in college?

I tried asking her, but by then she appeared distracted. She was looking around for a server. She should order us some food, she said. An early dinner, perhaps.

"Did you meet him in New York City?" I asked. I knew I was born there. That was all I knew. She leaned back a little and bit down on her lips, so they both disappeared entirely, leaving nothing but a thin line for a mouth. "You can't imagine what it's like," I said then, and I reached for her hands again. "Not knowing the basic facts of your existence. I wanted to know you because I want to know me—who I am." I wanted to know him, too, I explained. Didn't she get how hard it was, the not knowing?

She seemed to be softening. She gave me this look, her eyebrows scrunched together a bit, the kind of look you give someone when you're about to give them difficult news. A server showed up right then, and Amy rattled off a few dishes, ordering for us both.

When he left, she turned back to me.

"We didn't meet in college," she said.

I relaxed a bit then. She was going to tell me. I was going to figure this all out. She would tell me and I would know. The information she gave me would complete me, somehow, in some vital way, and I would be able to move on with my life. I wouldn't even need to have a relationship with her, with him, whoever he was. I just needed the truth. That's what I told myself, sitting there. I nodded at her, my birth mother, encouraging her to continue.

"I didn't go to college," she said. "All this?" She waved her hand around the interior of the restaurant, as if to indicate everything inside, the gilded mirrors, the chandeliers, the floor-to-ceiling windows looking out onto the streets of Seattle, dark now, wet with rain. "I did this on my own." Now, I knew this wasn't true—or at least not strictly true. I had read her bio. She and her husband worked together. She hadn't mentioned him, and I didn't bring him up, either.

I wasn't sure how I was supposed to respond to that. "That's great," I said.

"What about you?" Amy asked.

I opened my mouth to speak, but I had no idea what she was asking me.

"You never said what you were studying," Amy said. "What's your major?"

I shifted in my seat and cast my eyes over the room, hoping I might be rescued by the waitstaff coming to fill our water glasses. No such luck. I shrugged. "I'm undecided."

"Undecided?" Amy didn't like the sound of that.

"It was biology, but I wound up dropping it."

Amy was leaning in, focusing on me, as if she knew there was more to it than that. I sighed. "It's just—I always thought I'd major in biology, right? Ever since I was a little girl. But it turns out—it turns out I'm not interested in it at all."

When I was a kid, I used to accompany my mom to work every once in a while, when school was closed, I explained to Amy. My mom was—is—a scientist, a conservation biologist at the Missouri Botanical Garden. I could spend hours there on my own, wandering around in that geodesic dome, looking at the plants. At home, I would do the same. My mom would find me in the backyard on my stomach, observing a caterpillar through a magnifying glass. This got her thinking that I would follow in her footsteps. She bought me a microscope one Christmas, and I would press things against the plates and marvel at the cell walls on the blades of grass or rose petals.

"She seemed so happy that we had this in common," I confided to Amy. "That we were alike in this way. I didn't have the heart to tell her the truth. I even majored in biology, but I struggled to pay attention in class. If I really focused and studied hard, I could do okay on tests, but then all that stuff happened with Kate—anyway, I bombed my biochem final. That meant I had to drop the major, and I was relieved."

"So what was the truth?"

"The truth?"

"That you were afraid to tell your mom."

"That I had never been interested in biology. I admire my mom, what she does, but I just don't have the same passion for it that she does. I loved looking at plants up close, spending hours in the gardens or examining caterpillars, but it wasn't a *scientific* interest. That was the thing."

"What was it?" Amy was resting her chin in her hand, taking me in while I talked.

I felt relaxed. Relieved, in a way. I had never told anyone this—not really. I wasn't even sure I had thought about it before. I smiled a bit, encouraged by her interest in me. "It was the beauty of it," I said. "The way a leaf looked with a ray of sunlight shot through it. How everything under the microscope contained a whole different world. When I looked at something up close like that, I wasn't thinking of the structure of the cells or photosynthesis or whatever—I was making up stories, imagining myself the size of a grasshopper, like Thumbelina or *The Borrowers*."

"I love that book!" Amy exclaimed.

"I wanted to live in those miniature worlds," I concluded. "Not study them."

Amy was nodding as if this all made perfect sense. I felt elated, somehow. Lighter. "I know what this is all about," Amy said. She said the words with solemnity and authority.

"What?" This was why I came here, this was why I wanted to meet her. She would explain me to myself. Make it all make sense.

"You have a keen sense of beauty, a great imagination," she said. "You're an artist."

"An artist?" I had never thought of myself as an artist before. I didn't really like to draw, or to make things. "I did like the digital photography course I took freshman year."

Something flickered over Amy's face then, but I couldn't even say what it was. It was just a flicker, the wise and all-knowing expression blipping out for just a fraction of a second. "You come by it honestly," Amy said. "You come from artists, a long line of artists." She sighed. "You can't help it."

"Maybe I should major in art then."

"No," Amy said with finality. "There's no future in it."

Okay. So maybe Amy wasn't going to help me figure out my life after all.

"I was the daughter of artists," she said. She grew up in the foothills of the Siskiyous on a sprawling property her parents managed as caretakers, she told me. Elena Dodge, the owner, ran an artists' residency there, a place where artists could gather and create art and even live, sometimes for months. Amy and her parents and two brothers would tend to them, going into town to buy them supplies and showing up at their doorstep with clean sheets and batches of walnut scones.

Her childhood was perfect, but then, her senior year of high school, everything fell apart. Elena Dodge died, leaving the fate of the artists' residency in the hands of her son. A month after Elena's death, Amy's parents held a family meeting and announced they had accepted a management position at some seedy old apartment building in Medford. Amy and her fourteen-year-old brother would finish out the school year there. Her older brother, Robert, would continue his studies at the University of Oregon in Eugene.

"Switching schools in the middle of senior year, shutting down the residency, leaving my childhood home—all this was bad enough, but I was handling the news pretty well, all things considered," Amy said.

I nodded, unsure where this story was heading.

"My little brother was bawling. And my older brother was acting all stoic, his arm slung around our mom's shoulders. That's when they dropped the real bomb on me. My college fund—it was gone. Poof. They'd spent it." Amy raised her hands up the way a magician does after the rabbit disappears from the hat.

This was her origin story, I realized. That was why she was telling me this. She was, what? Seventeen, eighteen years old then? Still a couple years away from my birth. I listened patiently as she told me about the plans that had evaporated in thin air: UC Berkeley, then grad school to get her master's in hospitality.

"They said they would pay me back, but I didn't see how that was possible," Amy was telling me. For the last couple years, her father had been having problems with his manual dexterity, limiting his ability to build his sculptures, hulking human forms shaped out of metal scraps. At first they thought it was something minor, tendonitis maybe, but his symptoms never improved, and then he started having all these other problems—his balance was off, his speech came out wrong—but no one was giving him any sort of firm diagnosis. That was where the money had gone. Chasing a diagnosis. Hospital stays. Alternative treatments. That and her older brother Robert's college education.

Robert turned to her then, and that was when she knew he was in on it, this whole plan. The thing is, Robert told her, once he got his degree, he would go out and get a job as a software engineer. Did she know how much money they made? A lot. He would be able to help out the whole family. Pay for Dad's medical bills, anything he needed. And he would pay for Amy to go to college, too! Maybe not Berkeley, but somewhere in state. He had gone in state, after all. It would just require a little sacrifice.

She would just need to postpone college a year, maybe two. She knew, as he explained it all to her, that he was right. Her father needed her. He could fall over, hurt himself. It didn't help that he hadn't accepted his new reality and was constantly doing things like climbing up ladders to saw down tree limbs or taking too many muscle relaxers and getting into his pickup truck to run errands.

Still, even as her brother laid it out for her, she was spinning out an alternative narrative in her mind. Why should Robert be the one to finish college, to go out and get some amazing job that would save the family from ruin? He had a solid B average in college. She had been accepted to *Berkeley*! She imagined venturing off on her own, striking her fortune, and returning with enough money to find her father the best doctor, pay for her little brother's college, and buy her parents their own property, some cozy little cabin where they could make their art. Most of all, she liked to imagine the looks on their faces. Gratitude, of course. But also awe.

"It sounds so silly now," Amy said, laughing at her youthful ambition. "I had big dreams."

"It doesn't sound silly," I said, and I meant it.

Amy flashed me a look. She didn't think it was silly, either. I could tell. Even now, all these years later. "As soon as we moved to Medford, to that awful apartment complex, I started scheming," she said. Berkeley was a lost cause, but she found a scholarship that could be the answer to her problems. Participants would write an essay, and the semifinalists would deliver a speech to an audience and a panel of judges, who would choose a winner. The winner would get a tuition waiver for any four-year institution in the state. The essay topic had been practically custom made for her: "It Takes a Village." She had grown up in a thriving artists' community, built on collaboration and connection and stewardship! It was perfect.

In Portland, she sized up her competition. She was one of six finalists from all over the state. Four of them, she didn't have to worry about. She had heard all their speeches during the dress rehearsal. Hers was better. It was down to her or Jessica Jenkins, who went to Amy's old high school in Ashland. Jessica Jenkins had one of those tall, athletic bodies and heaving chests that made her look like an extra in *Baywatch*, or maybe even a lead. If that wasn't enough to distract the judges, her speech was actually good. She had spearheaded a team of other students to develop a community garden for underprivileged youth, getting half the town businesses to donate. She had been featured on the front page of the newspaper—only the *Ashland Daily Tidings*, but still!—and on some local news station.

"I had to beat her," Amy said. By this time we had already eaten through an order of truffle fries and some sort of elevated artichoke dip served with dark-purple endive leaves instead of bread or chips. It was that quiet, empty time in a restaurant, that lull between lunch and dinner, but a few patrons sat at other tables, each now lit with a votive candle. The candle on our table flickered between us. I hadn't noticed it before.

By then I was actually caught up in her story. She was leaning in, her eyes trained on me. At the dress rehearsal, she had passed around a tin of cookies from home. She had baked them herself, two kinds, oatmeal raisin and chocolate chip. Everyone took one or two—a kid from Salem took an entire stack, five at least—but Jessica Jenkins turned her down.

"She had a peanut allergy," Amy said. "I tried to tell her I didn't put any peanuts in the cookies, but she was like, 'you can't be too careful.'" Then Jessica Jenkins smiled at her. She said she loved Amy's speech. She said it was a real shame the artists' residency had shut down because Amy's mom was very talented—Jessica even had one of her paintings hanging up in her room! At first Amy was flattered by this. Her mom had local shows sometimes, and some of the little boutiques in Ashland sold her prints. Landscapes, mostly. Then Jessica said she had found the painting for sale at Goodwill for five dollars. Margaret Linden! she had exclaimed to her friends, reading the signature in the corner. Isn't that Amy's mom?

"I was furious, of course," Amy said to me. "Obviously she was just trying to psych me out, and it worked. I was shaking. Jessica had walked off, everyone else was laughing and joking around eating my cookies. I grabbed my bag and riffled through it. I was looking for my room key, so I could go up to my room for a minute, calm myself down. And that's when I saw it." Amy was smiling now. A tiny, mischievous little smile.

"What?" I asked, because I knew she wanted me to.

"A sign."

"A sign?"

"A little bag of peanuts."

I put my hand to my mouth. The light from the candle flickered across Amy's eyes, which were wide open, gleeful. It didn't seem possible that she would be confessing to attempted murder in a glitzy downtown hotel restaurant.

"Are you saying . . . ," I started. "What are you saying?"

"It doesn't take much to trigger anaphylactic shock," Amy explained. "You know they stopped serving peanuts on airplanes? People with severe allergies can get a reaction from the dust previous passengers left behind. From the scent of it."

"So that was your plan?" I couldn't believe what I was hearing. "Sprinkle her with peanut dust? She could die from that, Amy!"

"Oh, she wouldn't die. She had an EpiPen. She told me all about it when I offered her the cookies."

"Okay, so she'd just stop breathing for a few minutes. *That's* a relief."

"Ramona!" Amy shook her head, laughing. She was actually very beautiful. I used to search for my features in strangers on the street: that woman with my same dark curly hair, that man with my same eyes. Was she my mother? Was he my father? It haunted me, thinking I could pass them by and never be the wiser. How would I know? If I had passed Amy on the street, would I have recognized myself in her? I didn't think so.

She reached her smooth, pale arms across the table again, pushing the votive to the side. Our dirty dishes had already been whisked away sometime during her story.

Reluctantly, I brought my hands back up to the table.

"I didn't touch those peanuts," Amy said, her eyes still dancing. She laughed again. "Seriously, Ramona! I didn't want the scholarship that bad."

"But you said it was a sign."

"Yes! A sign I could beat her. A sign that my biggest rival, Jessica Jenkins, had a weakness. She wasn't invincible. She could go down with a particle of peanut dust. I didn't even go up to my room. I marched right out on stage and gave the best speech of my life."

Amy described the feeling, then, of owning that stage. She wore a red crushed-velvet dress with spaghetti straps and a black velvet choker—"very '90s"—and she captivated everyone in the audience. Her parents were there, in the front row, and she could see the looks on their faces, that look she had wanted all along. Pride and maybe even awe. She dazzled them.

"But good old Jessica," Amy concluded. "She beat me anyway."

"Well," I said, "sounds like you put up a hell of a fight."

Amy squeezed my hands once before letting them go, and then she ran her fingers over her hair, smoothing it down. She lowered her head and lifted her eyes to me, a conspiratorial smile hovering on her lips. "I actually got what I deserved," she said.

I had an uneasy feeling. "What do you mean?"

"I didn't sprinkle her with peanut dust," she said. "Of course not. But I may have shuffled her note cards right before she went onstage."

"Amy!"

"I know! It was awful. But they were right there and I—I don't know what came over me. I saw the opportunity, and I took it. Of course, it totally backfired on me because she had the opening lines memorized—most of us did, so you could look out at the audience, hook them in. She opened strong. And then when she did look down at her cards, that's when I thought she'd fumble. Anyone else would have panicked."

"Not Jessica?"

"It was like one of those scenes in a movie, where the person looks down at their notes and then back up at the crowd and goes, screw it, I'll just speak straight from the heart! And that was exactly what she did. She nailed it."

"Well," I said carefully, "I guess you did get what you deserved."

"So I never did end up going to college," Amy said. "You know what they say. Life gets in the way."

Like you wind up unexpectedly pregnant, for example, I wanted to say. But I didn't. For a few minutes, we sat in silence. Our drinks had been empty for some time. We were at a point where we needed to order another round or settle up. My stomach churned from the bar food—even if it was fancy bar food—and too many drinks. Somehow we had managed to talk for hours without her divulging anything I didn't already know about myself. I tried one last time. "Amy," I started, "maybe you don't want to talk about it, but—" I choked on the end of the sentence, about to burst into tears.

"Listen, Ramona," she said. "You want to know where you're from? You're from the most beautiful place in the entire world." And she told me about the lodge. She told me how she had worked there when she was about my age. She had been a lowly dishwasher when she started out, and look at her now! She ran the place. She was going to go back later in the year, this summer, for the entire season. It had changed a lot over the years. But so much of it was exactly the same. The beauty of the mountains, the glacial lakes an unreal shade of turquoise, the shaggy white mountain goats teetering on the edges of sheer cliff walls. There was nowhere else like it on earth. I should come and see it myself, she said, because that was where it all started. That was where it all began.

CHAPTER 3

RAMONA

Room 12 was on the first floor of the lodge, at the back of the building, with a "mountain view"—that is to say, it looked out toward the parking lot carved into the foothills instead of the lake. The room was small and dark, with a single narrow bed covered neatly with a wool blanket and a little bedside table with a lamp with a wooden base and a linen shade that didn't appear to be original to the lodge but looked like it was trying to be. It could have very well been the worst room in the park, like a medieval nun's cell, but I didn't mind it. I had come to Seven Glacier Hotel on impulse. It hadn't been easy booking a room last minute, but I called and begged the girl at the front desk to help me out, and she said she could give me a minuscule little room with a single bed and no view, which is why no one else really wanted it.

In September, I was supposed to be starting my junior year of college. That was where my mom thought I was going when I hopped into the car waiting for me outside our house. I had told her I'd arranged a ride with another student. Really it was an Uber taking me to the airport. I would miss the first week of school. So what. I couldn't think about college right now. All I could think about was going to Seven Glacier. It was where I was from, Amy had said. Not from New York City, where I was born, but this wild and—from the way Amy talked about it—almost magical place in the mountains. I hadn't spent much time in the mountains, or in the wild. It intrigued me, that I came from somewhere like this.

I didn't message Amy to tell her I was coming; I was afraid she would tell me not to. When I arrived, it was night, already dark, and when I woke up I saw nothing but the side of the hill jutting up from my tiny window. All the same, I had a tingling sense of anticipation. I walked through the hallways and up a narrow set of stairs into the main part of the lodge, which opened up into a grand room. My only reference point for a place like this was *The Shining*. Windows that spanned floor to ceiling looked out at the most idyllic view, a lake framed by snowcapped mountains that reflected into the lake's mirror surface. I stepped out onto the balcony and gawked at it for a good ten minutes before venturing down to the lakeshore, covered with pebbles instead of sand. I picked up a smooth, round stone. This pebble was from here. *I* was from here. I threw it into the lake.

I could have just emailed her. I could have called. Instead, I came to Seven Glacier. Part of it was because of what she said. This place was where I came from, this place would explain me somehow. I liked the idea of it, the simplicity of it.

The other part of it was Amy herself. I knew if I called, if I emailed, I wouldn't get the information I needed. She would have time to prepare her answers to my questions. I knew she had lied. Or—if not lied, then left out some very important information, information I was entitled to.

When she finally showed up, the first thing she did was sweep her eyes over my room. "Oh no, Ramona," she said. "This won't do at all." She had changed out of her cabaret costume and into long, high-waisted trousers and a brightly patterned silk blouse that tied at the neck. Her hair was out of that blond costume wig and meticulously styled, and her stage makeup replaced with regular makeup—eyeliner, blush, lipstick, the works. It was all so—so *Amy*, I realized. This was only the second time I was meeting her, excluding my birth of course, but already I knew this about her. She tried so hard to make a good impression. To impress me. That endeared her to me, despite everything.

I gestured for her to sit on a wooden chair by the room's only window, which was covered in thick, dusty curtains. Once again I felt underdressed next to her, in flannel pajama pants and a sweatshirt, my hair piled on top of my head in a messy bun. I sat at the edge of my bed and opened my mouth to ask her about what I knew, what I had found out about myself since I met her in Seattle half a year ago, but Amy was already marching to the phone and calling reception. "Georgia, this is Amy," she said crisply. She put her hand on the receiver and whispered to me, "We're going to get you out of here."

I tried to tell her it wasn't necessary, I didn't even plan to be here for that long, that I just wanted some answers, needed her to fill in some blanks, but she held up her finger to me, listening to the other end of the line.

"It's all sorted out." She put the receiver down and roved her eyes over the room again. She even popped into the bathroom and started gathering up my belongings. "We use the same brand!" she said, holding up a little vial of facial moisturizer. Within moments it seemed like she had packed all my things back into my small, beat-up rolling suitcase and carry-on bag. "Okay, I think this is it," she said. "I would have had a bellhop move this for you, but you seem to pack pretty light—"

"Amy!" God, I didn't want to change rooms. But ten minutes later we were settled into a new room on the third floor, with two queen beds, a private balcony, and—in the daytime—a dramatic lake and mountain view, according to Amy. We both stood at the windows and looked out, but it was pitch black, neither the jagged ridges of the mountains nor the surface of the lake visible. We looked back at our own reflections in the glass. I shivered, sensing a chill through the gaps around the window frames. Right then, a raindrop hit the window, making a tiny *thwack*.

Amy reached for the curtains and pulled them shut. "Winter's coming," she said. She may have meant the words to sound conversational, like most weather-related remarks—cold one out there, looks like rain—but it came out vaguely ominous, like she was a character on *Game of Thrones*.

We sat across from each other at the table by the windows, and Amy poured us each a glass of wine from the bottle she had had sent up. "To pleasant surprises," she said. She drained the entire cup.

I sat back in my chair, leaving my glass untouched. "Amy." I spoke slowly. Calmly. "I just want to talk to you. Answer my questions, and I'll go. I promise. No one has to even know I was here." She was married. She had a kid. She had this fabulous life, everything she wanted. She had shown everyone, made the fantasy she had dreamed up as a teenager come true. She could have it, as far as I was concerned. I didn't need to take that away from her.

She appeared to be thinking it over. She was studying my face. I met her gaze, staring at her, willing her to cooperate, like I was some hard-nosed cop intent on pulling out a confession from a criminal.

"What do you want to know?" she asked at last.

"Tell me about Frederick Bennison."

"Freddy?" Amy's voice came out thin and high-pitched.

I had found his name a couple months ago. Amy could have told me about him in Seattle, but she didn't. Why? I got it into my head that if I could find my biological father, I could talk to him, piece together this story of who I was. Through one of the adoption forums I participated in, I found a lead on a guy who could supposedly help me find him. He cost $500. I waited until summer and then I went home and got a job, and as soon as I had the money, I contacted him. And then, a couple weeks later, there it was: a photograph of my original birth certificate. Ramona Bennison, it said. Mother, Amy Linden. Father, Frederick Bennison.

"I know he's my father," I said. "I saw my birth certificate."

"I told you it doesn't matter," she said. "I told you—" She put her hand to her forehead and clenched her eyes shut.

I slammed a hand down on the table, and Amy jumped. "I'm sick of people telling me it doesn't matter. It matters. I have a right to know where I'm from."

"I told you, this is where you're from."

"Yes, and you told me I should come see it for myself. You said that, you said—"

She was nodding, trying to placate me. "I know," she said softly.

"I looked him up, you know. Frederick—Freddy Bennison. So I know he's rich—he's some big hotel family, right? And he's Black."

She paused for a second. "Half Black."

"You don't think that's, like, relevant information? Something I deserve to know about myself? I mean, all this time, I had no *clue*—"

I waited a week before I even googled him. Something about Amy's reaction when I asked her about my father made me hesitant. What was I going to find? Some rapist? An abuser? When I finally did look him up, I was surprised. He was biracial, the son of a Black mother and a white father. That made me part Black. It made no sense. All those ancestry sites I had registered for, and none of them so much as mentioned it. My hair was dark and curly, but my skin was pasty white. Still—I began to rearrange the way I considered myself.

"Oh, Ramona." Amy looked like she was struggling to find a way to explain all this and failing.

I didn't plan it. I didn't even expect it—but I burst into tears. "It's like just because I'm adopted, I should just shut up and be grateful for the life I had. Grateful I was raised by parents who didn't lock me up in a closet and starve me. Like I'd be rotting in an orphanage otherwise. And you know what, I am grateful. Of course I am. It's just"—our eyes met for a charged moment—"I wasn't completely honest when we first met, okay? I made my life so great, but it wasn't."

"It wasn't?"

"My dad," I started. I realized, as soon as I said it, how this sounded. She was probably conjuring up images of every bad father from literature and television: dirty white undershirt, cigarette dangling from his bottom lip, empty whiskey flask fallen to the floor.

The truth was, he left us. Or he left her, my mom—that's what they say when they leave. I was eight years old, and it seemed to come out of nowhere. My dad was the thoughtful type who bought my mom flowers for no reason, never forgot a birthday or anniversary. My mom was taken by surprise as well. She never saw it coming.

He met another woman at work, and they had a silent attraction to each other for a year. He never cheated on my mom—that was what he told her later, as if that made it so noble, to leave your life and child for another woman you hadn't even had sex with. Well, then he went off and married this other woman, and within a year I had a new little brother. I was supposed to visit my dad on the weekends, but it became more and more hectic. Then my sister was born and they moved to a suburb, and my visits stretched out until it seemed like I was just a periodic guest rather than one of my dad's actual children. I even slept in the guest room, a room decorated by my stepmother, with empty drawers for my things, folded towels on the end of the bed. Like I was a guest in their Airbnb. A nice Airbnb, I supposed. But still.

And yes, it occurred to me that he didn't really view me as his at all. I was just an awkward remnant of his old life.

"My dad left us. They got divorced," is what I said to Amy.

"Divorced?" Amy opened her eyes very wide. "They weren't supposed to get *divorced*."

"A lot of people get divorced," I said, suddenly defensive.

"Not your parents," she said. "I chose them. I chose them for you. You should have seen their file. Way better than everyone else's stupid pictures of wallpapered nurseries and piles of stuffed animals. Your parents, they had careers, a house—a mansion! They spent their time off summiting mountains, camping in a tent on the edge of a cliff or something. Skiing in the Alps!"

I couldn't help but marvel at this. This picture they had painted of themselves—according to Amy, anyway—was so far from how I knew either of my parents that it seemed almost entirely fictional. "I've never gone skiing in my life." I shrugged. "My mom never really got over it," I said. "Him leaving. It was quiet, just the two of us in that huge house."

Amy's eyes seemed unable to focus. She had downed quite a few glasses of wine at that point. "If I wanted you to be raised by a poor single mother, I could have done it myself!" she burst out.

I backtracked then. "No, no. My mom was a wonderful mom. Is." I paused for a long time before telling Amy about my mother's diagnosis. "She'll be okay," I said. "I think. It's me. I'm not handling it well."

She said she knew what it was like; she had been through it herself, with her dad. She reached her hands across the table, the way she had in Seattle, and I placed my hands in hers. They were soft and warm. She squeezed them gently and looked me straight in the eye. Her eyes were focused then, as if she had achieved a spontaneous moment of sobriety. "You belong here," she said, tears streaming down her face. "With Jonathan and Gabe. I'll introduce you to them, I promise. They're going to love you."

She freed her hands from mine and wiped at her cheeks with the back of one hand.

"And Freddy?" I added, unable to keep the desperation out of my voice.

"What about Freddy?" she asked, as if she had forgotten all about him.

"Are you ever going to tell me about him? I mean, I thought of just calling him up myself and asking him, but I thought—"

"Hasn't it occurred to you that maybe there's a reason I don't want to talk about this? That maybe some things are better just—tucked away in the past?"

I didn't answer right away. "I did wonder that," I said at last. "I thought maybe I don't want to know who my father is. Maybe he's some sort of lunatic. Maybe he—I don't know." I lowered my voice. "Amy, you can tell me. Did he—I mean, maybe it wasn't consensual, or . . ."

"No, no," she was quick to say. "Nothing like that." She tried to reach for my hand again. This time, I didn't let her. "Still," she continued, "it's painful for me to remember sometimes. The past. It has a way of—of haunting you."

"So why did you meet with me then? Last March?" Once I started, I couldn't stop. The rest came out in a rush. "Why did you sign up for that online DNA testing service? I never would have found you if you hadn't registered with them. You know what I think? I think you wanted me to find you. You know how long I searched for you? I mean, no one seemed to have any idea where I came from, like I was some baby dropped off at a fire station or something. I could have been placed in a basket and floated down the Nile for all I knew. The adoption agency had nothing on you. That's pretty weird, right? I mean, people have open adoptions these days. So of course my imagination went wild, trying to figure out what might have happened to you, to me. Then, all of a sudden, there you were—a biological match."

I exhaled and reached for my glass of wine at last. I drank it all in five gulps and then reached for the bottle—bottle number two at this point—and refilled my glass, stopping before the liquid reached the rim.

She reached once again for my hand. I let her take it. "I wanted to meet you because I wanted to make sure you were okay," she said. "I wanted to meet you because I wondered, too. All those years. I needed to know."

"Exactly!" I said. "It's like—have you ever done a jigsaw puzzle, worked on it for days or even weeks, watching the picture come together, section by section, and then found out at the end that a piece is missing?"

"We have puzzles down in the lobby for the guests. Pieces go missing all the time."

"Well, that's what it's like for me. Like my life is this puzzle, and I'm trying to put it together, but part of it is missing. Not just a piece but, like, whole *chunks*. And meeting you—it helped me. It's helping me. It's filling in those blanks. And now that I've started, I want to keep going, you know? And you can do that for me. I could call him up myself, but—"

"No!"

"Just tell me he's evil. A bad person. *Something*."

She shook her head sadly and let out a resigned sigh. "It's just that once you know something, you can't unknow it."

Our eyes met across the table. Our hands were still clasped together, her delicate, soft little hand pulsing in mine. "But that's all I want," I said. "To know."

CHAPTER 4

RAMONA

It was almost the beginning of a beautiful love story, the way Amy told it.

Soaking wet, sobbing, and kicking her ugly close-toed shoes into the dirt—that was how Freddy found her, the first time they met. She had just stormed out of the kitchen, bursting from the employee exit at the back of the building.

He came out the same doors a minute later, and he was singing. He wasn't just singing. He was caught up in his own performance, waving his hands, accompanying the sounds he was making with exaggerated facial expressions. When his eyes landed on Amy, he stopped midnote.

"Whoa, whoa, whoa!" He looked her up and down. "What happened here?" He said it the way a teacher would say it to kids on a schoolyard, like he was the person responsible for setting things right. It didn't seem possible that he might be flirting with her, not in the state she was in, a grimy bandanna covering her head, kerchief style, like some sort of pilgrim maid, a grungy apron emblazoned with the Bennison Hotels/Seven Glacier logo—an uninspired BH stacked over 7G—tied around her waist.

"I'm fine." She pulled the kerchief from her head and ran her fingers through her hair, suddenly aware of the guy standing before her, his long limbs, those kind hazel eyes. He hadn't been at Seven Glacier the previous summer, unless he had worked on the other side of the park. She would have remembered seeing him, tall and "boyishly handsome," as her mother might say, his hair in a loose Afro, tight curls springing out every which way. In addition to this he was wearing lederhosen with hiking boots, which should have looked ridiculous but instead seemed to enhance his charm, like he was some sort of rock star heartthrob who had for some reason decided to take up yodeling.

"Yeah, you look fine." He raised his eyebrows in that teacherly way: Are you going to tell me what's really going on?

She looked down at the bottom half of her body, soaked in water and now—thanks to the dirt-kicking a moment earlier—coated in a layer of grime.

She couldn't think of anything witty to say, so she just told him the truth: she had somehow managed to tip an entire bin filled with dirty dishes and scalding-hot water off the dish cart and onto the floor. And her feet. "Who needs skin, right?" she quipped.

He knelt down in front of her to take a look.

She lifted up one pant leg, then the other. Her left leg looked normal. The skin on her right leg was pink, but not alarmingly so. He inspected each leg carefully, instructing her to flex and point her feet.

"I can take you to the nurse if you want," he said.

"There's a nurse?"

He shrugged. "Probably. Or I could go in the lodge and yell for a doctor."

She almost laughed at that. "I'm not even supposed to be in the kitchen. I worked in the kitchen last summer. Apparently I did such a great job that the kitchen manager requested me by name this year."

"Oh yeah?"

"The thing is, Stuart *knew* I didn't want to work in the kitchen."

"No one wants to work in the kitchen."

"Exactly. The same thing happened last year. I told them I have experience—actual hospitality experience!" She was getting worked up. She could feel her face flushing with heat. "So you're a—bellhop?"

she guessed, based on the lederhosen. "Or one of those open-top bus drivers?"

"Bellhop."

"Lucky."

"Yeah."

She liked him for that. For not denying that it was luck. For not saying his job was just as bad as hers. Only guys—young, strapping ones, without fail—worked as bellhops. Yes, they had to wear lederhosen and hiking boots, and sure, they had to hoist suitcases up and down stairs and probably cater to fussy tourists' demands, but they also got to interact with the guests, cracking jokes and dispensing advice about the best hikes and scenic outlooks. Not to mention the tips.

"Freddy," he said. "Freddy B. Smooth."

"That's your name?"

"Or maybe Freddy B. Cool."

"These are what, stage names?"

"Freddy B. Ready? How's that?"

"Reminds me of Right Said Fred."

"The problem is, there are a lot of Freds in show business. All the cool names are already taken. Fred Astaire, Freddie Mercury."

"Freddy Kruger, Fred Rogers," Amy added. "Frederick's of Hollywood. I guess that's more of a store than a name."

"And you are?" He extended his hand for her to shake.

"Amy." They shook hands like they were completing a business deal.

"Do me a favor, Amy?" He cocked his head to the side and smiled. And then he asked her to listen to his audition. "You can give me notes."

"Your audition?"

"The cabaret audition! Can you sing? You should try out, too."

"The cabaret? Are you serious?"

Unselfconsciously, he sang a few warm-up notes, raising a hand in the air like an Italian opera singer.

"Seven Glacier is the only hotel in the park that still has a cabaret," he said. "It's like—tradition."

"But it's for tourists."

"Well—yeah. Don't tell me you were here all last season and never went."

"Not once." She held up her hands, pleading her innocence. "Blame Stuart Swiftcurrent."

"The bane of your existence."

"He said don't bother." What he had actually said was that it was lame, a way for egocentric theater kids to strut around in costumes for attention.

"Oh, I know Stuart," Freddy said. "I'm going to have a serious talk with that dude." Then he clapped his hands. "Ready?"

"Ready for what?"

"To rehearse."

"I thought I was giving you notes."

"We have to get through the song first. Here—stand over there." He took her by the shoulders and repositioned her so they were standing face-to-face, as if they were about to start a slow dance. Freddy started up with the background vocals of "The Lion Sleeps Tonight." "You know how it goes, right?"

She nodded and half-heartedly echoed him.

"A little faster. Good."

After she had repeated the lines a few times, he came in with the lead vocals, staring straight at her, smiling. His voice was good. Clear and bright. But then he stopped them both, making a little director's motion with his hand.

"Good," he said. "You should totally audition with me."

She laughed.

"How's your feet? Can you walk?"

She flexed both feet. Her socks and pant legs were both still soaking wet, but she no longer felt the pain from dropping the bin on them. "I'm good."

He took her hand and led her down the path from the back of the kitchen to employee housing. "Where are you taking me?" she asked as he led her up the stairs to the boys' floor.

He glanced up and down the hallway and then peeked behind the door of the bathroom. "It's empty," he said.

"I'm not going to the boys' bathroom with you."

"It's for the acoustics." He arranged the two of them in a tiled shower stall, standing face-to-face. Amy looked up at him and cleared her throat. Freddy was looking down at her, opening his eyes wide and then nodding, counting off. He pointed at her and she started singing.

This time when he came in, it sounded even better, his voice magnified and echoing, and then they were both getting into it, singing to each other like they were in some old-timey movie, snapping their fingers and shimmying back and forth in the tiny stall. When it was over, the spell broke and suddenly she felt foolish, standing in a shower stall with this guy she had only just met, and she stumbled out backward, mumbling something about needing to get back to work. The dishes were waiting.

~

At some point during Amy's story we had migrated from the little table by the window over to the beds. I sprawled out on the one closest to the window, Amy on the other. She had untied the elaborate bow at the top of her blouse and let the collar hang open a bit. Her head was propped up on one hand. I watched her as she talked, the way her eyes sparked when she talked about Freddy. My father.

This was all so much better than the nightmare scenarios I had come up with about my birth parents. Amy and Freddy's story—it was almost cute. I sipped at my wine, letting the warmth spread through me. We were comfortable here, Amy and I, just the two of us, talking. Cozy, curled up on beds tucked away in a rustic mountain lodge, talking deep into the night. It could have been like this, if I had grown up with her. We would have been the kind of mother-daughter who were best friends, gossiping and giggling. She would let me stay up late on school nights, pull me out of class to take me on spontaneous shopping sprees, feed me ice cream for dinner if that was what I wanted.

I loved my mother, of course, but I didn't have that type of relationship with her. Not at all.

I smiled over at Amy. "Freddy sounds cool," I said.

"I don't know if he was cool, exactly." She said this carefully. Conspiratorially.

"No?" I raised an eyebrow, and we both laughed.

"There was just something in the way that he looked at me," she said. No one back in Medford, Oregon, looked at her that way. It was this place, she realized. It changed her. And it wasn't just her, it was him, too. Freddy. She knew those kinds of guys in high school. She had grown up in Ashland, after all, a theater town. A theater town filled with theater kids and their overenunciation, their dramatic way of dressing, in scarves and berets. They practiced choreography when they walked through the halls and called each other "dah-ling." They weren't the cool kids—far from it—but they didn't care.

Freddy, in high school, was one of them. Amy could almost guarantee it. But here, at Seven Glacier, he was something else. He was popular. It wasn't him, and it wasn't her, not exactly. Seven Glacier could transform you, make people see you differently, like you were a character in a movie. Not just a character, but the *main* character. Amy had always wanted this. She craved it—to be looked at the way Freddy was looking at her. Even if he was drunk.

"He got the part in the cabaret," Amy continued. "He invited me to this bonfire at the cabins, to celebrate. I wasn't going to go—they're a mile away from the lodge—but I did. I tried talking my roommate into going with me, but she was a practicing Mormon who didn't work on Sundays and was saving herself for marriage. 'Not my scene,' she said. So I went alone."

~

"I'd like to make a toast!" From across the gigantic bonfire, Freddy stood up and raised an almost-empty bottle of beer. The fire sent crackling sparks into the night sky. Seated on a log between two other park employees, Amy took one last swig of her wine cooler and tore the gold foil off the lid of the next one. Premium berry flavor. Much better than the bitter, soapy taste of beer. Like drinking a Jolly Rancher.

"See that beautiful woman over there?" Freddy pointed across the bonfire at Amy. Freddy stumbled back, almost falling, and then he caught himself. "Whoa," he said. He was still pointing at her, and everyone raised up their plastic cups or beer bottles.

"Winona!" this guy yelled out because, according to him, Amy looked like Winona Ryder. The firelight flickered off their eyes and the sparks snapped in the air and then someone starting clapping and Freddy said, "She's my good luck charm!" At that, someone whooped and everyone drank.

Freddy made his way around the circle and flopped down beside Amy, flinging an arm around her shoulder. "Hey," he said. He smelled like beer and campfire smoke.

"You're drunk."

"*You're* drunk." He nudged closer to her, so the left side of his body aligned with the right side of hers. She could feel his leg hairs press into the skin of her calf.

Some of the guys stoked the fire with more logs and then an assortment of kindling, sticks, and damp pieces of wood. The flames died down for a moment, and that was when she turned to look at him. He cut his eyes to hers and smiled, and she smiled back right as the flames of the fire rose up again, and that was when he kissed her.

They made out, forgetting the bonfire, the others, the wailing of the harmonica and the strumming of the guitars receding into the background.

And then they were scrambling up. Freddy stood first and held his hand down to Amy. He pulled her up and she tipped into him, her hands on his chest. She could barely stand. Her head was spinning.

Her mouth felt puckered from all the wine coolers. How many had she drunk? Two, three—maybe even six.

They had agreed to "get out of here," to find somewhere to—

"Over there." Freddy led her by the hand, and she followed along a tree-lined path. The cabins offered more "rustic" accommodations for Seven Glacier visitors. Little brown houses with yellow shutters, arranged in circles in the woods behind a small motor lodge that housed a restaurant and a gift shop.

Freddy tried the handle of one of the cabins and she whispered for him to stop, yanking them both away. "What are you *doing*?"

"No one's in there."

"They're *asleep*."

He pushed her against the side of the cabin and kissed her, hard. She pressed herself into him and he lifted her arms over her head and when she moaned, a light came on in the cabin.

They ran away, laughing.

They climbed through a half-open window of what appeared to be the laundry cabin. Freddy propped her up on a washing machine, and she tore off her flannel shirt. His hands went under her tank top, pulling it up over her head. He kissed the top of her breasts, tugging at the cups of her bra.

She wasn't going to sleep with Freddy. That was what she told herself on the walk over. They had only just met, after all.

But then she was fumbling to undo the top button of his shorts and he reached down and yanked them off, and then her shorts were off and his hand was between her legs and their mouths pressed against each other, and then they were doing it, having sex right there in the laundry room, on top of the washing machine, frantic, jerky sex that ended with both of them breathing hard, collapsing into each other.

She woke up a few hours later face down in an unfamiliar bed, Freddy's arm slung over her back. It was still dark, so dark she could barely make out where she was. Her head was pounding and her stomach lurched. She needed a shower, a solid meal, and about five more hours of sleep. She sat up and craned her neck around. Gradually, her eyes adjusted to the darkness of the room. They were in a bunk bed, on the top bunk. Below them she could make out a lump beneath a pile of blankets. She had no memory of arriving there.

Freddy slept beside her, his face pressed into the pillow. She extracted herself from the weight of his arm and attempted the climb down the wooden ladder, but her foot missed the last step and she clattered to the floor. In the bottom bunk, the figure huddled under a pile of blankets groaned, and then the bundle writhed and flopped for a moment before settling back down. From the top bunk, nothing. She felt around the floor for her shirt, her socks and shoes, and crept out the door and into another tiny room, furnished with a built-in table and sink. By then she had figured out where she was: in one of the employee cabins. It was so small, like a child's playhouse almost, and suddenly her lungs seized up and she struggled to take in another breath. She had to get out of there.

Outside it was dark and so still she could hear the rustling of the trees. She walked slowly away from the cabin, tiptoeing to avoid the snap of a twig. Her desire to flee undetected was instinctual rather than logical. What did she expect, Freddy to come springing off the top bunk and out of the cabin, demanding her return? All the cabin employees to peer from their windows to witness her doing the walk of shame back to the main lodge? One circle of cabins led to another, and then another, and she started to panic, imagining herself trapped in some maze, but after a few minutes, she reached the main road.

She felt terrible, her body at odds with the beauty of the landscape. The sky just beginning to lighten at the edges of the horizon, the snow atop the rocky peaks in the background glowing eerily. She debated briefly between going along the paved road and cutting over to the walking path. It must have been almost five in the morning, and no one was up yet, but if she took the main road, she would risk getting run down by some early-bird tourists in their rental cars. The walking path would be shorter, cutting through some woods and a field of tall grasses.

She entered the dark woods and quickened her step, looking back over her shoulder at every rustle in the brush. Ahead, a clearing, like a light at the end of the tunnel. She was almost running by the time she burst out of there, panting and relieved to be out in the open, where the first light of dawn shone on the long blades of grass. She leaned down with her hands on her knees, trying to catch her breath, her eyes closed tightly. They stung with sleepiness. Her drunkenness hadn't worn off yet; she could still taste the memory of those wine coolers, their boozy, fruity sweetness. She would never drink those again. Never.

And worse, she could still feel Freddy on her. That tang of beer and smoke, his hands pressing against her. Between her legs felt sore, used. She liked Freddy—she did. But she was so drunk. So was he. Stumbling-back-from-the-fire drunk. Having-sex-on-a-public-washing-machine drunk. She would never be able to look him in the eye again.

At that point in Amy's life, she had romantic ideas about love. If you put out on the first date, they wouldn't respect you. That was an idea she had internalized at some point early in her teen years, and no amount of *Sassy* magazine articles encouraging her to stash condoms in her medicine cabinet or Madonna "Express Yourself" videos had been able to dislodge it. She hadn't even been out on a date with Freddy. They had staggered into a laundry room, had sloppy, unprotected sex on a washing machine, and then crashed on the top bunk in someone's cabin. Who had seen them at the bonfire? Everyone. That guy in the Tibetan sweater. The braless girl in the homemade patchwork tank top. Dave, the line cook. She worked with him. What would her Mormon roommate think if she heard about this? She would faint from shock.

Keep going. That was the only thing to do. When she stood and opened her eyes, the sky had brightened and she sallied forth. Life went on. In the distance, Seven Glacier Hotel loomed over the edge of the lake, so kitschy and charming, with the little balconies outside every window, the large stone chimneys, all set into the valley. Postcard perfect. Really, everything would be okay. She had learned a valuable lesson, a lesson about sobriety and—

She froze. Out of the corner of her eye, she saw something move. Something large and dark and covered in fur. A bear. He didn't see her, not at first. She stayed still as a statue, frozen in walking position, one foot in front of the other, her arms midswing. Only her eyes moved, tracking his slow amble through the thick grass.

Just walk on by, she pleaded with the bear telepathically. Walk on by. Never mind her, a young woman all alone at the break of dawn, walking by herself through bear country despite the warnings, despite the signs at the foot of every trailhead suggesting hikers stick to groups of three or more. Those signs were for tourists. All last summer she had worked at the park, and yes, she had seen bears, but they were tiny brown dots in the distance, viewed through binoculars.

She had read about bears and what to do if she were to encounter one. In that moment, though, her mind went blank. Lower your eyes or make eye contact. Make yourself huge or cower into a ball. Stay completely quiet or make a huge racket, scare it away. She couldn't remember. All of those responses seemed logical. Instead she just stood there.

The bear made his way out of the tall grass and stepped one paw onto the walking path. Amy didn't breathe. She prayed for that bear to just keep walking, but when his second paw landed down on the path, he stopped. His ears pricked up. He was that close—so close she could see him twitch, not even ten feet away from her.

Her head continued to spit out jumbled facts about bears. In the last five years, there had been only two bear attacks resulting in death. Both victims were nineteen-year-old girls hiking alone. Both grizzly attacks. *Please* let it be a black bear. The bear turned his head and observed her frozen in place on the path. His fur was reddish brown. His snout prominent. A grizzly.

He raised himself up on two legs and her eyes—only her eyes—traveled to take in his full height. What was he going to do? Pick her up and bat her around? Tear her apart with his claws? Maul her? It was the beginning of the season. Huckleberries were less abundant now than they would be later in the summer. Maybe he was hungry. He was waving his paws through the air, thrashing, and finally Amy fell to the ground, rolling into a ball. Protect your face and neck. If he picks you up, play dead.

Blood pounded through her head, and she was sure he could hear it, the rush of it, all that blood pumping through her body, her heart thumping. He could smell her, he probably smelled her before he saw her, her young body, reeking of premium berry wine coolers and sweat and sex. That was it, the sex. Bears were drawn to it, that primal animal smell. A couple on their honeymoon one summer had been awakened by a bear tearing apart the nylon fabric of their tent. She had heard this story so many times she assumed it was made up. Some sort of nonurban legend. The bear had smelled the sex on them, sniffed them out, stalked them, maybe, torn the tent to shreds and then—

The bear was panting, grunting, and then he let out a roar. She waited to feel the claws sink into her skin. Waited to feel herself lift up and bounce through the air like a beach ball.

She couldn't see it, but she could feel it, the earth vibrating as the bear fell back down to all fours. He would charge her now, jump on top of her. But nothing happened. She didn't know how long she crouched in crash position, her eyes screwed shut, praying Oh please, God, please. I'll never drink again, I'll never have sex again, before it occurred to her that it was over. Slowly, she raised her head, just enough to peek out from underneath her eyebrows and see the bear shuffling into the grass on the other side of the path.

~

When she went back to the kitchen for her shift a few days later, she was determined to make the best of it. She had cheated death. It was a sign. Some mystical force was watching out for her. It was this place, Seven Glacier. She adjusted her kerchief and tied her apron on.

"What are you doing here?" Stuart Swiftcurrent leaned against the edge of the industrial sink where she had just started spraying down the employee breakfast dishes. Stuart was in his midtwenties, with thick, jet-black hair in a 1970s shaggy style, and this was his fifth season at the park. Offseason, he lived in St. Anne, a plains town twenty miles east.

"I work here, remember?"

"Not anymore you don't."

She didn't stop what she was doing. Stuart was always joking around with her like this, giving her a hard time.

"You've been reassigned," he said.

Only then did she stop spraying and turn around to look at him. He frowned and raised his eyebrows as if to say, Yeah, surprised me, too.

"Reassigned? I thought you requested me special."

"Get over it, Linden!" He swatted her with a bar cloth. She had already given him an earful about how not happy she was to be back in the kitchen for a second summer in a row.

"Wait, so where am I going?"

"Hell if I know. Talk to human resources."

Over in human resources, an office the size of a closet on the main floor of the lodge, the guy didn't seem to have any idea what she was talking about when she asked where she had been reassigned. "What did you say your name was again?" He was a young guy dressed as a middle-aged engineer—weird gold-rimmed glasses, an ill-fitting short-sleeve polo shirt with snaps instead of buttons. His desk was piled high with files and books and papers, and he shuffled through them, patting his hands around as if in search of some magical piece of paper that would give him the information he needed.

She repeated her name.

"And you want to be reassigned."

"I *was* reassigned."

"Why would you get reassigned right at the start of the season?"

"Stuart Swiftcurrent told me—maybe something got written in my file?"

"You're the one who wanted to work at the front desk!" he said, suddenly recognizing her. Two years in a row now, she had given him her spiel about growing up in the hospitality business. I'm majoring in hospitality, she told him, which wasn't exactly true as she was only taking general education courses at the community college while she stayed home taking care of her father, but it seemed like it could have been true, or *would* have been true, if she had been able to go to Berkeley as she had planned.

"Yes!"

She had been standing awkwardly in the door, but now she sat herself down in a hard wooden chair while he shuffled through more papers and then swiveled around to thumb through files in a dented metal file cabinet. He swiveled back, opened her file, and read it with a look of deep concentration, nodding, raising his eyebrows, and exclaiming little things like, "Huh!"

"Did you bring in the black pants and white button-down shirt? Close-toed black shoes?"

Amy shot forward in the chair, an eager little pupil. "Of course."

"Put them on and report to the front desk. Meghan will train you."

"The front desk?" It seemed like a mistake. A joke.

"That's what it says," he said, tapping the contents of the manila folder.

"But—why?" She almost didn't want to ask. She had begged him two years in a row for that job, and now it was getting handed to her for what seemed like no reason whatsoever.

Back in her room, she changed out of her kitchen garb and into the black pants and white button-down shirt. She had spent a lot of time picking it out from the J.Crew catalog. More expensive than any of the other clothes she owned, but worth it. Black stovepipe pants. A cotton poplin shirt with shirred detail at the shoulders and darts at the bust, not some shapeless button-down from her dad's closet. At home, modeling the clothes before the mirror, she looked businesslike yet elegant, exactly the kind of person they needed at the front desk. Travel-weary guests, missing reservations, misplaced luggage—nothing she couldn't handle.

She entered the lobby of the hotel and looked around as if for the very first time. The lobby was enormous, an open atrium that looked up at all three stories of the hotel. The Douglas fir beams, Swiss balcony railings, wrought iron and glass light fixtures—this was where she belonged now, right here.

She introduced herself to Meghan, a tiny girl about her age with a pointed chin, expressive eyes, and very small lips, like a silent movie actress, Clara Bow or Louise Brooks. She even had the right hairstyle, a short bob with blunt bangs straight across her forehead. If she was surprised to hear that Amy had been assigned to work alongside her, she didn't show it.

The morning went quickly, with guests checking out or coming up to the desk to ask questions or request services. She put in an order for fresh towels in Room 214, sent a couple off with a pamphlet for a boat tour, and suggested a half-day hike for a family of four. "Great job," Meghan said, observing her. Her voice was high and squeaky, like a little girl's, but unenthusiastic.

During a lull, Meghan dragged a heavy binder up to the counter and the two of them bent over it, studying the lodge's policies and procedures.

A loud thump on the desk startled them both. "Freddy!" Meghan exclaimed in her chipmunk voice. Amy hadn't seen him since that morning she had left him in the top bunk of the cabin. Three days ago.

"Hey, Meghan," he said, but he directed his dazzling smile at Amy. Adorable even in his lederhosen. "Hey," he said. "The front desk suits you."

After her near-death experience face-to-face with the grizzly, she had vowed to turn her life around. She had vowed never to drink another drop, to so much as look in Freddy's direction. She had made a solemn promise to—well, if not to God, if not to some omniscient being watching over her, a fairy godmother or guardian angel, then to Seven Glacier itself, her own little universe. Despite all this, she smiled back. She couldn't help herself.

When he was gone, Meghan turned to her, suddenly much more interested in her than before. "So." She smiled and dipped her chin conspiratorially. "How do you know Freddy Bennison?"

Amy blinked back at her, unable to disguise her shock. "Freddy . . . Bennison?"

"He's so nice," Meghan said, rolling her eyes to emphasize just how nice he was. "Not to mention very easy on the eyes."

"We met at the bonfire a few days ago." Wait, no. She started to correct herself, but Meghan cut her off.

"Too bad he has a girlfriend, right?"

This didn't even register with Amy. Her mind was still catching up. "Wait, Freddy Bennison, as in—"

"The Bennison Hotels."

"So he's the son of Charlotte and Mason Bennison?"

"I guess so."

"I've *seen* her," Amy told Meghan.

"Cool," Meghan said, though she clearly didn't understand the significance of the event.

"That's his *mom*?" The first time Amy saw Charlotte Bennison was last summer, shortly after she had arrived at the beginning of the season. She was sitting on one of the couches in front of the gigantic circular fireplace in the hotel lobby playing cards with a friend. Charlotte Bennison strode by with a pack of businessmen in suits and ties trailing behind her jotting down notes on clipboards. She stood out, and not just because she was a statuesque Black woman among a sea of pasty-white tourists. While the guests clomped around in dusty hiking boots, shorts, and layers of flannel and fleece, she looked like a rich lady in a soap opera, in a brightly patterned silk blouse tucked into navy-blue wool trousers, tailored perfectly to her slim frame.

Oh my god, Amy had whispered to her friend. Do you know who that is? That's Charlotte Bennison. She runs this place—she's the CEO of this entire hotel group. Her friend didn't get it. Only Amy would recognize the CEO of the hotel group—she had done her research before arriving, after all. Only she would feel awed in her presence. She admired the way Charlotte strode through the lobby with purpose, as if she knew exactly what needed to be done and who needed to do it.

Amy knew Charlotte ran Bennison Hotels with her husband, a nerdy white guy, but she had no idea she had a son. A son her age. A son who worked at Seven Glacier Hotel and seduced young women at bonfires. Freddy Bennison.

"Excuse me a minute." Amy left Meghan to fend for herself at the front desk and ran after Freddy, who had disappeared down a hallway with a large brass luggage rack.

She found him waiting for the elevator. "Freddy!" she called out.

Freddy smiled at her with an ease that surprised her. For some reason, she thought he would want to avoid her as much as she had wanted to avoid him. Wasn't that the decent thing to do, when you've humiliated yourself in front of someone? They had been drunk out of their minds. The sex they had was frantic and messy and not exactly something either of them would want to remember, let alone relive. Or so she had thought. The way he was smiling at her made her wonder.

"How's the new job treating you?"

"Did you have something to do with that?"

The elevator dinged, and the doors opened.

~

Amy paused in her narration. This must be it—the part of the story that would veer off in an unexpected direction, explain why Amy seemed so rattled by the mention of Freddy's name. The reason she hadn't mentioned him in the first place, back in Seattle, when I had asked about my father.

"Well," I prompted, "what happened next?"

Amy made a show of raising her wrist to her eyes and trying to read the time on her watch. "Listen, Ramona, it's late."

"But what's the rest of the story?"

"The rest of the story?"

"I assume this is the part where you reveal that Freddy turned out to be some major asshole. A violent psychopath."

Amy was sitting herself back up and straightening her clothes. Her eyes had widened at the words "violent psychopath," but now her expression was calm. "Oh, Ramona!" she said. "Freddy Bennison, a psychopath? No, no, no. He was—Freddy was—" She bit down on her lips, as if she was trying to come up with the perfect description for him. "Nice," she concluded.

I sat up, too. Amy appeared to be leaving. It was late. She had to go. "I'm going to call him," I blurted out.

That stopped her. "It's the middle of the night."

"First thing tomorrow. He's on East Coast time, right?"

"Ramona—please. You can't call him."

"Why not? You said yourself—he's a nice guy."

"We should get some sleep," she said. And then, right before she slipped out the door, she added, "Trust me, Ramona. He won't necessarily be happy to hear from you."

CHAPTER 5

AMY

Jonathan, Gabe, and I lived in a cabin tucked behind the lodge when we stayed at Seven Glacier. Originally, it had been designed for the winter caretakers who lived here after all the roads closed and the snow came. It was rustic but charming, with the same fake Swiss woodwork as the hotel, down to the little yellow shutters and wooden windows adorned with window boxes spilling with geraniums. We wanted to raise Gabe with a sense of adventure, to engage with the world. That was what our whole hotel brand was about—memorable adventures, unique accommodations. I had been raised much the same way, at the artists' residency.

I crept up the ladder to the little loft where Gabe slept. It had a skylight overhead, and I could make out his features by starlight. He slept on his side, in the fetal position, one cheek pressed against the pillow. He was breathing deeply. I leaned over and kissed his cheek. "Night night," I whispered. When he didn't stir, I felt the back of his head, locating the tangled clump of hair that seemed to grow larger and denser with each passing day. Silently, I tried to unravel the knots with my fingers until he must have sensed me there, hovering over him, and he flipped around, away from me.

In my bedroom, I undressed and slipped into bed beside Jonathan. I pressed myself against him, the front of my body against the back of his, and ran a hand down his arm. "Are you awake?" I waited for him to groan or roll over, but all I heard in response was the steady, familiar sound of his breath.

I rolled back over and checked my phone for the time: 2:18. I set my alarm for six, and what seemed like mere seconds later, the high, hollow sounds of pan flutes lured me from my sleep—if I had slept at all. I didn't have that same sense of time passing I usually did after a full night's sleep. I didn't feel rested, exactly, but I didn't feel groggy and hungover. I felt like—a machine, perhaps. I went through the motions, briskly, more briskly than usual. I almost leaped out of bed. Beside me, Jonathan turned around and adjusted the blanket around himself, but he didn't wake up.

Five minutes later, I was dressed and out the door, rushing into the main lodge and pounding on Ramona's door. "Rise and shine!" I announced when she opened the door.

Ramona's eyes were half-shut, her hair spiraling out in every direction. She was wearing the same thing she had on the night before—a few hours earlier. I tried not to show the relief on my face. I had wanted to get her up and away from the lodge before she had a chance to call Freddy. If she never called him—if I could somehow just convince her to stop digging into this—everything would be fine.

Back when we first met in Seattle, she asked about her father. I could have just made up a name, told her a story that made sense. A story that left no more room for questions or further investigation. Maybe her father was an Austrian alpinist I'd met on a trail, made love to in a cave, and last saw rappelling into a canyon. Or—no, this was what I should have done—I should have said I had no idea. That I'd slept with half the park employees, a handful of tourists, and a few townies from the surrounding area as well. It could have been any one of them, there would be no way to know.

It hadn't occurred to me to have a story in place, and then she had to come back here asking about Freddy Bennison, and now—what? I wasn't one of those chess geniuses who could map out every possibility in my mind. Inept as I was, I could plot only one move at a time. My plan was to take her out on a hike very early, take her somewhere with no cell phone reception, and bring her back very late, so she couldn't call Freddy. That was it. It bought me some time, at least.

On the drive to the Ridgeline Loop, we sipped coffees and nibbled on breakfast sandwiches I'd bought us from the café at the lodge, along with packed lunches. At first Ramona was quiet, still groggy with sleep. Maybe even still drunk—between us we had polished off two bottles of wine. By the time we pulled off the gravel-covered road leading out from the lodge and onto the highway, though, she had perked up. "All right," she announced after I had finished a little monologue about the geology of the region. "I'm ready."

"Ready for what?" I asked innocently.

"For the rest of the story."

"Oh yeah." I drummed my fingers on the steering wheel and then squinted through the windshield. "I can barely see through this thing!" A feeble delay tactic, to be sure, though it was true: the windshield was covered in dust and the splattered remains of insects, their delicate wings and pale blood. I made a production of spraying windshield fluid onto the glass and turning the wipers on.

"I wouldn't even know where to begin," I said.

"Just start where you left off. He got you a job at the front desk," Ramona prompted. "Then—what? Something must have happened."

"Nothing happened. I stayed away from him."

"Wait, so you and Freddy never—"

"It was just that one time," I insisted. "In the laundry room."

"Oh my god." Ramona chuckled and turned her head to look out the window at the view. We were driving on the highway, through the plains, but out the passenger-side window, the mountains of the park jutted up, looming in the distance. It was an odd sight. In Oregon, where I grew up, mountains tapered down to foothills. They didn't just end. "Pregnant from a one-night stand," she said. "What are the odds?"

~

At the front desk, I had ascended to the top of the seasonal worker hierarchy, among the waiters and the boat guides and the bellhops. I didn't make any more money than before. Even less, actually, because as a dishwasher, every once in a while the waiters on the floor would tip out the kitchen and I'd wind up with a few rumpled dollars after my shift. But up at the front desk, I finally felt like I was learning something, a part of something, a tiny but vital cog in this machine that kept the hotel running. It was a position with some dignity to it.

Every moment I spent behind that desk, handing guests their room keys or arranging a wake-up call, I tried to imagine Charlotte Bennison walking by in one of those richly patterned blouses and impeccably tailored trousers, flanked by a posse of execs in suits, writing down her commands on their clipboards. In this fantasy, so consumed would I be by my front desk duties that I wouldn't even see her coming. She would be the one to notice me. She would stop in her tracks and stare. Who is that? she would ask the execs, who would look at each other and shake their heads. Or, in an alternate version, she would say, That young woman is the very embodiment of the Bennison Hotel Group. Somehow this would lead to our introduction, an instant promotion to some unspecified but important position in the head offices in New York City, where I would also double as the model for the hotel's new advertising campaign.

In my fancy new hotel job (the fantasy continued), I would live in one of those gigantic lofts artists always seem to live in when they move to New York in the movies. I would move my parents and little brother in with me—the loft would have all these extra bedrooms—and my dad would get the finest medical care money could buy. His health would return, slowly but surely, and when I came home from a long day at the office, dressed in a Chanel suit or whatever it was rich executives wore in New York, I'd find my dad up in the loft, surrounded by his sculptures, all those life-size human forms he made out of found metal remnants.

The dexterity back in his hands again, through some miraculous new experimental treatment he was trying, he'd be strong enough to hammer old tin cans out into sheets for a new piece. My best work yet, he would say. A masterpiece, I would agree.

Of course that fantasy never came true. Charlotte Bennison didn't set foot in Seven Glacier that summer. I used my ambition as an excuse, though, to stay away from Freddy.

It was impossible to avoid him after getting reassigned to the front desk. The bellhops reported to the front desk when they arrived and checked in regularly in case we needed someone to run up a set of towels or deliver luggage to a room. Every day, he walked past me in those fake lederhosen, always greeting me with some pithy line or a nod and a smile. He was always asking me to join him and his friends on hikes or gatherings, and I would demure. We should just be friends, Freddy, I tried to tell him.

I had been successfully avoiding hanging out with him for a couple weeks when I somehow wound up sitting beside him on the steps outside the lodge by the employee entrance on a work break. "You're avoiding me," he said, squinting down and smiling at me as if he took this not as an insult but a personal challenge.

"I'm not avoiding you."

"So come see me at the cabaret tomorrow night."

"I have plans."

"Saturday then. You could hang with us after. You know some of them already." Freddy listed off some names, only some of which sounded familiar.

"Maybe next week."

"So you *are* avoiding me."

"Right." I gave him what I hoped was a friendly yet mysterious look.

Freddy lowered his head so he was speaking directly into my ear. "We had fun, though, right? At the bonfire?"

I could feel myself blushing, the blood rushing to my cheeks. "We were drunk. You have a girlfriend."

"Is that what's bothering you? It's not like that; she's cool." He explained that he and his girlfriend, Sam, had been together since freshman year, how she was a very serious person (I'm a very serious person! I wanted to interject, nonsensically), how they had a real connection but when they were apart, as they were this summer, with her in Washington, DC, and him up here in the mountains, they had "an understanding." "If something happens, it happens," Freddy explained. He said some other stuff about not needing to subscribe to old-fashioned views of relationships that were all about ownership and labels. He and Sam weren't like that. They were free, they didn't try to pin each other down.

"That's not very romantic," I told him.

He said it was very romantic, giving someone complete freedom. If they came back to you, you knew it was because they wanted to, not because they had some misplaced sense of loyalty or obligation, a ring or a piece of paper.

It's just that, I countered, if you loved somebody, it seemed like you wouldn't want to hook up with anyone else. It seemed like one person should be enough. If two people really connected, there was this current running between the two of them, why would they want anything else? Anyone else?

After I delivered this impassioned speech, I laughed self-consciously, afraid he would think I was talking about the two of us, me and him. At times like this I wished I smoked, just so I had something else to do with myself, some purpose for being here on the steps with Freddy besides chatting about our philosophies on love. Cigarettes could also punctuate these conversations, give them an end point. The cigarettes eventually burned out, and then it would be over. I could stamp the butt into the ground and then throw it into the old coffee can in the corner, signifying an ending.

"I'd better get back to work," I said awkwardly.

"Hey," Freddy said. As we talked, his leg had edged closer and closer until it brushed against mine. I could have stood up or shifted my position, but I didn't. "I've felt it before," he said, and then he nudged me playfully, crashing his whole body into mine, almost toppling me over on the step.

I took that as my cue, standing up and then stepping behind him, climbing the stairs and reentering the building. "I've got to go," I said. I could already hear the conversation play out. Felt what before, he wanted me to ask. I wasn't going to take the bait. That current, he would say. This current running between us. It's there. Don't you feel it?

But the conversation hung in the air, unspoken.

Of course I felt it, that current running between us, but I didn't want to give in to it. The shame from our first sordid encounter still hung over me, and I wanted more than anything to erase it. The more I resisted giving in to him, the temptation of him, the purer I felt. Also, I couldn't get over the fact that he was Charlotte Bennison's son. He was the reason I had the front desk job, that was clear. What if someone found out? Yes, it was a job standing behind a counter at a hotel, not a starring role in a Hollywood blockbuster, but I had my pride. In my mind, this job could take me where I wanted to go, but I wanted to do it on my own, not because I had slept with a Bennison.

I tried to stay away from him. But I didn't always succeed. We took our breaks together on those back steps more and more frequently. At first accidentally-on-purpose, and then by design. We would sit side by side, our legs touching, and when no one else was around, I let him kiss me. Weeks went by and that was all we would do, like two characters in a romance book aimed at twelve-year-olds. The days went by and one day our shifts ended at the same time, and it was raining outside. His roommate wouldn't be back until after dinner, he told me, so we could go into his room. If I wanted to. It wouldn't be any different than sitting on that stoop. We could talk.

And that was how it happened, inch by inch like that, late afternoons in Freddy's room, lying face-to-face on his narrow bed, talking, and then kissing, but only with all our clothes on. And then one day I let him take my shirt off, and then another day, okay, all our clothes could come off except our underwear. I drew the line there. From that point I would not go further, I told him. I remembered the bear, the promise I'd made to the universe when it had spared my life. I would never touch Freddy Bennison again. Was that what it was? Or never sleep with him again. I could touch him but not have sex with him. Yes. Yes, that was right. That fulfilled my promise.

Freddy didn't mind at all. Maybe he even liked it, the challenge of it.

I hated how I kept giving into it, my desire for him. We shouldn't be doing this was my refrain that summer. Near the end of the season, late in August, we lay side by side on his bed, just a zipped-open sleeping bag slung over us. Naked except for underwear. I still hadn't let him slip my cotton underwear down my hips, but he worked around them, kissing me down my bare chest, running his hands down my hips, slipping his fingers under the seams and touching me, and it was at this point that I made him stop, usually, but this time he moved his head down, pulling aside the fabric, and I let him keep doing what he was doing until I whimpered in pleasure.

Afterward we nestled together on the bed, his arm slung around me, and he kissed me on the side of my head. "I've been wanting to do that all summer," he said. When I didn't say anything, not right away, he asked if I had wanted it, too.

"I wanted it," I admitted.

Freddy hadn't mentioned his girlfriend since that first time we had discussed her, and I never asked about her. I tried not to think about their "arrangement." It didn't matter to me, I decided. It had nothing to do with me at all.

Freddy asked me what I was thinking about, and I didn't want to remind him of his girlfriend so I said the next thing that popped into my head: "I'm thinking we both kept our underwear on, so it's okay. We didn't break the rules." Then we both laughed, and I started to wonder what I was doing, exactly. What kind of game was I playing? I couldn't even explain it to myself.

He asked me then, as he had several times throughout the summer, if I was going to go see his next performance. "Is that the only reason you came here?" I asked him. "So you could be in the cabaret?"

He said it was as good a reason as any.

"So you aren't going into the hotel business then?" I asked him. "I mean, eventually?"

He told me about his father, who had come from a long line of hoteliers. "He wants me to carry it on." Freddy was lying on his back staring up at the ceiling, just rafters and beams. "Who knows, maybe I will one day."

"And your mom?"

"What about my mom?"

I wondered a lot of things about his mother. Did she come from a long line of hoteliers, too, or was she more like me, from humble beginnings? Had she clawed her way to the top? Tell me everything about her, her whole life story, I wanted to say. Instead I just said, "Does she expect you to work in the industry, too?"

"Why are we talking about my *parents*?" Freddy rolled on top of me and kissed me. "Listen, if you don't want to see me in the cabaret, just tell me," he joked.

I told him what I always told him. I couldn't. It would be bad luck. Break the spell.

~

I didn't see him perform at the cabaret until the very end of the summer. It was one of the last performances of the season, or maybe it was the last. At any rate, it was Freddy's last, the Saturday of Labor Day weekend. I never saw Freddy on Saturdays, but I needed to see him—I was *desperate* to see him. I ran through the lodge in search of him, hoping to find him carting luggage around. I had lost track of time, barely noticing that the sun had already set behind the mountains. The sky glowed electric blue, the surface of Seven Glacier Lake dark. He wouldn't be working, not now. He would be at dinner, maybe, and I searched for him in the employee dining area. He wasn't there, either. The kitchen crew was already starting to clean up, carrying the trays of food back into the kitchen. I followed them back there.

Someone was calling my name. It was Stuart. "Amy," he said again, impatiently, as if he had been trying for a while to get my attention. "What are you doing here?"

"Oh, hey," I said, fake-casual.

"Are you okay?" The way Stuart was looking at me alarmed me. What did I look like, in that moment?

I raised a hand to my hair. Tangled. From the nest of my hair, I pulled out a small, shriveled leaf. "I was on a hike," I said.

"Here." Stuart was setting a plate of food in front of me, pushing me onto a stool at the end of the stainless steel prep counter. "Eat this."

Once I started eating, I couldn't stop.

"What happened?" Stuart said, and I didn't answer, my mouth full of buttered biscuit.

Stuart left to get me a glass of water, and when he returned, I smiled at him, attempting to seem normal. "I'm fine," I said. "Just hungry."

His eyes had narrowed, and he studied me carefully and then reached out to pluck yet another leaf from my hair. Never had I seen Stuart in this mode. What did you do, Linden, fall into a ditch? I expected him to say something like that. I told him I was looking for Freddy. He hadn't seen him, by chance, at dinner? He had. Earlier. The cabaret always gets to dinner early on performance nights.

The cabaret! Of course. Of course that was where I could find him. I thanked Stuart and went straight there. Back then, the cabaret took place in a little theater in the basement. Guests sat on hard wooden chairs and looked up at the stage that had been erected sometime in the 1950s.

The show had already started, and it was a full house, so I stood in the back and leaned against the wall. Freddy was the star, or so it seemed. He wore a white T-shirt tucked into dark jeans folded up at the cuffs. For most of the songs, he also wore sunglasses, though he would remove them at dramatic moments as the songs required. What songs they sang, how well they sang them, I couldn't say. I closed my eyes, willing for it to be over.

A smattering of applause and my eyes opened, and then the sounds of chairs scraping across the floor, bodies shuffling past me and out the doors. It was over. I pushed past the crowd, going against the stream, made my way to the stage, which was now empty.

I found him behind the stage, laughing. Still, I didn't call out to him. I was careful not to draw attention to myself. I hung back there until he noticed me. And he seemed so happy to see me standing there, his eyes lighting up, that I knew I was making the right choice, that everything would work out for me after all.

He planned to go out with the others after the show and invited me to come, too, but I told him I had been looking for him. I needed to talk to him. Alone.

My roommate had already left, back to Utah, so I took him up to my room. Out the window, the moon was so big and bright that it illuminated the room, casting strange shadows. As soon as I had him inside, I threw my arms around him and kissed him. "Amy, what's wrong?" he said, but I didn't answer, pulling off his clothes.

"I just want you," I said, and I pushed him down on the bed.

We kissed, stripping off our shirts, his cuffed jeans, my cutoff shorts.

"What's this?" Freddy pulled back and took me in, running his hands along my arms, my legs, feeling the crosshatches of lines rising up from my skin like braille. Visible even by moonlight, bruises bloomed on my limbs, and Freddy reached over to switch on the light, but I stopped him.

"I went on a hike." I pointed at the long, angry scratches on my arms and legs. "Bushwhacking." I pressed a finger into the largest bruise, the size and color of a plum, forming on my right bicep. "I got banged up trying to ascend a rock wall."

"A *hike*?" The way Freddy said it made it sound like it was the last thing he ever expected me to do.

"I go on hikes all the time." I reached a hand down into his boxer briefs, and he settled back down on the bed, resting his head on my pillow.

"Oh yeah?" he said, but his eyes had closed as he responded to my touch. "With who?"

"By myself."

"You shouldn't—" But before he could finish I pressed my lips to his and began pulling at his underwear.

"Let's do this," I whispered into his ear, and then his boxer briefs were off, for the first time since we'd been playing these puritanical little sex games, and then I straddled him and placed his hands on my hips, on the fabric of my practical cotton underwear, and told him to take them off. He pulled at them eagerly, and I had to lie down for him to slide them over my legs and untangle them from my feet.

I was back on top of him again, and he said he didn't have anything, not on him, he hadn't been expecting this, and I said it didn't matter anymore, and then I sank down onto him. And with Freddy, pressing myself against him, feeling him, all of him, I could forget everything but him, I could forget everything about that day, the hike, the scratches, everything that happened, the tangled brush and the rocks and the lake.

When I came I cried out, and Freddy tensed up and said he was almost there, he would pull out. "No," I said. "Please."

When we were finished, we both lay panting on the bed, side by side, our hands entwined. Freddy looked over at me, and I smiled back at him. I felt much better then. Calm. "What was that all about?" he asked.

I turned on my side to look at him, that beautiful face of his. I kissed him lightly on the forehead. "I have something to tell you," I said.

He blinked back at me, his eyes wide open and innocent. I could tell him anything. That was what his expression said. Anything.

"I'm pregnant."

CHAPTER 6

—

AMY

Ramona and I had pulled off the highway and onto the steep, winding road up to the trailhead. I slowed down, the car bumping over rocks, branches scraping against the metal sides of the vehicle. The entire car would be coated in a taupe layer of dust by the time we returned.

The parking lot was quiet, with just a few cars left by backpackers or day hikers who had somehow managed an even earlier start. "It's a bit of an ordeal but it's worth it," I told Ramona as we prepared for the ascent. Sunscreen, water bottles, daypack filled with our lunches, trail mix, and protein bars. "Ridgeline Loop is one of the most spectacular hikes in the park," I said, as if I was quoting from a brochure. "The views from the top—they're unparalleled."

The beginning of the hike was the hard part and also the boring part, just straight up a trail through the forest, no scenic overlooks. We trudged up in relative silence. Every once in a while I might call out the name of a plant, showing off my knowledge of the region. Trillium, queen's cup, glacier lily.

"Hey, can I ask you something?" Ramona called out from behind me. The way she delivered the line, the oh-so-casual cadence to it, made me think she had been summoning up a way to say it for some time, formulating and reformulating the words in her head as we marched up the trail.

I turned around to face her without slowing my stride, walking backward. She had pulled her hair back into a ponytail, and she was breathing hard from the exertion of the climb. I turned back around. "Do you hike much in Missouri?" I asked, stalling.

"Not much." She told me about the suburban neighborhood where her father lived with his wife and other kids, a big white two-story house with Ionic columns. The house was set among other similar houses in a hilly subdivision with wide streets and even a pond with a permanent water feature in the middle. At night, Ramona would walk alone along the limestone sidewalks, and she could spot wildlife, even out there in the burbs. Deer pranced over the mowed grass, owls flew from the limbs of the deciduous trees, frogs chirped their mournful frogsong.

Finally, after a few silent minutes, my curiosity got the better of me. "What did you want to ask me?"

"You don't have to answer if you don't want to."

I didn't turn back around. Maybe, whatever she wanted to ask me, it was easier to ask with us walking single file like this rather than face-to-face. "I can handle it."

"I've been wondering—I think it's normal for me to wonder—why you went through with it. The pregnancy, I mean."

"Right," I said. "Good question." I could hear Ramona's labored breathing over the sounds of our boots crunching along the path. "You ready for a rest?"

At the base of a scrubby fir tree, we pulled off our packs. Once we'd arranged ourselves, catching our breath, taking long gulps of water from our bottles and fishing out the M&M'S from the bag of trail mix, I told her. I told her the truth, as well as I could remember. "You know how most people find out they're pregnant because their period is late?" Ramona was listening carefully, nodding. "I mean, I guess that's not something you've had to worry about, right?"

Ramona narrowed her eyes at me. "Right."

"I just mean . . ." I wanted to tell her that it was cool with me, if she dated girls. That it didn't matter. No, that it mattered, it definitely mattered, but that I didn't have a *problem* . . . no, that I thought it was wonderful. Okay, there was nothing I could say about her dating life that would sound remotely normal. Best to move on. "Okay, anyway, I didn't find out that way. I mean, I missed my period, but I totally spaced it. It's like, I didn't keep track of it, and it didn't come whenever it was supposed to, and I just didn't notice."

"You didn't notice?" Ramona repeated skeptically.

"I had other stuff on my mind. And so I didn't just miss *a* period. I missed a *lot* of periods. All those boxes of tampons I'd packed were just lying there unopened in my suitcase under my bed. So by the time I went to the pharmacy in St. Anne I was already, what? Four months along? I couldn't believe it. I even went back there, bought another test. The first one had to be wrong, I thought."

Ramona didn't say anything, but she watched me carefully. I had this strange feeling, sometimes, when I looked at her. The past and present coming together. It was happening now. That summer—when I found out I was pregnant, I was having a baby—was connected, directly linked, to this moment right here. That clump of cells multiplying inside my womb had grown bigger and bigger until she emerged from my body, and now look, here she was, sitting beside me on a rock, a rock not far from where it all began.

"The pharmacist was this woman, a woman in a white lab coat and these huge glasses. I still remember that. She had this little plastic wheel thing, like a little chart that figures out your due date based on your last period, which I figured must have been early May, right around my birthday, just a couple weeks before I'd left home to come to Seven Glacier. I used to read about those girls who don't realize they're pregnant until they're giving birth on a toilet seat. Is this what I had become? Someone so out of touch with her body that she doesn't even know she's pregnant? I asked that lady—this was a small town, you know. St. Anne. Still is. I asked her what I could do, and she said it was too late to do anything but go through with it. I know now that wasn't the case, but at the time, I believed her. It made sense. And back then, especially during the summer in the middle of nowhere, it wasn't so easy to go online and do my own research. According to her little calculator, I was eighteen weeks along. Well into the second trimester."

"And according to the time of conception."

"What?"

"I mean, you could have just counted back the weeks to when you had sex with Freddy, since it was just that one time."

"Oh, right. Right. So I go to Freddy and I tell him what I learned. I tell him that I'm pregnant and it looks like we're going to have this baby—" I shot a quick glance at Ramona. "Sorry, I mean—"

Ramona waved her hands at me. "No, no, trust me. I get it."

"We were your age, pretty much. Freddy was still in college. And I was supposed to go back home and take care of my dad." We both fell silent for a moment. "We should get going," I told Ramona, "if we want to make it back before dark." We had a long hike ahead of us.

Farther up the trail, the scenery shifted. We emerged from the narrow path through the forest, and the sky opened up overhead. We were on the back side of a mountain covered in rocks in varying sizes from pebbles to boulders as big as cars. "See up there? That's where we're headed." I quickened my pace, eager to get to the top, to the view I wanted to show Ramona.

"Amy!" Ramona called out, and I turned around to find her trailing behind me, struggling to keep up. "Slow down."

"Sorry."

Ramona was breathing hard, and I waited while she wrangled her water bottle from her pack and took several glugs, sloshing the water over her face and onto her shirt.

"It's okay," I said. "Take your time. I forget sometimes. I'm used to it here."

When we started back up again she asked me about Freddy. Just forget about him, I kept wanting to tell her. He's truly not important. Nothing I could tell you about him matters in the least.

It matters, don't tell me it doesn't matter, I kept hearing her cry out at me. And so when she asked me how he reacted to the news that I was pregnant, I relaxed. This, I could talk about.

~

The night I pulled Freddy away from the cabaret and told him I was pregnant, he held me in his arms and told me not to worry; he would take care of me. Of us.

That night, I fell asleep beside him for the first time. I didn't remember struggling to fall asleep the way I usually did, tossing and turning, distracted by the heat or the moonlight streaming through the windows or the creaks in the floorboards of that old building. I slept deeply, without dreams, and when I woke up it was morning and there I was, and Freddy was still there beside me.

"Come with me to New York," he said as we got dressed. I had woken up ravenous. We could make it downstairs for the employee breakfast if we hurried.

From the very start, we didn't discuss ending the pregnancy. It was too late for that, I had told him, and he had accepted it as readily as I had. We didn't discuss adoption, either, not at that point. All that was left to decide then was where we would live, how it would all play out.

At a table in the back of the dining area, we sat with our heads close together, hovering over our plates piled with scrambled eggs and toast and pale-green cubes of melon. Freddy had a year left of college. I had my dad to take care of; back in Oregon, everyone was counting on me to return home. If I didn't . . . what then? Still, showing up pregnant, with a boyfriend, would only make everything more difficult back at home. Either way, I had screwed it all up for them.

"The whole reason I came here was for them," I said ruefully. Despite everything, I hadn't let go of that dream of returning home triumphant, fistfuls of cash in my pockets, saving us all from ruin.

Freddy tipped my chin up with a finger and smiled at me. "I know."

~

"The thing you have to know about my mom is that she is a very head-strong person," Freddy told me the first time I met his parents. We had arrived in New York right before classes started, and I was staying with him in the apartment he shared with two other guys. He had his own room and the guys shared the other. This was because, Freddy admitted sheepishly, his parents owned the apartment, though they did charge him rent. When I asked him how much, he refused to give me a straight answer. "Below market" was all he said.

"Oh, I know," I said. I should have been nervous, but I wasn't. I was excited. Charlotte Bennison, in the flesh! I dwelled less on the fact that I would be meeting Freddy's parents for the first time (which would be stressful enough in ordinary circumstances, but had the added complication of a pregnancy announcement) than on the idea that I would be in the same room as Charlotte and Mason Bennison of Bennison Hotels.

Freddy and I walked the fifteen blocks from his place to his parents', and as we got closer, the apartments got nicer, the sidewalks cleaner. It was evening, a beautiful night.

"Have you met my mom?"

"I didn't meet her. But I saw her my first summer at Seven Glacier. I told you that. Besides, she's famous."

"My mom? Famous?" Freddy grabbed my hand and swung it as we traipsed down the sidewalk. He was in a good mood. Wait until you see my mother's face, he kept saying, cracking up each time. We had gotten in a bit of an argument then, with me asking if the only reason he brought me to New York was to ruffle his parents' feathers and him insisting no, no, he brought me here because he loved me and we were having a baby together *but*, all the same, he did love messing with his mom, just a little bit. It was just that she was so perfect all the time, and she expected him to be perfect, and it got so tiring. He loved his mom, but every once in a while he just wanted to test her, push her limits. He had been like that since he was a kid. It was all in good fun, he insisted. Just the way he and his mom interacted. I would see.

We approached a stately building where two doormen, both dressed head to toe in burgundy uniforms complete with two rows of brass buttons and matching felt hats, greeted us. "Hey, welcome home, Freddy," one of them said, actually tipping his hat. Freddy had prepared me for this, and I smiled at both of them and nodded as if all this was normal for me. I didn't want to be one of those rubes who bugged out her eyes and gawked, mouth open, exclaiming, You grew up here?! No.

I had dressed carefully for this occasion, which was difficult, because my clothing options were dwindling as my abdomen grew bigger. At twenty weeks, I still was barely showing, at least not with the right outfit on, but none of my pants fit right. I settled on my black J.Crew pants I had brought to Seven Glacier for the front desk job, the top button unfastened, and a billowy white button-down shirt, so large it could almost qualify as a dress. On the plus side, it did an excellent job of hiding the pregnancy (not to mention the unbuttoned pants). I just hoped I pulled the look off, more Uma Thurman in *Pulp Fiction* than service industry worker in her ill-fitting black and whites.

Freddy's parents' apartment was exactly how I had imagined it, down to the deep-red Persian rugs, the floor-to-ceiling bookshelves filled with hardcover books, the large but tasteful floral arrangements, and the eclectic collection of furniture, a blend of Danish modern and more contemporary pieces.

Freddy and I sat across from his parents in the living room, where two identical white-upholstered sofas faced each other in front of an ornate inoperable fireplace that housed yet another floral arrangement instead of logs and kindling. Freddy's father, Mason, was tall and lanky like Freddy, with the same long nose, but otherwise looked nothing like him, with a full head of auburn hair and pinkish freckled skin. He wore small, gold-framed glasses, just like in the pictures I had seen years ago, when I first looked them up. "Can I interest you in a drink, Amy?" he asked as he stood over one of those wheeled gold drink carts that rich people on television—and apparently real life—all seemed to have.

Unlike Charlotte, he had not appeared to dress up for this occasion. He was barefoot, in navy-blue shorts and a loose button-down shirt rolled up at the sleeves. "Water is fine for now," I said.

"Still or sparkling?"

I hesitated, not expecting a follow-up question. "Sparkling." I hoped the hesitation came off as me weighing the pros and cons of each choice rather than unworldliness.

On the coffee table between us sat a single bowl of mixed nuts. No one ate any.

"So, Amy," Charlotte said, leaning forward and looking straight at me, almost through me. She was drinking a gin and tonic. I registered that little fact about her the way I registered every other detail of her. She wore a powder-blue short-sleeve sweater and cream-colored trousers, probably her idea of casual loungewear. What struck me most, though, were her hands. Piano-player hands, my dad would have called them, thin and graceful. Her fingernails paradoxically appeared perfectly natural and impeccably manicured, shiny peach ovals. "Where did you come from?"

This struck me as a strange way of phrasing the question, Where are you from?

"I'm from Oregon," I said.

"And your parents, what do they do?" Charlotte asked.

"My dad was a sculptor, up until a few years ago. My mom's a painter. She was—is—pretty good. You might have even heard of her—Margaret Linden?"

They shook their heads politely.

I pointed to the artwork hanging over the fireplace, a large-scale portrait of Rosa Parks made out of hand-knotted pieces of reclaimed fabric. "I was just admiring that piece. Jo Harrington stayed at our residency one summer."

"She's very talented," Charlotte said, seemingly unimpressed with my insider knowledge of her art acquisitions.

"Your parents ran an art residency?" Freddy's father asked, smiling encouragingly.

"I grew up there. We—uh, they were caretakers there, so we did a lot of the behind-the-scenes stuff. That's what brought me to Seven Glacier, actually. I have a real interest in hospitality. It's in the blood, you could say."

"Are you a business major?" his dad asked. He was leaning back, one arm slung along the couch, the other hand swirling his drink. Even seeing the two of them sitting right next to each other, it was hard to picture them together. Charlotte so poised and glamorous, Mason so relaxed and almost impish. A lock of his reddish hair flopped into his face, and he blew it up with a puff of breath.

"Oh, Amy doesn't go to college," Freddy piped up.

I turned my head slowly to Freddy and gave him an icy look. Then I turned back to his parents. "I'm more focused on hands-on experience," I said. "At the moment."

I couldn't tell how this little introduction was going. During the transition from the living room to the dining table, I pulled Freddy aside and whispered, "We shouldn't tell them—not yet," but he just placed a hand on my back to steer me to my seat.

"It's going great," he whispered back. "They love you."

We sat down to a dinner of a casserole that appeared to be made out of wild rice, broccoli, and pieces of chicken. "Chicken Divan," Charlotte announced. "Freddy's favorite." I wondered idly if she had made it herself. It was hard to picture her in the kitchen. In addition to the casserole was a large glass bowl filled with a green salad and a basket of buttered rolls. If I had harbored any anxieties about dining with the rich and famous, they had dissipated. No complicated place settings, overabundance of silverware, or obscure delicacies to navigate here. The Bennisons would have been more out of their element at the artists' residency where I grew up. Tofu scrambles for breakfast, avocado and sprout sandwiches on whole grain bread for lunch, and eggplant moussaka for dinner.

The evening passed pleasantly, and I was beginning to feel more at ease. Freddy had said they loved me. I saw no indication of that, but maybe this was how they expressed their love, with stilted dinner conversation and mixed drinks and simple, down-home food.

And then Freddy announced, "Mom, Dad, we're having a baby. Amy's pregnant."

Freddy had said he couldn't wait to see the look on her face, so maybe I was expecting something more dramatic, her head swiveling around to glare at Freddy or choking on her drink. Her expression, as far as I could tell, remained completely neutral. A very small smile, so small it was almost undetectable, hovered on her lips. "A baby," she said. Then she turned to me. "Amy, how far along are you now?"

"I'm due on February fifth."

"And you have . . . explored your options?"

"Mom!" Freddy snapped. "Listen, we've worked it out. I'm finishing school. Amy can stay with me in the apartment and then—"

"She certainly can NOT," Charlotte said.

"Charlotte," I said, and then she did give me a look, as if I had slapped her in the face. For a millisecond, I couldn't understand what I had done. Then it hit me. "Mrs. Bennison," I amended. It sounded false to me. Growing up with my parents, among artists, I called all adults by their first names. Honorifics were reserved for elementary school teachers and maybe the stray octogenarian. "It's just until Freddy finishes school. By the summer—"

"You plan to raise a baby in a student apartment? Are Jeremiah and Michael aware of this plan?"

"Mom, we figured it out—" What we had figured was that I could stay with Freddy in his room and Jeremiah and Michael could continue staying in the second bedroom up until winter break. By then I'd be almost due and we would ask the guys to find other living arrangements for the last semester, and we could turn the second bedroom into a nursery. Freddy explained this to his parents, though he had lost some of the resolve he had had on our walk over, making the whole idea sound childish and ill-conceived.

"That was not the agreement, Frederick," his mother said. "You have an obligation to those boys. You really expect them to move out over winter break? How is that going to work?"

Freddy shot me a look that said See what I have to deal with?, and then he turned back to his mom, straightening up. "Mom, we have it taken care of."

"You obviously do not" was all she said.

"More chicken anyone?" asked Mason. He lifted the casserole dish up and raised his eyebrows. I let him dish more onto my plate and exclaimed over how delicious everything was.

Freddy was looking over at me. This time, his look said, Remember what we said. Stick to the plan.

"Mrs. Bennison," I started again, keeping my voice light.

Freddy relaxed in his chair, smiling at me encouragingly.

"You are absolutely right." I didn't look at Freddy. I knew what his expression would say this time: What are you doing? This is not what we planned. You are going rogue! I had originally imagined buttering up to Charlotte slowly, perhaps starting with asking if I could shadow her on the job. I would impress her with my shrewd observations, maybe even swoop in with a brilliant suggestion that would save the day—"a simple plated menu instead of a buffet cuts down on food waste"—and Charlotte would be so impressed that she would hire me on as her personal consultant. But now I saw another way in. A quicker way in.

"It wouldn't be right, asking Jeremiah and Michael to move out. And Freddy should enjoy his senior year. He doesn't need his pregnant girlfriend tagging along with him everywhere."

"Amy—" Freddy interjected, but I ignored him.

"I may have a solution that works for all of us," I suggested. "I've already talked about my interest—passion, really—in hospitality. And

I worked at the front desk at Seven Glacier all summer; I already know what goes into the work there."

Freddy got up then, pushing his chair back with such force it almost toppled over. He raised his hands to his head. "Amy, no, this wasn't the plan!"

But Charlotte and Mason exchanged a look. With that look, I finally saw it, what linked them together. She was all business, cool and decisive. He was the fun one, the people person. Together, they were a business powerhouse, making decisions together. That was how we could be one day. Freddy and I. Only he didn't see it yet. He didn't have the vision.

Gently, I reached over, placing a hand on Freddy's leg. He sat back down.

"You want a job," Mason stated. He looked pleased with himself.

"I think we could manage that," Charlotte said. "We have just the place."

CHAPTER 7

AMY

By the time we reached the summit, Ramona was visibly distressed. Cheeks flushed, shirt drenched in sweat, the side of her face plastered with tendrils of hair. I led her to a wide, flat rock and instructed her to breathe deeply. "We should have rested more along the way," I said. "I always forget how difficult the ascent is." I handed her a second bottle of water and she drank from it in large gulps. "Careful," I warned.

After she had caught her breath and I plied her with dried fruit and the sandwiches I'd packed from the restaurant, I pulled her back up to standing. "Look at that." I couldn't keep the tremble from my voice, and I swept my arm over the view dramatically, like a game show host. Like a religious figure from an old-time movie. *The Ten Commandments*, maybe. Look at this splendor before us! I wanted to cry out. Behind us were the switchbacks traversing the rocky terrain we had just ascended. The rock we stood on sat on a strip of land no wider than an old country road. Ahead of us, the land dipped down, a steep ravine plummeting thousands of feet to the valley floor. From this vantage point, we could see the entire park spread out before us to the west, an intricate quilt of forests and mountain ranges stitched together with silver threads of rivers. And then on the east, the mountains ended and the plains began, spreading out for miles and miles until they dipped down below the horizon.

"Best view in the park," I said. "But a bit of a trek."

"It's incredible," Ramona agreed.

We stood there for many minutes, letting it sink in. Wind whistled past our ears, whipped our hair back. I wanted to tell her how happy I was to be here with her, to show her this. I wanted to say something trite, something like, it really puts everything into perspective, doesn't it, standing on top of the world like this. You stand up there, just a tiny little speck, and the world is so big, bigger than you ever imagined. Nothing you could ever do makes a difference, in the end. No matter how good. Or how terrible.

I didn't say anything, though, and after a while Ramona asked how we were supposed to get back down.

"It's a loop," I said. "Hence the name." I pointed along the ridge and said we were coming up to the easy part, a two-mile walk along the ridge, on even ground. I didn't tell her that some of the path would be very narrow, carved out of the sides of the cliff. I was keeping her spirits up. Then four miles back down to where we started.

As soon as we had rounded a bend, out of the wind, Ramona began to prod me for more details. "Freddy's parents were going to get you a job," she prompted.

"Right."

"They were supportive."

"Not exactly."

"They didn't get you a job?"

"Sure, they got me a job. But Charlotte . . ." I trailed off.

"What?"

"She's a bitch."

"Amy!"

"I'm just saying, I admired her so much, you know? I basically wanted to *be* her. For me, she was like a celebrity. It's like if you met . . . I don't know. Harry Styles."

"You think I'm into Harry Styles?" Ramona was laughing.

"You know what I mean. I idolized her."

"Charlotte Bennison," Ramona mused. "Is she still alive?" I caught a hint of hope in her voice. "She probably isn't even that old!"

I knew where this was heading. "I doubt it," I said. "She's probably long gone by now. Or senile. And even if she wasn't, trust me, you wouldn't want to meet her."

"That's my grandmother."

Ramona was getting all excited again. Somehow I was always leading the conversation down these roads I didn't want to go down and didn't know how to get off. If we had had any sort of reception way up here on the top of the world, I knew Ramona would be whipping out her phone and looking her up. Oh look, here she is, oh great, I think I'll just give her a call right now. I imagined accidentally knocking the phone from Ramona's hands, where it would smash into a million pieces. No, better: I imagined grabbing it from her hands and hurling it down the ravine. Whoops.

"Listen, Ramona, it was tough, taking care of a newborn. After everything I had been through—I went through a lot, those last few months. And Charlotte—"

"Wait, what?"

Ramona had been walking ahead of me, and she stopped dead in her tracks so fast that I crashed into her. Our boots slid on the gravel path, and her foot slipped out from under her, down the ravine. With both hands, I grabbed her by the pack and righted us both, pulling us back to the center of the path.

Down the ravine, loose pieces of earth had broken free, were still plummeting down below.

"Careful!" I said needlessly.

Ramona turned to face me. "What do you mean?" she asked.

"What do I mean about what?"

"You said it was hard taking care of a newborn."

"Right," I said slowly, not understanding her confusion.

"I was adopted as an infant."

"I thought you knew all this stuff. You found the birth certificate. You must have adoption records or something."

"It was never a secret or anything. I mean, we celebrate my adoption day every year. April fifteenth."

"And your birthday is February fifth. You were born on your due date. Right on time."

She bit her lower lip, trying to work out the math.

"So you knew you weren't adopted right at birth," I prompted. "Who did you think took care of you, in the beginning?"

"I just thought—I guess I thought it was just paperwork. Like it took time to process the adoption papers, or . . . I don't know."

"I did. I took care of you."

~

I wrote my parents a postcard because I couldn't bear to call, and a letter left too much room for elaboration. The postcard was one of those illustrated vintage ones, with "Greetings from New York City!" in block letters over a silhouette of the skyline, a different tourist attraction in every letter. I wrote in my tiniest writing with a black ballpoint pen:

> Hi Mom and Dad (and Alex!), Greetings from NEW YORK! Great news. My hard work at Seven Glacier finally paid off. Charlotte Bennison (of Bennison Hotel Group) took a special interest in me and offered me a job at one of their boutique hotels in Brooklyn. You would love it. Art on the walls in every room (a mural by Duncan Jones!!! in the lobby), views of Manhattan from the rooftop. So sorry for the late notice. Terrible timing but great opportunity! WILL SEND MONEY SOON! LOVE to all, Amy

Yes, I left out some details. I left out the part about moving here with Freddy, the arguments he had with his parents, who didn't exactly hand me the job at the Hedgewick because of my reputation as a hard worker at Seven Glacier. I left out a return address, a phone number. And the part about being six months pregnant. I wanted to tell them, and I would tell them. I was just trying to figure out the best way to go about it.

One shock at a time, I figured. First, I wouldn't be coming home to take care of my dad when Alex started high school. I had no idea what they would do without me. Alex would go back to school. There was no question about that. He had to finish high school. My mom could be around most of the time, but not all the time. When I had last talked to my mom, she said my dad was responding well to a new treatment. Some days, he was almost back to his old self, full of energy, going out to his studio and working on a new project. Wasn't that what she had told me? I tried to remember. "Almost back to his old self." I was sure she had used those exact words.

My dad was not a reliable reporter. Every time I asked him how he was doing, he said the same thing: "Same old, same old." He didn't want to spend our phone calls going over his medications, symptoms, or alternative therapies, so we didn't. We talked about our lives, about art. He gave me the report from my older brother, Robert, who was now, according to my dad, living with his girlfriend on a cooperative farm in Idaho or somewhere. So much for that degree in software engineering.

If it was true what my mom had said ("Almost back to his old self"), then maybe me moving off to New York wouldn't be such a horrible thing. Maybe, after they had gotten used to this new development, I could spring the second shock on them: Guess what, Mom and Dad? You're going to be grandparents!

～

January, the tail end of the holiday rush. I worked alone at the front desk at the Hedgewick, checking in the occasional guest, answering phones. Freddy called near the end of my shift, asking if I wanted to meet him near campus when I got off. "A bunch of us are getting together. Should be a good time."

Outside the glass front doors of the lobby, snow fell. It was beautiful, I supposed, the way the snow lit up through the amber glare of the streetlights. "It's snowing," I said. It was freezing out. While technically the distance between us was less than three miles, in this weather, it felt insurmountable. Bundling up in the gigantic coat I had found in a thrift store, stepping into ill-fitting boots, trudging to the subway stop, etc., etc., all while nine months pregnant, just so I could sit in an overpriced bar with Freddy and his college buddies did not strike me as "a good time" at all.

"I could send a car," Freddy said. "Or I could come to you." He lowered his voice then, and I could picture him in the common space in his apartment, at one end of the floral hand-me-down couch draped in a striped Mexican blanket. Chatter in the background, Jeremiah and Michael laughing.

I softened then. He wanted to see me. After all this, he wanted to see me. He wasn't embarrassed to hang out with me, his twenty-one-year-old girlfriend from southern Oregon, heavy with child. When his friends looked at me, they viewed me as a curiosity. They asked probing questions, as if trying to get to the bottom of it, my whole "situation."

"Is Sam going to be there?"

Long pause. "I think so. She's cool, though. She likes you. She told me that."

I laughed. "Right." Freddy had broken up with Sam as soon as we moved here. Their "arrangement" didn't accommodate knocking up another woman, he assured me. It was over between him and her. From now on, it was just the two of us. Freddy and Amy forever. And soon, the three of us. She took the news well, Freddy had reported. In fact, she wanted to meet me. And so I had spent an awkward night out in a bar with Freddy, his ex-girlfriend Sam, his roommates, and a handful of other people I was introduced to and promptly forgot. We met in some hole-in-the-wall college place with dartboards, pool tables, and cheap beers that came by the pitcher.

I was expecting someone outgoing and flamboyant, the female version of Freddy. I expected her to be blond and bubbly, though later I wasn't sure how I had created that impression. Instead she was sensible, almost plain, her hair pulled back in a messy knot with a stray hair elastic, as if she had done it in thirty seconds without looking in a mirror. She wore no makeup. She was double majoring in political science and social work.

It was funny that Sam—with her total lack of pretension, her serious green eyes trained on me, as if she really wanted to get to know me, to understand me—gave me an inferiority complex when Freddy's parents' lifestyles-of-the-rich-and-famous didn't. Her disheveled hair and lack of makeup had a curious effect, somehow making her seem thoughtful and worldly, as if she were above all the usual petty trappings of femininity. She asked me questions about where I grew up, about working at Seven Glacier, and listened carefully to my answers, never breaking eye contact. She wasn't condescending, not in the least. If anything she came off as interested—*very* interested, the way an anthropologist might take notes on a newly discovered tribe.

It was hard to explain, then, why I didn't want to hang out with her again. I wished I could say she treated me like a charity case, but it was more as if, around her, I *felt* like a charity case. Sam—like Freddy, and the rest of their friends—was heading down one path, and that path was closed to me. They were effortless and cool, and I was pathetic and dowdy in my pregnancy uniform, the voluminous button-down and black pants that I thought made me look like Uma Thurman but maybe made me look exactly who I was, a college dropout who got pregnant too young and didn't have the money for any cute maternity clothes.

"You sure you don't want me to come to you?" Freddy was asking me. "I could bring dinner."

"It's okay," I said. "You should go out. Enjoy yourself while you can." We made comments like this a lot these days, as we prepared for the baby's arrival. Although Freddy's life wouldn't be changing so much, would it? At least right away. He would stay in the apartment with Jeremiah and Michael until he finished college, graduated. That was the plan. I had signed off on that. I had practically orchestrated the whole thing! If I ever started feeling resentful, I would remind myself of that. I wanted it this way.

"I'll come over tomorrow."

"I have to work tomorrow. You could study in the lobby, though. We could head out after my shift. There's a new Ethiopian place that just opened down the street."

As soon as we hung up, the phone rang again. "Hedgewick Hotel," I answered in a singsong voice. I thought it was Freddy again, calling to deliver some extraneous piece of information, or some new detail that would lure me, his heavily pregnant girlfriend, out into the cold and snow. Despite everything, Freddy still wanted me, wanted us to be together. I almost couldn't believe it sometimes, my good fortune. If you could call it that.

"Amy?" A young male voice was on the other line.

"Alex?" My little brother. "How did you find me?" Not the most elegant greeting. "I mean, I forgot to give you my phone number. I'm sorry; I've been trying to pull together some extra cash—"

"You didn't make it easy," he said. And then, in the same breath: "Dad's sick."

"What?"

"He's in the hospital. You should probably come home."

"What happened? I thought he was doing better!"

"What made you think that?"

"He was back to his old self," I said stupidly, though I couldn't remember if my mom had actually told me that or if I had just imagined her saying it because I wanted it to be true. These months in New York, growing bigger by the day, I had been picturing the three of them at home. Better off without me, I reasoned. One less mouth to feed. My teenage brother didn't have to share a bedroom with his own sister in that crappy apartment—I was actually helping out more this way, by leaving home, by making money. Not that it had exactly worked out that way.

And also (my imagination continued), my dad was getting better by the day in my absence. Back to his old self. The flare-ups dying down to nothing. His agility returning to his hands. His balance so good he could not only stay steady on two feet, he could balance on one leg with his hands spread out like wings.

"He was doing okay, maybe," Alex was saying. "Same old, same old, like he always says, right? But then he got pneumonia. He's on a ventilator."

"Will he be okay?" My heart was beating too rapidly now. A thirtysomething couple opened the lobby doors, sending in a gust of ice-cold wind. They rolled their bags over to the side and appeared to be consulting with each other.

"You should come home," Alex said. "At least for a week or something."

The couple came up to the desk. Into the phone I chirped, "Thank you for calling!" and placed the receiver back in the cradle.

That night I couldn't fall asleep. Freddy's parents had offered me a room in the basement floor of the Hedgewick, a ten-by-twelve-foot room with concrete walls painted white, with exposed pipes that snaked up the sides and across the ceiling. Along one wall was a kitchenette consisting of a dorm fridge, hot plate, microwave, and sink. In the corner was a single bed that barely fit me and my protruding abdomen and definitely not me and Freddy. Perhaps that was by design. Up by the ceiling were two windows facing an alleyway with bars on them for safety. It was warm, very warm. That was the only good thing about it.

Once the baby was born, Freddy and I were going to find our own place. I could hardly raise a baby in a hotel basement reminiscent of a prison cell. Is that what Charlotte Bennison would want for her granddaughter? It was a girl. I found out after my first prenatal appointment, soon after I met Freddy's parents. They handled all that. I was grateful, too. I really was.

I tossed and turned on my narrow cot, trying to find a comfortable position, arranging and rearranging the pillows, elevating my feet, then my back. Nothing helped. I was working up a sweat. Every night, the pipes creaked and clanked, like I was living in the boiler room of some Victorian dungeon. If someone flushed in one of the rooms above, I could hear it, hear the water rushing. I closed my eyes and tried not to think of anything, tried not to think of my dad. Especially not that.

Inside me, the baby mimicked my struggles, twisting and turning in her dark pool of amniotic fluid. She pressed her hands and feet to the walls of my womb so hard I could make out their shapes, the tiny little fingers and toes. I fell asleep sometime in the middle of the night, exhausted, overheated, and I had the dreams I'd been having since I moved into this place, spurred by the sounds of water gushing and then dripping down the pipes. Dreams of water. My own face, sinking below the surface, my eyes open in terror, unable to breathe. Every time, I shot straight up in bed, gasping for breath. I covered my ears with my hands like a young child and tried to block out the sounds. The clanking and the gushing and the incessant drip, drip, dripping.

I called home every day and talked to my mother, my two brothers, but not my father. He was always resting, they said, or in the middle of some procedure. When would they release him from the hospital, I kept asking, and they didn't really answer. They said I should come home. I told Freddy and he told me to go, he would pay for the plane tickets, but I couldn't fly, not when I was full term. I could take the train, maybe. But that would take four trains and three days. I imagined giving birth in a train bathroom, the car jostling over the tracks, somewhere in the middle of North Dakota. Showing up at my dad's bedside with a newborn swaddled in an Amtrak blanket.

Five days later my mother called the front desk of the hotel at ten o'clock at night. I was already in my cell, thrashing on my cot with dreams of drowning. Janelle was working at the front desk on her own. We were never supposed to leave our stations, but my mother insisted, and so Janelle came down and pounded on my door.

I ran upstairs in drawstring sleep shorts and a man's tank top stretched taut over my abdomen. No one was in the lobby then, to see me in my panic. No one but Janelle, who stood by my side and placed a hand on my arm as my mother told me the news. My dad had died. My mother seemed so calm about it, as if she had been expecting it, but I hadn't been expecting it at all. He would be back to his old self! Same old, same old! That is what she had told me, and I had just kept repeating those words over and over until I believed them.

I missed my dad's last days. I missed the funeral. I missed moving out of that basement room at the Hedgewick Hotel and into a new place with Freddy. I missed my own baby's birth. Oh, I was there, obviously. But afterward, I truly couldn't remember anything about it. I pieced together the details later, from what people told me. The pregnancy and childbirth books I had been reading had prepared me for the pain, given me the vocabulary to understand all the ways the medical establishment might interfere with what should be a natural process. I had been prepared to reject the drugs, the episiotomy, the forceps. I had a birth plan. What they hadn't prepared me for was how to articulate that birth plan when, blunted from grief, I could barely string together a coherent sentence.

I wasn't screaming or crying out in pain, they told me later. I wasn't barking orders at harried nurses or thrashing around on the bed the way women giving birth did on television. My eyes stayed closed and I sat clutching my abdomen as it contracted, the entire rounded belly clenching, changing shape beneath my fingers and then rounding out again. I stayed so still through the discomfort they wondered if I had fallen asleep. And maybe I did fall asleep, in a way, in a waking dream, because when the contractions got closer, I started to dream, that same dream about sinking underwater, deeper and deeper. If I remember anything from childbirth, it was that dream, that terrifying dream.

Freddy said my eyes shot open when the baby was coming, when it was time to push. The doctor told me to push and I did, but it was all on instinct, a primal response, because I was still dreaming. I was sinking to the bottom of a lake, to the murky slime forty, fifty feet below the surface, staring up to the top as if through a tunnel, with only a tiny pinprick of light at the end.

The next thing I remembered was being home, in our new apartment. Freddy placed a baby in my arms. Ramona. We named her Ramona. I had chosen it after my favorite character in the books I had loved as a child.

I felt like I was dreaming all the time, then, whether I was asleep or awake. And it wasn't just me anymore, drowning. It was the baby. The baby with her dark curls—a full head of hair, right from the beginning!—her large trusting eyes open and staring up at me, floating in the water. In a lake or maybe in a bath, the warm water lapping around her. My hands on top of her, pushing down—

NO! If I was asleep, I would jolt up in bed. If I was awake, I would startle, find myself on a chair, the baby in my arms, safe. Safe. My heart would take minutes to settle down. I would hold her closer and whisper in her ear, You're safe. I would never hurt you. Never, never.

This went on for weeks. I was going through the motions, changing diapers, changing clothes, breastfeeding. I didn't feel what I was supposed to feel, though. So much of what we do is ruled by the hormones surging through our bodies. Adrenaline fires us up, surges through our veins and allows us to perform superhuman feats. Dopamine infuses us with happiness. Pheromones pull us toward one another, fill us with desire.

And then there's love. Oxytocin warms the heart. After sex, or after childbirth, there it is. For women, it comes in stronger than with men. That's what they say. Have sex with a stranger and think you're in love? That's the hormones talking. They come in most powerfully, though, after childbirth, bonding us instantly to our newborn babes. Or that was what was supposed to happen.

I didn't feel it, that surge of love. It's indescribable, the feeling of love you have for your baby, the women said in all those books. It's like nothing else on earth, this sense that you would do anything for this baby to protect it, to nurture it.

When she cried, I picked her up. When she was hungry, I fed her. But I couldn't feel it, that warm rush of love and devotion, that motherly instinct. I wondered if I was broken.

One day when Freddy was in class and I was left alone with the baby, Charlotte paid me a visit. She had visited many times before, but always with Freddy around. She would hold the baby, even smile down at her and admire her beautiful curls, but she would always hand her right back the second Ramona writhed or fussed. I came to the door with my hair a mess, spit-up dried on my shirt. "Freddy's not here," I said by way of greeting, assuming she would apologize for her mistake and get going. Instead, she wormed her way inside the apartment.

I hadn't been expecting her visit and therefore hadn't done my usual preparation. The place was a mess: the sink piled high with dishes, the countertops cluttered with open food containers and unopened mail, the floors littered with limp laundry. Charlotte put her hands on her hips and surveyed the destruction. Not disapproving, exactly. More like she was assessing the damage the way she might do for one of her hotels, tallying up a to-do list and preparing to delegate tasks to a team of experts. "Amy," she said after a lengthy pause. "You've got to pull yourself together." And then she started bustling around the place the way people are always doing in books when someone has been laid up in bed for far too long, withering away in some dark room at a forgotten wing of a crumbling old mansion. She opened up the blinds, letting the sunlight stream in the room. She wiped down counters and gathered dirty clothes into a pile. All the while I sat on the couch—a brand-new couch, purchased by Freddy's parents—with the baby in my arms. I watched her with curiosity but didn't get up to help. I was too tired.

That evening, I put Ramona to bed in the little bassinet we kept in the corner of our only bedroom, and then Freddy came home with a pizza, which we ate straight out of the box, sitting on the couch in front of the television. He ate an entire slice before bringing up his mother's visit.

"She told you about that?" I asked.

"Don't be mad," Freddy said, holding his hands up. "I asked her to."

"Asked her to what?"

"To check on you."

"I don't need anyone to check on me."

We both stared ahead, looking at the television. It was early in the evening, so we were watching *Entertainment Tonight*. I never used to watch these shows. Oscar buzz. Brad and Jen. More speculation on Princess Di's death, a year and a half later. After a while I could feel Freddy's head swivel to look at me, and when I looked back, he turned off the television. "Amy," he said, and by the way he said my name I knew I was in for some sort of serious discussion.

I sighed. "I'm doing better. Ramona's sleeping in longer stretches—that helps."

"Yeah, that's good."

"The house was a mess when your mom came over, but that's because I had no warning. I would have tidied up a bit—"

"It's not about being tidy. You think that's what I care about?" Freddy raised his voice and I shushed him.

"The baby!" I whispered.

"You were saying some crazy things."

"When?"

"After the baby was born."

The weeks leading up to the birth, the birth itself, the first—what, month?—after delivery all blended together, leaving me only with scraps of memory, a jumbled blur of images and sounds. Even after we moved to our new place, I swore I could still hear the water rushing through those pipes in my basement room at the Hedgewick. *Drip, drip, drip, drip—gush!*

I knew I was out of it, barely going through the motions, but this is the first I had heard of incoherent ravings. "Like what?" I was curious, mostly. But also, I will admit, nervous.

"There was something you kept saying, over and over. Every time you said it, you got more upset."

"I wasn't in my right mind. I was having all these dreams."

"You kept saying 'I did it all for them,'" Freddy said. "I kept trying to ask you what you meant but you wouldn't explain it. 'I did it all for them. I DID IT ALL FOR THEM!'" Freddy did a passable impression of me in my delirium, the way I crumpled my face in anguish, my hands grasping at my hair. He really should major in theater arts. I had assumed he *was* majoring in theater arts until we moved here and he informed me he was getting his degree in business administration, just like his dad.

I shrugged. "Who knows what was going through my mind at the time? It's just—you know, I told you this already. Like working at Seven Glacier. Coming here to New York, getting the job at the hotel. It was all this big plan I had to work my way up in the world, you know? I never finished college, like you. My parents can't give me all these opportunities, get me the right job or buy me an apartment or whatever. But I thought—I guess I thought I could do that, for them. For the baby. I had this crazy plan that I would, I don't know, make it to the top somehow, make all this money, and then I'd save them all. I'd get the best medical care money would buy and get them out of that awful apartment . . . on one level I knew it was stupid, but part of me really believed it, deep down."

Freddy said, "You moved here to be with me. Because you were pregnant."

"Yes, I know, but—"

"Are you saying you got pregnant on purpose? All so my mom would get you a job in a hotel?"

"Freddy, don't be ridiculous. I don't even remember saying that. I'm just trying to come up with a plausible explanation for some stupid thing I was screaming during a fever dream. 'I did it all for them.' It could mean anything. It could mean nothing."

Freddy didn't look as if he believed me, but his expression softened. "Look, I'm sorry."

"What kind of plan would that be, anyway? I don't need to get *pregnant* to move to New York or make minimum wage at the front desk of a hotel."

"No, you're right. You're right."

"And if I was *trying* to get pregnant, I would have had sex with you more than that one time, don't you think? I mean, to increase the odds."

"Babe! You're right. You win."

"But it's like—whatever I did, whatever I did to get where I am today, I did it for my dad. I did it for Ramona, so she wouldn't go through what I did growing up, having to leave the only home I ever knew, sacrifice my education, all that. I did it because I was trying to make things better." I felt myself getting worked up. The pressure in my sinuses, the tears welling up. This time, I let them spill down my cheeks. Every time I thought of my dad, this happened. It could come out of nowhere. I had been in denial right up until the end. It wasn't terminal, his condition, so I kept thinking it would eventually get better. I kept thinking there would be some treatment he hadn't tried, or some new miracle drug that would get him back to his old self. Or, if I was trying to be realistic, I might have conceded that he might never get better—he might lose more independence as his condition worsened, might lose his balance more often and have to move around in a wheelchair—but I didn't think he would *die*.

I would have done anything for my dad to make it better. And Freddy didn't know—how could he?—the lengths I would go to help my dad. The lengths I had gone. Whatever I did, I did it for him, but then he died. It was too late. So what was the point?

Freddy put his arms around me, and I wilted onto his chest, heaving with sobs.

"It's okay," he said. "I've got you."

CHAPTER 8

——

AMY

There's an art to telling a story. A good story has interesting details. Not all the details. As a storyteller, it's up to you to decide what to leave in, what to leave out to make the most compelling narrative. You have to consider your audience. And so I told Ramona I struggled after my father died, and I had a hard time those first few weeks after she was born ("You probably had postpartum depression," she said, with the air of authority young people educated by the internet always have), but I didn't tell her I had been afraid to be alone with her. That I let Freddy bathe her because if I heard so much as the taps turn on, I would get that vision, a glimpse into that nightmare that she was drowning, her innocent baby face, eyes wide open underwater, and my hands pushing her down.

How can you tell someone that? You can't. And so you don't. You leave that out. I couldn't tell how Ramona was taking it, hearing about how difficult it had been for me, how ill-equipped I had been to take care of her, my first baby. It was hard to gauge her reaction while we hiked. She rarely interrupted me as I talked. When I did get a look at her face, to get a sense of her reaction, her mouth was set in a thin, tight line.

∼

We reached the most treacherous section of the trail, where a fifteen-inch ledge was carved out of the side of a cliff and you had to shimmy along it with your back to the rock face, hanging on to a rope guardrail fastened into crevices of the rock with heavy-duty bolts. It was terrifying but exhilarating, inching along this ledge with the whole world spread out beneath you, all those snowy mountain peaks and ripples of foothills.

"I'm not going on that," Ramona said, her hands clenching each strap of her backpack like it was a parachute.

"It's not so bad," I said. "And we won't be on it very long—five minutes and we're around the other side."

"I can't do it."

"I was scared, too, the first time I did it. But there's no other choice."

"We could turn around and go back down."

"We could," I admitted. "But that would add four miles to the hike. We get around this ledge, and we're home free. Three and a half miles back down to the parking lot. Look, we'll take it slow, one step at a time. We'll hang on to this rope." I gave the rope a couple strong yanks. "See? It'll hold us."

I moved my backpack to the front of my body and stepped onto the ledge. Then I sidestepped along it, my hands behind me, holding on to the rope. "See? No problem!" I announced.

Ramona appeared to be deliberating. Then she slung her backpack around her body and stepped up beside me. I guided us along, narrating our advancement to the other side. "So just a few more steps, and the ledge will get a lot wider. This here is the narrowest part. Another ten feet along the ledge, and we'll be on the other side."

Beside me Ramona breathed heavily, inhaling and exhaling with such force she was almost hyperventilating. I placed my hand over hers, which was clinging to the rope for dear life. *"Shh,"* I said. "It's okay. Just a few more steps."

The narrow path opened wider, and when we both arrived there safely, Ramona let out a relieved "Whew!" and then laughed nervously.

"You did it!" I looked over at my daughter, her beautiful young face, the dark tendrils of hair that had fallen from her ponytail floating through the thin alpine air. She was taking in the view, that magnificent view, and she was smiling then, amazed at herself for what she had just accomplished, what we had just done.

And then it came to me in a flash, unbidden, like a subliminal message slipped into a filmstrip, a flicker of an image that pulses by you so fast you barely register it all, the image of my hands reaching out and pushing, Ramona's body slipping off the edge of the cliff and hurtling down below, wheeling down.

I gasped and stepped as far away as I could from Ramona, as far as I could possibly get on this wider section of the ledge the size of a twin bed.

"What?" Ramona looked over at me, alarmed. "What happened?"

I tried to laugh it off. "I forgot to tell Jonathan where we were going," I said. "I didn't even leave a note." Oh my god. That made it worse. No one knew we were here. No one on earth. If Ramona did have an accident on this trail, what then? There would be no one left to ask any more questions. No one to tell this story to. Everything that happened would stay exactly where it belonged. In the past.

I closed my eyes shut, very tightly, trying to rid myself of the image, the image of my hands on her back—

"Amy, what's wrong?"

The image of her face, her little baby face, sinking underwater—

"I'm fine." I opened my eyes, perhaps a little too widely, and tried to smile. "I'll go ahead first. We shouldn't be standing so close together on the ledge. Wait until I disappear around the corner before you start."

"Why?"

"It's standard procedure," I said. "I should have remembered for that first stretch. Along this ledge, we need to space out. Way out." I made my way along the ledge, my heart pounding. Ramona followed my instructions, waiting until I rounded the bend. A few more steps and I was off the ledge, back on solid ground. "Okay!" I yelled.

I scampered up the path, away from the cliff, so that when Ramona emerged, I was far ahead of her. "Hey," she said once she caught up to me. "What's the rush?"

"We did it!" I exclaimed, raising my hand up so she could slap it. Then I threw my arms around her. My heart was still beating wildly, like a trapped bird, so fast and loud I feared she could feel it, but I didn't let go. I held her, pulled her in as tight as I could. "My beautiful girl," I said. "We made it. We're safe."

~

By the time we returned back to the lodge, it was past seven, right before sunset. She wanted to go back to her room to shower and change, but I insisted we head straight to the dining room. "We need to replenish," I said. If we went back and changed, we might tire out and miss dinner, and it was essential that we get a good meal in after a long day of hiking. This is what I said, and it was true, of course, but also, I wanted to keep her from making any telephone calls. There was only so long I could hold her off. I knew that. Nothing I had told her had convinced her to just forget about Freddy Bennison.

We straggled in, our hair tangled from the wind, our hiking clothes limp and rumpled, and we ran straight into Jonathan and Gabe, right in the middle of the lobby.

"Amy!" Jonathan was typically an extremely easygoing person, but his eyes darted over me, frantic, as if he were inspecting me for injuries. "Where have you been?" He rushed toward me, embracing me, and then I felt little arms circle my waist and heard Gabe's high, sweet voice.

"Mom!"

I hugged them both, rumpling Gabe's hair. "I'm so sorry," I said. "I should have left a note."

The two of them stepped back, and only then did Jonathan register Ramona standing next to me, a tentative smile hovering on her lips.

"This is—ah—" I hesitated.

"Ramona." Ramona extended her hand for Jonathan to shake. "Ramona Crawford." She leaned down and smiled at Gabe, a real smile, warm and inviting. "And you must be Gabe!"

Gabe inched closer to his father, but he looked up at her with a friendly, curious expression.

"I ran into Amy in the lobby this morning when I was asking the front desk for a good hike recommendation. She told me I had to see Ridgeline Loop—"

I nodded, playing along. "But she needed a ride to the trailhead, and I offered to take her there myself."

Jonathan was frowning slightly. This story was not coming together very well. Since when did I volunteer to offer chauffeur and hiking concierge services to guests? We weren't even working here, not exactly—we were supposed to be on vacation.

"Full disclosure, I'm a huge fan of Amy's work. She's like—like Harry Styles for me."

"Harry Styles?" Jonathan repeated.

"I mean, she's famous. I'm a hospitality major," Ramona said.

Jonathan's face lit up then, as if this *did* make sense. "Oh, right!"

"Right!" I said. "She wanted to pick my brain about Adventurprise Hotels and I was telling her about the Ridgeline Loop and one thing led to another and I was offering to drive her—I really should have left a note, though. I got all swept up—I mean, it's not often you meet a fan."

"Her number one fan," Ramona added, gilding the lily a bit, if I could be completely honest, but still, I looked over at her and smiled gratefully.

"Have you eaten dinner yet?" I asked my husband and son. They had not. The four of us found a table in the dining room. By the time our food arrived, it was dark outside and many of the other diners had already finished, leaving us in the cozy glow of the lantern light.

Dinner went great, better than I could have imagined. Gabe seemed taken by Ramona, who listened patiently as he regaled her with his latest obsession, ducks. "I like all animals of course," Gabe was telling her. "But ducks are my *particular* favorite." We ordered dessert, with all of us insisting that Ramona try the huckleberry cheesecake, a house special. Gabe had his usual, a huckleberry milkshake, which he let me take spoonfuls of.

"My birthday is coming up," Gabe told Ramona. "If you want to get me a present you could get me a duck egg," he said. "I would watch over it and raise the duckling as my own."

"Any kind of duck?" Ramona asked, and she smiled over at me.

"So, Ramona," Jonathan started, talking over Gabe's recitation of his favorite duck varieties. "Where are you going to college?"

"Oberlin," she answered.

Jonathan looked thoughtful. "I didn't know they had a hospitality program. Is it new?"

"Relatively new," she said.

"Are you interested in management specifically, or going into the marketing side of things?"

"Jonathan! What's with the third degree?" I said. "How's that cheesecake, Ramona? Good, right?"

"Delicious," she said. And then to Jonathan she added, "I'm still exploring my options."

"You're smart to come here, get some real boots-on-the-ground experience." He just wouldn't stop! To be fair, it wasn't often that we met someone as passionate about the hotel industry as we were. I would probably be safe in saying that we had never met anyone as remotely passionate about hotels as the two of us, and that included Charlotte and Mason Bennison. Ramona was born, and I never went back to college. After my stint at the Hedgewick in Brooklyn, I worked at another hotel and then another, and another, each time climbing my way up another rung on the ladder.

By that time, the Bennison Hotel Group no longer had a contract with the accommodations at Seven Glacier. I applied for a position on the board of the company that did. It was as hard and as simple as that. I always knew I would come back to Seven Glacier. From dishwasher to board member. I liked to imagine myself walking through the lobby and up and down the halls, a team of hotel workers behind me taking notes on clipboards, just like Charlotte Bennison that first time I had seen her. In this fantasy I'd be wearing a floor-length gown. This was silly, of course. I knew it was. Why would I be wearing a gown? But I could picture it. I could picture it clearly. I imagined all the young seasonal workers, maybe some young girl like I had once been, watching me in admiration. Somehow, in this fantasy, Charlotte would witness me. She would be shocked but grudgingly admiring. She would turn to me and say something like, I underestimated you, Linden.

As a board member, I visited hotels around the world. When you worked in hotels, you always had somewhere to go. Somewhere comfortable and beautiful. Hotels were always someplace you might really want to go—unlike apartments, which got plunked down somewhere practical, even in the most depressing parts of town.

I was in my early thirties at that point in my life, staying at a charming little hotel in Spain, with a white stucco exterior and wrought iron balcony railings. That hotel was managed by a handsome, scruffy American. He had already worked in a hotel in Bali and another in Argentina. "Geo-arbitrage," he called it. He had ambitions to start his own hotel group one day, specializing in unique hotels in beautiful, possibly remote locations all around the world.

On that trip to Spain—that fateful trip!—I canceled my other stops and stayed in the white stucco hotel with the handsome young American, and we spent two glorious weeks together. I felt like I could tell him everything. I felt like I could . . . but I didn't. I didn't tell him about my past. It didn't seem relevant. Not exactly. And I didn't think I'd see him again, did I?

We kept seeing each other. For two years we met in hotels all around the world. Our epic romance! Two years later, I was pregnant. We met up in London for New Year's Eve, and that was when I told him. We were lying in bed, in a room with a view of the St. Paul's Cathedral, and I delivered the news gravely but matter-of-factly: I'm pregnant. This time, I knew right away. The missed period, the queasy, carsick feeling every morning, the way everything smelled stronger and worse somehow. He surprised me, though. He didn't seem upset by the news—he seemed excited.

I was the one who didn't see how it could possibly work. My job was in danger. I feared I'd be voted out soon. I was the youngest person on the board by far. I had new ideas, exciting ideas, and they were stuck in the past. He could see it very clearly, though, our future. He would join the board, and the two of us would take over. Together, we'd run the entire hotel group. Eventually, we would rename and rebrand: Adventurprise Hotels, we would call it.

He proposed right there, on our rumpled London bed, and I said yes.

In the dining room at the Seven Glacier Hotel, sitting around the table with my long-lost daughter, Jonathan was still at it, quizzing Ramona about her dreams and ambitions. He couldn't help himself. The cover story Ramona had come up with had worked, but it had worked too well, and Jonathan was getting a little *too* enthusiastic about meeting a young protégée.

"She didn't come here to learn about hotels, Jonathan," I blurted out. "She doesn't care about hotels at all."

I didn't plan on doing what I did next. The idea came to me and in an instant, I knew it was the right thing to do. Running around with Ramona, keeping her a secret, what was the point? Jonathan loved me. He would do anything for me; I was sure of that. No matter what.

I tapped my fork against my glass. "Jonathan, Gabe, I have to tell you something." The air was charged, I could feel it, a little electric spark zipping back and forth, binding us together, the four of us. This was my family! My husband, my son, my daughter. Ramona could move in with us, travel with us! Come back to Seattle with us, go to college there. She said she might drop out anyway. What else was she going to do? She needed to know who she was and where she came from. She needed me, she needed us. I was holding back from her, but

I didn't have to. We could be a family, and she wouldn't need anything or anyone else. Just us.

I placed a hand on Gabe's shoulder, and he gazed up at me the way kids do when you tell them you have a surprise for them and they think you're going to give them something they've been wanting a long time, a new toy or a spontaneous late-night trip to the ice cream shop. "Gabe, you have a new sister!"

He had always wanted a sister. He had asked Santa for a sister the last four Christmases in a row, even though by last Christmas he didn't "technically" believe in Santa Claus anymore. He wanted a sister and not a brother, he explained, because he didn't want to have to share his toys, logic he had picked up from some of his contemporaries.

"You're *pregnant?*" asked Jonathan.

"No, no, no," I clarified. "It's Ramona." I lifted up my palm and gestured over our empty dessert plates, the way one might introduce a queen. "Ramona is my daughter." I looked over at Ramona when I said it. She looked stunned, a deer in the headlights, but then her eyes—still wide from the shock—glistened. She was happy. I knew she would be.

Jonathan did a comic double take, as his understanding of our dinner guest recalibrated from aspiring hotelier to his wife's grown-up daughter. "You have a daughter?"

"It's a long story." I turned to face my son. Gabe sat quietly in his chair and tapped the tip of his spoon against the bottom of the dessert plate. "What do you think about that, Gabe? Pretty cool, right?"

He looked up at Ramona with a pained expression.

Ramona bent toward him. "I'll bet you were expecting a *little* sister."

"I mean, I kind of was," Gabe said to her. "No offense."

"None taken."

"Babies are no fun anyway," I said, as if I had planned this entire surprise from the beginning, all for Gabe's personal benefit and enjoyment. "An older sister is way better."

I would have to explain everything to her later—I hadn't *planned* on telling them, and not like that, not in the middle of the Seven Glacier dining room. It was just a gut instinct. I wanted to get it out in the open. I wanted to fold her in, I wanted her to be a part of the family, a part of us here, in this park where she was conceived.

Jonathan had already recovered. "Ramona," he said. "Wow. I'm so happy to meet you." This defused some of the tension and we all laughed. Well, all of us except for Gabe, who still sat with his arms crossed in front of him.

"You wouldn't want a baby sister anyway," Jonathan said to him now. "You wouldn't want to change diapers, would you?"

"That would be disgusting," I added.

"I wanted to teach her stuff," he said. "I would be a Good Example."

Ramona placed a hand on the back of his chair and leaned down to confide in him. "You can still teach me stuff," she said.

He perked up a bit at this. "Can you ride a bike?"

"Well, yes," she admitted.

"I'm sure there are plenty of things you could teach Ramona," I said. "And she can teach you things, too. That's what brothers and sisters do."

"I know!" Ramona said. "No . . . I couldn't ask you to do that."

I had never seen Ramona at this age, it occurred to me then, observing the two of them. My two children, twelve years apart. They didn't look anything alike, but they seemed to feel something between them already, a bond. Maybe that's what Ramona meant, how it mattered where you came from. Bloodlines connecting you, drawing you home.

"What?" Gabe was asking.

Ramona shook her head sadly. "Nah," she said. "Never mind. I couldn't ask you. It would be too hard."

"Just ask me."

"Well, all right. What if I asked you to teach me how to swim? Could you do that?"

"Yes! I can teach you right now!"

"It's almost time for bed, buddy," Jonathan said.

The dining room had cleared out. The four of us were the only ones left, sitting around the table. Sometime in the excitement of my announcement, our plates had been cleared. All the other tables had been cleaned off, and the waitstaff hovered patiently on the sidelines, waiting for us to leave so they could stack the chairs up on the tables and clean the floors. I would need to tip extra well, make up for the inconvenience.

We had already left the dining room, about to make our separate ways to go to bed, when what Ramona said hit me. Everything went silent. The lobby was hushed and quiet at that hour, but my mind went quiet, too, as if all the chatter in my brain, the excitement of our day, of the secret I'd been keeping all these years rushing out into the open turned off with the flick of a switch and all that was left was darkness, a black void. "You don't know how to swim?"

~

The next day we took Ramona to Gabe's favorite swimming spot along the shores of Seven Glacier Lake, a ten-minute walk along a shady path to a little swimming area next to a boathouse where guests could rent rowboats and paddleboards by the hour. The weather was cool, almost too cool for swimming at this time of year, but the sky arced huge and blue above us and the sun shone down, warming our skin. We had just started out, with Gabe in the lead, eager to show Ramona the way, when Gabe's foot caught on a tree root, sending him flat on his face. When he turned around, covered in dirt, the skin scraped off one knee, I could tell by the way his brows knit together that he was summoning all his energy not to cry in front of his new big sister, and I swooped in. "Oh no!" I exclaimed, bending over him and surreptitiously wiping a few errant tears from his eyes.

Little beads of ruby-red blood had begun to form on his knee. "Jonathan, do you have your pocketknife? We may need to amputate."

Now a little smile formed on Gabe's lips. He rolled his eyes up at Ramona. *"Mom."*

"I should have never let you walk down here yourself. It's too dangerous." I helped my son up to standing.

"Don't worry, I'm okay," he said, and he took a few experimental steps to demonstrate. "See?"

"We should have carried you," I said. "Or put you in one of those clear plastic bubbles and rolled you."

He was laughing by then, and we continued down the path, with Gabe instructing Ramona on the fundamentals of swimming. "You have to get comfortable in the water," he said. "You have to put your face in."

"Got it," Ramona was saying, a good sport.

"Some kids are scared to put their face in the water," he said.

"Not me," she said.

"Then why can't you swim? You're a grown-up."

"I'm not a grown-up! I'm still a kid," she said. "A college kid."

"Oh, okay." Gabe seemed satisfied with this.

Ramona told him that she was supposed to learn how to swim when she was about his age, but that was around when her parents got divorced, and it didn't wind up happening. Then the next summer, her dad's new wife had a baby, and everyone sort of forgot about swim lessons, and that just kept happening and eventually she was a teenager and it was too late to take lessons with all the other kids.

"My friends used to try to teach me, but by then I was a lost cause," Ramona told him as we spread out our towels and blankets at the base of a pine tree. Its long, dry needles coated the ground. Jonathan and I sat next to each other on the blanket as Gabe instructed Ramona to get ready for her first lesson. Obediently, she pulled her oversize T-shirt up over her head. Underneath she was wearing a simple navy-blue one-piece swimsuit.

"It's never too late," Gabe said with authority.

"I can't even float."

"Everyone can float."

"Are you wearing sunscreen?" I asked.

"I put it on at home!" Gabe cried.

"I'm asking Ramona." Her skin was very pale and smooth, as if she had spent her childhood locked up in an attic. Her dark curly hair flew through the breeze, and she lifted her hands to pull it up into a messy bun.

"Yes, Mom," Ramona joked.

We all laughed. All this subterfuge, this secret I had kept from my family, my own parents, my husband, my child, and for what? It had worked out fine. Jonathan and I stayed up late last night, and I told him about the pregnancy, about moving to New York with Freddy, about how his mom wanted me out of their lives and so I made the difficult decision to put Ramona up for adoption. My voice broke at the end, telling him that part, and Jonathan held me and whispered in my ear: I've got you, I've got you. He said I could have told him, and I said I knew that. No more secrets, I heard him say as I drifted off to sleep.

Gabe took Ramona's hand and led her into the water. She screeched from the cold.

When we got home, back to Seattle, I should throw a party for Ramona. I thought about this as I sat beside Jonathan on the shore. A "welcome to the family" party. I would invite everyone. My mother, who lived in Portland now in an artists' collective with her longtime companion, George, this weird guy with a ZZ Top–style beard who had retired from the automotive industry and now spent his time tinkering on old cars to run them on cooking oil. I'd invite my brothers, of course, and their partners, and Chloe and Zannie, Gabe's cousins. Jonathan's family could come, too, to this party, and I'd introduce Ramona to everyone and everyone would love her, welcome her right in.

This party took shape in my mind, from the dress code (I'd wear a gown, of course—all my fantasies seemed to involve gowns!) to the menu (six courses, like a royal wedding) to the decor (tasteful floral arrangements, maybe an ice sculpture—do they even make ice sculptures these days?) when I heard a splash and a shrill cry.

Gabe stood waist-deep in the lake, holding—or attempting to hold—Ramona's body on the surface of the water. Ramona's feet kept sinking down, and she laughed and splashed as she righted herself.

"Be careful!" I yelled out to them as they started the process over again, with Ramona attempting to lie down on the water, Gabe holding her up with his little arms, giving her pointers on the correct way to breathe, holding the air in her lungs to make herself buoyant.

"The water is shallow," Jonathan said to me.

"You can drown in less than two inches of water."

I leaned forward onto my knees, watching my two children in the water. Constant vigilance. That is what parenthood was, wasn't it? How many stories had I read over the years? You couldn't leave a child alone for a minute without disaster striking. I spent those first few years of Gabe's childhood bracing for impact. Don't take them down the slide on your lap—they'll break a leg. Anchor the dresser to the wall or it will tip over and crush them. They could get their little heads caught between the slats of a crib, the balusters of a handrail. Anything could happen at any moment.

"Good—good!" Gabe was coaching, and for a moment, Ramona's body seemed to hover on the surface of the water, but then her heels weighed her down and her legs slipped underneath, and then the rest of her went down, all of her, until she was gone.

I shot up and raced across the shore and straight into the water, straight toward the two of them. By the time I got to them, Ramona was already standing back up, laughing, squeezing the water from her hair with her hands, and I felt foolish.

"Mom," Gabe scolded me. "You're interrupting the lesson."

She was fine. They were both fine. I was the one breathing hard, standing up to my thighs in the lake with my clothes on. "That's enough swimming lessons for today," I said briskly.

"It's cool," Ramona said. "Gabe's a great teacher."

"No, that's enough," I said firmly. "I want you both to come in right now. It's time for lunch."

It wasn't even noon, but something about the edge in my voice convinced them to follow me back to the shore. Only after the two of them were completely out of the water, bundled up in towels and snacking on grapes, did I feel like I could relax again.

After lunch, Ramona asked if we could rent one of the rowboats. I answered, "No," at the same exact time Jonathan said, "Sure!"

"I don't know if we have time," I said.

"We have all day," Ramona said. "Come on, Amy, let's do it. Just you and me."

"You should do it," Jonathan said. "Gabe and I will rent a pedal boat."

Gabe shouted, "Yes!"

"Ramona doesn't know how to swim," I said.

"I'll wear a life jacket."

I was clearly outnumbered. "All right," I conceded. And then, not very convincingly, I added, "Let's do it!"

Ramona sat across from me and took the oars. "I'll start," she said. Almost immediately, she seemed to get the hang of it, and soon we were gliding away from the shore, away from Jonathan and Gabe in their little pedal boat. For a few moments, all I could hear was the sound of the oars pushing the water away. Dip, *swish*, dip, *swish*, dip, *swish*. I closed my eyes and tried to block it out. I gripped the sides of the boat as hard as I could to steady myself, to keep myself calm.

Then I opened my eyes and smiled at my daughter, who was still pumping away at those oars like she was born to do it, like she was paddling away from an island of cannibals or ghost pirates. "We're lucky to have this kind of weather so late in the season," I said brightly, just for something to say. "One year it even snowed on us at the end of August. The elevation is higher than what you're probably used to, so the weather is unpredictable."

The weather. I was actually talking about the weather.

Ramona stopped rowing and let the boat drift. We were in the middle of the lake. Gabe and Jonathan were a tiny dot near the shoreline.

Ramona was staring at me with a serious, almost menacing look, and that was when I knew. I knew she knew.

CHAPTER 9

RAMONA

Something Amy had said to me on my first night at Seven Glacier kept nagging at me: Trust me, Ramona, she had said. He won't necessarily be happy to hear from you.

From what I could figure, there could be two main reasons why Freddy wouldn't be happy to hear from me: either he had residual feelings of guilt about giving me up, or he wanted to forget about my existence.

Amy had said he was a nice guy. From how she told the story, it certainly sounded as though he had risen to the challenge. He could have simply left Amy on her own or handed her a couple hundred dollars and told her to "take care of it." He didn't, though. He moved her to New York with him, I was born, and then they put me up for adoption. Cue the guilt. You know what, I told myself, if that was the case, it wasn't my problem. He needed to deal with it; he owed me that much.

Or, maybe he had some great new life now like Amy did. When we finally reconnected, she didn't tell me about Jonathan or Gabe. Even in Seattle, when mentioning her new life, her family, would have been the natural thing to do, she didn't. I couldn't say I wasn't hurt by it, but I also, at some level, understood. I was a secret.

Perhaps Freddy wanted to keep me a secret, too. He was, according to my online sleuthing, successful. The son of rich hotel magnates, of course he was. He sat on the board of Bennison Hotels, he worked as the chief marketing director at the New York headquarters, he undoubtedly made bundles of money and would inherit millions more. His long-lost daughter's return could throw him off his game, remind him of days gone by, when he was young and foolish.

There was something about this that didn't quite add up, though. Despite all his success in the business world, he didn't seem to have settled down for some ordinary life with a wife and kids. From what I could deduce from his social media accounts, he had remained single. His life, or what he showed of his life, was a series of charity balls—a different woman on his arm each time—and backpacking trips with groups of friends all over the world: Nepal, Austria, Canada, Peru. A guy like that—carefree, single, on the top of his game in a very secure job—this didn't seem like the type of person to get bent out of shape by a phone call.

The dinner was what finally convinced me to contact Freddy. I had been perfectly willing to pretend I was a stranger with her family. I didn't come to Seven Glacier to worm my way into Amy's life. Did I entertain fantasies that we would meet, become best friends? That she would immediately introduce me to everyone she cared about and they would become my instant second family? If I did, it was a fantasy I kept tucked very far back in my mind. I was too busy imagining the worst.

No, I had come to Seven Glacier for answers, not a new family. So I was surprised when Amy tapped her fork on her glass—as if she was preparing to make a speech at a wedding—and let it all out in the open.

The funny thing was, all day as Amy drove me farther and farther from the lodge toward the trailhead for Ridgeline Loop, the oddest sensation came over me. No one knew I was coming here, to Seven Glacier. What if I never showed up at college? How long would it take before anyone even knew I was missing? Amy had so much to lose, with me turning up here. Her perfect little life, the job she had always wanted in this place that transformed her into the person she always knew she could be, with her extremely good-looking husband and adorable little son.

Amy dragged me out of my room at the crack of dawn to take me on that hike. At first I wanted to give her the benefit of the doubt: she wanted to show me something amazing while she told me "the rest of the story," whatever that was. As we marched along the ridge, I could feel her edging closer to me, her eyes on me, and I thought she might be psyching herself up to tell me something momentous, something important about Freddy, about me, about life itself, and so I whipped around to face her and I swear—I swear her arms were outstretched, palms out, a desperate look in her eyes, wide open.

But of course she didn't push me. She didn't even touch me, not until later, when she pulled me into her and hugged me close. My beautiful girl, she said.

And then what could I do but keep going? Along a narrow ridge on the side of a cliff that dropped down a thousand feet below. A single push and I would be gone. No more digging into the past, whatever secrets she was hiding.

Don't be silly, I told myself as we ventured on. She's your mother! She told you to come here. I would will myself to breathe steadily, to focus on moving forward, the crunch of my boots.

So later, at dinner, when she introduced me to Jonathan and Gabe, a profound sense of relief washed over me. She didn't want to *kill* me— she wanted me to be a part of her life! She wanted me to love her, I realized. And if Amy, who had so much to lose by revealing this twenty-year-old secret to her husband and child, was willing to do that for me, then Freddy, who had basically nothing to lose, could, too.

~

By the time dinner was over, it was too late to call New York City. I hadn't planned on calling him, anyway. How could I? What was I going to do, dial up the Bennison Hotel reception and ask to speak to him?

If they asked me what the call was regarding, what would I even say? Oh, this is his daughter. The daughter he had with Amy Linden twenty years ago and put up for adoption? Yes, I'll hold.

No. I sent an email. His address was right there on the "contact us" page of the Bennison Hotels website. I made it short and to the point, with no greeting or closing:

> My name is Ramona Crawford, and I was born on February 5th, 1999. I have some questions about the beginning of my life I hope you'll be able to help me answer. I don't want anything but a conversation.

Ten minutes later I received an incoming call from Freddy Bennison—a video call. My phone was in my hand when it started vibrating, and when I saw his name on the screen, I dropped it on my bed in panic. My heart was racing. I put my hand to my hair. What did I look like? I was meeting my father for the first time, and I was a complete wreck.

The phone continued to vibrate, and then, a moment later, it also began to ring. "All right, all right," I muttered. I tried to smile and then accepted the call.

Freddy looked exactly how Amy had described him. Boyishly handsome, with a loose Afro. He was in his early forties, but I might have mistaken him for someone much younger.

Neither of us spoke at first. We were taking each other in. He gave a surprised little laugh, and I swear I saw tears well up in his eyes before he blinked, willing them away.

I laughed, too—what else could I do, in a situation like this? Meeting my father for the first time!

"Ramona?" he said, his voice incredulous. "Wow," he said, and he laughed again. "Is that really you?"

Amy's words ran through my mind again: Trust me, Ramona, she had said. He won't necessarily be happy to hear from you.

He was happy to hear from me.

"I really wanted to meet you," I said, and I found my eyes prickling with tears as well. It was so good to see him. He was in his apartment—or what I assumed was his apartment—in what looked like a large loft, with high ceilings, brick walls, and exposed ductwork. He was sitting at a table and leaning toward the camera, as if he were trying to get a better look at me.

He asked me how I was doing, was I a college student, and I answered a series of questions about myself before I told him the reason I needed to talk to him: I had recently found Amy Linden and that I was here in Seven Glacier now because she had invited me here. "She said coming here—she said it would help me understand. To explain—how it all began." It sounded so flimsy now. Why *had* I come here?

Freddy was nodding as if it all made perfect sense, and I kept going, the words coming out in a rush. "It's just that—I know something happened. Something must have happened, something she doesn't want me to know about, but she won't just say it, and I feel like if I just knew, I could move on with my life, you know? It's like there's this big mystery surrounding this beginning part of my life, and I want to solve it."

"Wow," Freddy said, and he looked away from the camera and ran a hand over his hair. He looked back at me, his eyes scrunched in concern.

A fatherly look, I wanted to call it. I did the same thing I did when I first met Amy, studied his face, his mannerisms, trying to locate myself in them. You always hear things like this, among family members: she has her father's eyes, she has her mother's smile. I didn't get that growing up. I didn't look anything like my mother. She even tried to force it, dressing us up in mother-daughter outfits on Christmas and Easter, and still, it never fooled anyone.

"Whatever you need to know," Freddy was saying to me. "I'm not sure how much help I'll be, though. It was a rough time—I'll tell you that. You should really ask Amy."

I *have* asked her, I wanted to whine, like a child. I closed my eyes for a second and took in a deep breath. This was my chance. I opened my eyes and blurted out the first question that popped into my head: "Why did you give me up?"

I braced myself for something—his guilt maybe. Anger. Or maybe he would shut down the conversation entirely: That's enough of that. Instead he just looked . . . confused. "You'd have to ask Amy about that."

"But you had a part in it, too, right?"

"Not really. It was up to her."

"But you had to have signed something. Waived your paternal rights? Isn't that how it works?"

Freddy looked away from the screen and then back at me. Something was happening with his face, something I couldn't quite interpret. "Ramona." He said my name slowly and glanced away again. "You know I'm not your father, right? Amy told you that?"

I must have remained silent for half a minute at least, trying to process this. It made no sense. "Your name is on the birth certificate."

"I thought Amy would have told you what happened."

"What happened?" I was panicked now, trying to go over everything she had told me. Was she lying to me this whole time? What was the point? "She told me how you met. You went to New York—"

Freddy was running his hands over his hair again. "Listen, Ramona, there's a lot she's leaving out."

"She lied to me," I said, more to myself than to him.

"What did she tell you?"

I stood up from my bed and started pacing around, holding the phone out in front of me but not really looking at it. "How you met outside the kitchen, the cabaret, the bonfire," I said. "The one-night stand—something with a bear."

I returned my attention to Freddy, and his eyes were half closed. He was nodding along.

"She found out she was pregnant at the end of the summer," I continued. "And you went to New York and then I was born and—I don't know. I don't know." I was having a hard time controlling my voice then. "I don't know what happened after that."

"Okay," Freddy said. "Yeah. I mean all that—it's accurate. To a point."

I tried to let this sink in. Are you sure you're not my father, I wanted to ask him. Because it sounds like you are. Or if you aren't, you could be—

"I thought I was your father. I had no reason to—I mean, I believed her. I had no reason not to believe her. And you know what, I liked being your father." Freddy looked as if he were trying to put on a cheerful expression and failing.

"Well then, how did it ever come out? The truth."

"My mom—she got a paternity test. After that, it was all over. I never talked to Amy again. I found out later she had put you up for adoption, and it killed me, but what was I supposed to do about it? I figured—I don't know."

"What?"

"She couldn't—she had a hard time adjusting. You know? Her dad had died and it was all so much for her and . . ." Freddy trailed off, but I understood what he was trying to tell me: maybe it had all been for the best after all.

"God," I said. "I'm such an *idiot*."

"No, no!" Freddy said. He reached a hand out and then let it fall back to the table. "I believed it, too. I wanted to believe that beautiful baby girl was mine. That beautiful, white baby." He gave me a wry little smile.

"So we're both idiots," I said. The two of us laughed because what else were we supposed to do? Freddy wasn't my father. These last few months, ever since getting that photograph of my birth certificate, I had tried to make it work, make this piece fit into the story of my life.

Now it was just an empty hole again. "So who is he then?" I asked. "Did she tell you?"

He shook his head.

"She wasn't dating anyone else that summer?"

"I went over and over it, after she left. It wasn't as though we were really together—I mean, there was just that one time, and then she acted so guilty about it. That there was someone else . . . explained it, in a way. And she did disappear every weekend."

"Disappear?"

"We had different days off, so it wasn't so strange—not at the time. And like I said, it wasn't as though we were even together. But you know, I kept trying to get her to watch me perform. I was in the cabaret—"

"Oh, I know all about that."

"Yeah, well, I performed two nights a week, and she never once showed up. Those were her days off, and like I said, she was never around."

"Where did she go?"

"She always had plans with friends. Hiking, backpacking trips, up to Canada. A lot of people did stuff like that."

"So my father—maybe he was one of them? One of the friends?"

"That was the thing," Freddy said. "She didn't have any friends. At least, I never met any of them."

There wasn't much more to discuss after that. Before we ended the call, he asked me what I planned to do next. He told me to pack up my bags, go back to college. It wasn't worth it, he told me. I could talk to Amy, come at her from every possible angle, and I still wouldn't find the answers I was looking for. I should move on, he said, for my own sake. It sounded like I had a good mother back home, a good life. Focus on that.

"You're right," I told him, and at the time, I meant it.

~

The next morning, Gabe was supposed to teach me how to swim. I tried my best to act normal around all of them, cheerful. I watched how Amy interacted with Gabe, nervous and flighty. But she did love him. She took care of him in her own way, joking around with him, making him laugh. She was the kind of mom who would promise to bake you a cake for your birthday and then almost burn the house down and end up taking you out for ice cream instead, laughing the whole time, telling you it was all a big adventure. My mom—the mother who raised me—wasn't like that at all. She was organized, cautious. I was her only child. After my dad left us, she never dated again. I thought about what Amy had told me about their files. How my mom had had a career and went skiing in the Alps. When she got better, I should take her somewhere. Anywhere she wanted.

I needed to confront Amy, but I wanted to do it in private. I kept thinking there had to be a reason Amy hadn't told me who my father was—or why she told me it was Freddy when she knew for a fact he wasn't. Considering the lengths she had already gone to to obscure the truth, what made me think she would start being honest now?

But then I thought about the first time I met Amy in Seattle, standing at the back of the hotel restaurant, her arm raised. Wearing that floor-length blue velvet gown in the middle of the afternoon. Or when she bustled into my room and insisted I move somewhere better, nice. She wanted me to admire her, to be proud of her, even. I would give her one more chance, I decided. If she didn't tell me what I needed to know, I would leave. It was that simple. I had nothing to lose.

I rowed us out to the middle of the lake and rested the oars on my lap. I was breathing hard from rowing and Amy was looking back at me with what I could only imagine was a guilty expression.

I came right out with it. "You lied to me."

"I didn't lie," she said, as I knew she would. "Not exactly."

"I know Freddy Bennison is not my father. You lied about that."

"I never told you he was your father!"

This threw me. "You told me the whole story, about how you were working in the kitchen, right over in the lodge." I waved my hand in the general direction of the hotel. "How he was auditioning for the cabaret. The bonfire, the one-night stand. He got you that job at the front desk, you moved to New York—"

"Right," she answered slowly. "But I didn't tell you he was your father." I must have shaken my head or murmured something in my bafflement because she continued, "You found your birth certificate, remember?"

"Yes . . . ," I said, failing to see her point.

"You said, 'Tell me about Freddy Bennison.'"

"Oh my god." I looked to my left and my right, as if searching for an audience who could witness this.

"So," Amy ventured, "I told you about Freddy Bennison. But I never told you he was your father."

I closed my eyes for a moment, trying to remain calm. Then I snapped them back open. "Are you fucking serious?"

Amy flinched.

"You knew what I meant! What, I just want to hear the entire story about some random guy?"

"He wasn't a random guy! Everything I told you was true. He could have been your father—I thought he was your father! I mean, I thought it was a possibility. Why else would I tell him that, move to New York with him. We were raising you together! And we probably would have, too, if his mom—"

"Do you know how much of an idiot I made of myself? I reached out to him and—"

"I told you not to contact him!"

"I've been going around these last couple months thinking I'm Black. What if I'd tried to join the Students of Color group at school? Like I'm—I'm—what's the name of that white lady who—"

"Rachel Dolezal?"

"Right, like I'm the next Rachel Dolezal or something. Can you imagine?"

"I would have advised against that" was all she managed to come up with.

"Well, jeez, Amy, you think? You think maybe when I said I was part Black you might have mentioned that I'm not? Or wait—*is* my father Black? I don't even know."

"No," she said quietly.

"Well, are you ever going to tell me? Who is he? What's the big mystery?"

"This is such a mess," she said. "This whole thing."

"Why did you even agree to meet me then?" I lashed out. "What was the point of all this? You *told* me to come here—you told me I was from here, that coming here would—I don't know, explain everything to me."

She hid her face in her hands. At least she had the sense to be ashamed of what she had done. "I don't know what I'm doing half the time," she said. "I don't know what I was thinking."

"So you regret it." My voice was hard and flat. "You wish everything had just stayed the way it was. The birth certificate sealed away, me back in college with no clue."

"No!" She reached out her arms as if to grab me, to bring me into her, hug me to her, but she was sitting too far away from me. "That's not what I want at all."

"But you refuse to tell me anything about myself. And what you do tell me is just—lies."

"I wasn't lying." She said this with her head bowed, almost too softly for me to hear. "Look, I told you about Freddy because he's a part of your story—he is! He helped take care of you and when I left, he was devastated. You have to believe me."

"And my father?"

"Your father didn't want anything to do with you." She said it sharply. "So you can see why I wanted it to be Freddy! It makes a better story, doesn't it?"

"But it's not the *true* story!"

"You want to know the true story? I never loved anyone the way I loved your father. And I thought he loved me."

"How did this even happen? I thought you were with Freddy all summer, working at the front desk, flirting with him, all those 'puritanical sex games' . . . and now you're saying there was this whole other guy, and this *other* guy got you pregnant?"

The air was still, out on that lake. Suddenly Amy was twisting around in the boat, craning her head around as if to take it all in, the majesty of it, the outlines of the mountains crisp against the backdrop of the sky, the sunlight glinting off the water. When she turned back to face me, she had rearranged her features, and her expression was calm. Serene. "Did I ever tell you why I came here?" she said. "I mean why I first came here, to Seven Glacier."

I shrugged. I was growing tired of her stories, which may or may not end up being at all relevant to me and my life. I wasn't sure why I had thought Amy was capable of doing it, of helping me fill in the gaps.

"By 1997 I was twenty years old—your age!" Amy said.

I didn't meet her eye, but I could feel her gaze anyway. I let my eyes rove over the landscape. A slight breeze rippled across the surface of the lake. It really was beautiful here, I conceded. But only in my mind.

"My dad still couldn't be left on his own," Amy continued. "So that's what I was doing with my life. Taking care of my dad, doing odd jobs around the apartment complex, hounding tenants for rent checks, taking the odd class at the community college when I had the chance."

It was at the community college where Amy saw the brochure for seasonal work at Seven Glacier. For weeks she just looked at the pamphlet. She took it home and hid it under her mattress like it was porn, taking it out to lust over the pictures of the mountains and lakes, the grand old lodge, the young people with their big frame backpacks. And then she started plotting—it was just one summer. Her brother could stay home with their dad during his summer break. She could do this. When she told her family about it, about this plan, she made it sound as if it could change everything, not just for her, but for all of them. It was very naive, of course, but she found herself truly believing it—this job would turn it all around for her. For them.

"I wasn't going to make the same mistakes my parents made," Amy continued. "I didn't want to work for Elena Dodge—I wanted to *be* Elena Dodge. And Seven Glacier was how I was going to do it. I was convinced." She shook her head at the memory of it, young Amy. Young, delusional Amy.

"Well, it worked out, didn't it?" I said, my voice flat. "In the end."

She met my eye. "I got distracted."

"What do you mean?"

"I mean I lost sight of it, that goal."

"Because of Freddy?" I looked at Amy then. She was looking back at me, her eyes very still and serious. She was trying to tell me something. Something important. Something actually important.

"No, no." She waved her hand impatiently. "I met Freddy in 1998. My *second* summer at Seven Glacier. I'm talking about 1997. The beginning. My first summer."

I nodded, trying to follow. She had come here two summers in a row. Yes, she had said that.

"I was going to work at the front desk, somehow get discovered as a hospitality prodigy, move up that career ladder, blah blah blah. But then what happens?" Amy paused dramatically.

"What?" I asked, hating myself for getting sucked in once again, sure she would just feed me another line, rattle off some vignette that would tell me absolutely nothing I needed to know.

"I get stuck in the kitchen," she said. "Washing dishes with Cory."

"Cory," I repeated. She had said the name with an air of drama, as if I should understand the resonance of it.

"Cory Duncan." She looked at me straight in the eye and held my gaze. "Your father."

Amy leaned in. "Nothing was going according to plan. I just had the summer to do it, one summer. Then I would have to go back to take care of my dad again. I thought coming here—I thought it would change things. But nothing changed. Nothing would ever change for me. And then Stuart—Stuart told us all about this secret place, a secret hike tucked way up in the middle of the park. Cory and I—we decided to go there. That was where it all started."

I kept my face very still, watching her.

"And that was where it ended, too," she said. "On the shores of Shangri-La."

CHAPTER 10

RAMONA

Amy had never been in love before—or never been in love with someone who loved her back. That was what she told me, as the boat drifted across the surface of the water. Her eyes were shining in a way that had become familiar to me now, the way they sparked when she told one of her stories.

For most of high school, she had been head over heels for Anthony Dearborn. She thought that was love, but she didn't know anything then. Anthony, with his scraggly blond hair and expressive blue eyes, stood at his locker, piling books into his backpack, when Amy heard him swearing softly. Amy looked over from her neighboring locker. For months she had lingered there, hoping to cross paths with him, but it hadn't happened. Until now. Until his ballpoint pen burst in the pocket of his flannel shirt right before the bell was about to ring. Ink began to spread from the pocket, blooming out from the plaid shirt and onto the white T-shirt underneath.

"Oh no," Amy said, and that was when Anthony noticed her for the first time, noticed she was standing there, observing him in his crisis.

He had to take a test, he said. An essay test, in English. "I'm already late." His eyebrows rose over those soulful blue eyes. "And I don't have another pen." The bell rang through the now-empty halls.

"Here," Amy said. "It's my lucky pen."

He took the pen from her hands and smiled. "You saved my life," he said. "I owe you."

"I'll need it back!" she called after him, because it really was her lucky pen. It was expensive, a gift from her grandparents. It had her name engraved on it.

It was almost too perfect. If he aced the test, he would look at it and think of her. She didn't see him again the rest of the day, but that was fine. It gave her time to come up with some good lines. "I'm going to need my lucky pen back," was the lead contender. She imagined him smiling and handing it back to her. He would want to invite her out to coffee, to thank her, or maybe even dinner, and then—well, what then? She let herself take this fantasy to its logical conclusion. Love, probably. Marriage.

The next time she saw him, she used that line on him, and he looked momentarily surprised, but then he smiled and said she had saved the day. Still, he didn't give her back the pen. She had to remind him again the next day. "Oh, sorry!" Anthony appeared to be digging around for it in his backpack. He produced a clear ballpoint pen, the kind with blue ink, half used.

Was this a joke? "My pen—it has my name on it," she stammered.

He dipped his head down to hers. "I know," he said in a low voice. "I'm keeping it to remember you by."

And the really dumb thing was, the worst part of this whole story, was that she actually fell for this. She imagined that he was keeping that pen somewhere special, somewhere safe, as a memento of her, a token of their bond. And that half-used blue ballpoint pen he gave her in exchange? She kept it at the bottom of her underwear drawer as a keepsake. She held on to it for years, though they barely exchanged more than a few words after that.

Time went by. Her family moved away, high school graduation. And then, one day, she ran into him at a record store in Medford. This was months before she went away to Seven Glacier for the first time. She saw him flipping through the records and approached him. This was her chance. All these years, they had been secretly pining for each other. "Hey, Anthony," she said to him.

He looked up and smiled at her. "Hey yourself," he said.

Amy had a Cat Stevens record in her hands. It was for her dad. She was about to ask Anthony to join her for coffee.

His sunglasses were perched on top of his head, pulling his hair from his face. In a romantic impulse, she plucked them from his head and put them on her own face. "How do I look?" she said.

Then a girl sidled up to him and put her arm around his waist. "Ready?" she said to Anthony.

Instantly, Amy deflated. Mortified, she removed his glasses and handed them back to him. He slipped them into his front pocket.

"Jules, this is just a friend from high school, uh—" And then he paused. He didn't know her name! Her name that was engraved on that pen.

~

With Cory, my father, it was different. She didn't even notice him, not at first. He noticed *her*. He was just there, washing dishes by her side at the Seven Glacier Hotel, from that first day. He was easy to talk to, their voices obscured by the sounds of the kitchen. She didn't think of him as a romantic interest—more like a confessional. He made her feel like she was fascinating. He would ask her a question and she would give him a long, rambling answer, and then she would stop, embarrassed, afraid she was talking his ear off, but he would still be listening, watching her carefully. He had a crush on her, maybe, and she was flattered by that.

One of those days, that first week, he told her he wanted to be a photographer, and she told him to forget it. It was a hard life, she explained. She should know, after what happened to her parents. He didn't seem dissuaded. He wanted to be a wildlife photographer, he clarified. That was why he was spending the summer here, in the park. Wildlife photographers weren't ordinary artists. They went to great lengths to get the perfect shot. They dangled from the sides of cliffs, faced off with lions, swam with sharks. Amy struggled to picture Cory—quiet, unassuming Cory—doing any of those things.

So she didn't like him, at first, but she liked that he liked her. And so, when they had their first day off, they spent it together.

"We don't have to do this, you know," Cory said. He looked much different outside the kitchen, his hair falling rakishly over his forehead, freed from the bandanna kerchief he had taken to wearing while he worked. He was dressed in a faded black Slowdive T-shirt, black jeans, and well-worn Doc Martens that seemed to be repaired around the toes with duct tape. He had a camera slung around one shoulder and a small daypack that looked like a carryover from high school, a backpack covered in buttons and patches. He wore sunglasses, knockoff Ray-Bans with a safety pin holding them together on one side. He looked more like he was touring as a roadie with some indie band than someone who was about to embark on a strenuous hike through the wilderness.

They had caught a ride with a member of the kitchen crew, who dropped them off at the visitor center at the foot of the main road that wound through the park. From there, they needed to find someone who could take them five miles in.

"I want to do it." Amy said the words with great confidence, chin held high, shoulders back. The way she said those words—"I want to do it"—made her realize she was trying to impress Cory. That first week in the kitchen, she had treated him the way she treated her younger brother, Alex. Like her little pal. Her default mode for hanging out with guys her age was to joke around with them, trying to make them laugh, maybe punching them in the arm. Showing off a bit maybe, like she wanted them to be impressed by how cool and tough she was compared to all the other girls. It wasn't the best strategy. No—it wasn't even a strategy. And it wasn't even the true her, either, just this weird way she had started acting, maybe to fend off any sexual attention, make them regard her as one of the boys.

One time Amy was at summer camp, about thirteen years old, and she was splashing around with a bunch of other kids at the lake. Two of the boys found a dead fish—completely white and slimy and bloated with water. They gripped it by the tail and flopped it around, making the girls squeal in disgusted delight. Amy swam right up to them and inspected the fish up close. She took a finger and traced it along those bloated scales. Let me hold it, she said to the boys, and they handed it over. She's not afraid, one of them murmured. They were impressed. Then she arced her arm back and pitched the fish out, into the deeper part of the lake. It flip-flopped through the air as it sailed, and then it disappeared under the waves with barely a splash. You shouldn't play with dead things, she told them, and she swam away.

The point of the story: It did make them impressed with her. But it didn't make them like her.

Stuart and this other guy from the kitchen, Jake, had written down directions on an unfolded paper napkin. Cory and Amy stood in the parking lot looking over it, trying to decipher the directions. "Hitch to this mile-marker sign," she said, pointing at a spot on a hastily sketched map. "And head east. How will we know which way is east?"

"Maybe it will be obvious when we get there." Cory didn't seem overly concerned.

"Did it occur to you that maybe this is all some sort of joke?"

"No." Cory looked sideways at her. She could tell he was trying not to smile. It was as if, all of a sudden, their roles had flipped. She was the one with the crush, and he was just playing it cool. "Like what kind of joke, exactly?"

"Like a hazing ritual! You know, they give us this fake map, make us wander all over the park, lead us into a trap or something."

"A trap?"

"I don't know. Quicksand maybe."

"Who would wash the dishes then?"

"I don't mean they're trying to kill us. Just jerk us around a bit. For laughs."

"It's not too late to turn back."

"I want to do it. I'm just making sure *you* want to do it."

Cory ran his hands through his hair and grinned at her, and she found herself getting flustered and averting her gaze. He looked different, out of the bandanna and the heavy-duty apron, and he was acting different, too. More self-assured. "I think we can handle it. Whatever it is."

Hitchhiking sounded daunting but was actually very easy—they just asked a family in a minivan if they were heading down the main road through the park, and when they said yes, Amy and Cory asked if they could tag along partway. The family was Norwegian, all yellow-blond hair and ruddy skin, parents and a set of identical twin girls in braids. Amy and Cory learned, on that winding ride deeper into the park, that the family had been staying at a campground, taking in all the major hikes. "Even the girls, they love to hike," the mother told them.

"Oh yah?" Amy responded, unintentionally mimicking their accent.

"Yah," the husband said. "We saw a bear, didn't we, girls?"

The girls blinked at him from the back seat. Amy was sitting next to them, and Cory was crammed into a single seat behind them. The dad said something in Norwegian and growled. His hands lifted from the steering wheel and he clawed through the air, pretending to be a bear.

"Yah!" the girls screamed. They lifted their little hands and growled and clawed at the air, too. Then the wife joined in.

"Hey, the road!" Cory shouted from his spot in the back.

The minivan was veering out of their lane as it careened around a bend. Just then another car coming down honked its horn. The dad gripped the steering wheel and swerved back into the lane, almost grazing the other car. "Whoo!" he whooped in excitement. The wife and daughters cheered merrily.

"I wasn't expecting to almost die before reaching the trailhead," Amy said. The Norwegians had deposited the two of them on the side of the road, where they now stood on the shoulder, behind a guardrail.

It didn't look like a trailhead, even a secret one, and once again Amy began to question whether Stuart and Jake were messing with them, but she kept her worries to herself and pointed to a tangle of bushes about a half mile up a hill covered in flattened, dry grass. "That's on the map." She marched toward it in her new hiking boots.

The boots were one size too big, making her legs look cartoonish, disproportionally spindly. With two pairs of wool hiking socks, they fit. She had broken them in as well as she could the week before she arrived at Seven Glacier, taking walks around her neighborhood wearing a weighted pack.

Confidently, she headed toward the bramble. They hiked in silence, the only sound their boots crunching over the terrain, hard-packed earth dotted with tiny stones. When they reached the bushes, they stopped. The bushes were taller than they had appeared from a distance, with thin red branches reaching ten feet into the air. When you get to this part, Stuart had advised them, just bushwhack through it.

Amy stepped into the bramble, parting the branches with her hands. She cast a look back at Cory, who was right behind her. Their eyes met and seemed to communicate something then. Something like, There's no going back now, or We're doing this.

"When does it end," she moaned. She couldn't tell how long they had been trudging through it, the branches snapping under their feet, thwacking them as they waded through the tangle. It was dark in there, too, the sunlight barely filtering through the brush. Sometimes they would hear rustling—birds' wings flapping, trying to free themselves. Little creatures gnawing on grubs or scuttling underfoot. She wanted to stop, to rest, to drink some water or eat some trail mix to refuel, but there was nowhere to stop. The only possibilities were to just curl up into a ball and let themselves become permanently enmeshed in the bramble, overgrown with vines, or to keep going forward—or what seemed to be forward—parting the branches with their hands and forcing their legs through the gaps between the roots.

Then it happened—they emerged. They stumbled out and landed back on the dry ground, the sky arcing huge and blue above them. They looked at each other and laughed. Their skin was crisscrossed with red lines, and their hair looked like they had stuck their fingers in a light socket. Amy wrapped her arms around him. "We did it!" He didn't hug her back, or she didn't give him the time to hug her back, so she released him and busied herself with adjusting her clothes, running her fingers through her hair, dusting off her shorts with her hands.

Cory cleared his throat and pointed up to a grouping of rocks that created a steep cliff wall. "That's where we're headed." The sun was shining on the rocks, beckoning them forward, out of the darkness. "You go on ahead. I'll catch up." Cory was already crouching down, changing out the lenses on his camera. Ignoring his suggestion, she observed him at work, staring through his viewfinder at a bee dancing around the bowl of a scrubby golden wildflower.

"You didn't have to wait for me," he said when he was finished.

"I know," she said, impressed despite herself. She never would have looked twice at that flower, let alone noticed the bee buzzing inside it.

Eventually they reached the base of the cliff wall, which turned out to be fairly simple to climb—not sheer rock face but more like a super-steep staircase, with obvious hand- and footholds. Amy climbed up first, at Cory's insistence. Despite his decidedly nonathletic appearance and inappropriate footwear, he seemed to know what he was doing, and he said that if she went first, he would be in a better position to guide her if she got stuck. "Don't look up my shorts," she chided him.

She meant it as a joke. Once she had said it, though, it was the main thing going through her mind as she climbed up those rocks: What was Cory looking at? Could he see her underwear? What underwear was she wearing? The blue striped ones? She hoped not. Maybe the dark-red ones from Victoria's Secret? They were cotton, but in better shape than the blue stripes. Her mind obsessed on this topic for what must have been ten minutes straight, jolted back to reality only when her foot skidded on a bit of loose gravel and dislodged a stone about the size of a teacup, sending it down below. "Rock!" she screamed, hugging the wall and looking down at Cory, who leaped to his right in a graceful, almost lazy movement, letting the rock whiz by, not even grazing him. It bounced off one of the stone steps, smashed in half, and the two rock shards disappeared from view.

"You're doing great," Cory yelled up to her. "You're almost there."

Only then did she take in breath. For the rest of the ascent, she concentrated on her breathing. Then they reached the ledge. Just looking at it gave Amy a terrible feeling, acrophobia and claustrophobia combined. The ledge was barely wide enough to crawl on all fours, a narrow pathway that dropped off into nothingness below. If they slipped, that was it. They would tumble off the edge of the cliff. And they had to crawl, not walk, because there wasn't enough room to stand up straight. The cliff face jutted over the ledge, creating a low ceiling.

Cory was transferring his camera into his daypack, which he put on his chest in preparation for the crawl. He didn't look worried. Amy copied his movements, slinging her backpack onto her chest and tightening her ponytail. "I'll go first," she said, as if she did this kind of thing all the time.

She crawled forward, refusing to look down the side of the cliff. She focused only on the ground beneath her or right ahead of her. Cory was calling after her, but she didn't listen. She crawled faster, the end in sight: there it was, a wider ledge with no ceiling where they could stand up again. She crawled her way to it and stood up triumphantly, almost giddy with adrenaline. She did it. She did that.

Cory came up behind her, and she reached out her hand to help him stand beside her. Their eyes met and they laughed. He had such unusual eyes, Amy noticed then. Like nothing she had ever seen before. Silver almost, with a dark limbal ring. When he looked at her, his gaze was intense, as if he were boring holes through her, possessing her. She remembered a book she had read as a child, *The Girl with the Silver Eyes*. The main character had silver eyes and special powers—ESP or kinesthesia or something. Amy read a lot of books like that back then, in the '80s. Cory's eyes were like that.

After that the hike was easy, just like they promised. Up over the ridge and onto a grassy knoll. By that time they were running. The knoll was lit up by the sun behind them, the light glinting off the yellow-green grass, the wildflowers just beginning to dot the terrain. It was different up there, lusher, as if they had entered an entirely new ecosystem. The air felt cleaner, charged with excitement.

"Come on," she said, and she grabbed Cory's hand. From the top of the knoll, they could see it: Shangri-La. A lake nestled in the valley below, its mirror surface reflecting the clouds above. It seemed to glitter when the light hit it. It wasn't a trick after all—that was her first thought. It was real. Shangri-La was real, and she was there. She was there and so was Cory, and at that very moment, they were the only two people on earth seeing it, this miraculous sight, the most beautiful vision she had ever seen.

Cory's hand was still in hers. She squeezed it tightly and then took off, pulling him after her. She ran down to the shore and stood at the water's edge. She looked over at Cory, who was staring out at the lake. He had a small smile on his face, as if he were secretly contemplating something. His hand slipped from hers and he was reaching for his camera, fiddling with the settings.

"Let's go in," Amy said.

Cory didn't look over at her, seemingly engrossed in whatever he was seeing through that viewfinder. It was so quiet up there she could hear the click of the shutter.

In one swift movement, she yanked her shirt over her head. The cool mountain air nipped at her skin. Still, the blood pumped through her veins, warming her. Her heart pounded in her chest, her lungs took in gasps of air and pushed them back out. She had never felt more alive, so filled with energy, like she could dive in headfirst and swim to the other side.

She was scrambling out of her clothes then, kicking off her boots, pulling off her wool hiking socks, unbuttoning her shorts. "Come on!" She turned to Cory, prepared to strip him down and drag him in with her, but he stepped back.

There she was, half-naked, breathing hard—panting, practically—smiling. She expected him to react to that somehow, lustfully take in the sight of her near-naked body, pull his own shirt over his head and start making out with her—something. Instead he held his camera out between them and gave her an apologetic little shrug, like he would just love to go in but *unfortunately* the camera wouldn't allow it. "You go," he said. The wind whipped around them and she had to force herself not to shiver, though her skin betrayed her, prickling with goose bumps. It no longer seemed like such a great idea, tearing into a glacial lake at the top of the season. He smiled at her then. "I dare you."

And so she went in. She went tearing into the water, her feet barely registering the rocky bits of gravel—not sand—underneath them. As soon as she hit the water—so cold it hurt, as if it was sucking the life from her bones—she knew it was a mistake, but she kept going. She ran until that frigid water went up past her knees and then she jumped in all at once, shocking her system. She gasped and swam fast, trying to warm herself up and failing. Those guys in Finland or Iceland or somewhere who would heat themselves up in saunas and then jump into holes in the ice. Is that what they did? She had read about that somewhere. That was what it felt like, as if she had fallen through ice and into the murky dead waters underneath.

Cory looked very small, sitting there on the shore, the lens of his camera directed at her. "Come in!" she yelled out over the lake, but the wind carried her voice off in the opposite direction. "You get used to it!" she lied.

Cory didn't respond, and she swam back, stumbling on dry land like some waterlogged sea creature, her skin mottled and blue, her hair tangled and scraggly, pasted to her body. Her underwear—the dark-red ones, thankfully, still opaque—sagged off her hips.

Cory was pointing his camera at her. The shutter clicked. She grimaced and plopped down beside him. She hugged her knees into her chest, trying to warm herself.

"Hey," Cory said, and when she turned to look at him, he snapped another picture.

"Isn't there a moose or something you could take a picture of right now?" She dropped her head onto her knees, forming her body into a ball. "I must look like a drowned rat."

He said, "Hey," again, but more softly that time, and then she could feel his hands on her, trying to unravel her, opening her up. She looked at him again, and he was looking back with a serious, intent look in his eyes, and he said she didn't look like a drowned rat. She looked entrancing.

"Entrancing?" she repeated, smiling despite herself.

He leaned in and kissed her once, his warm lips pressed against her cold ones, briefly, testing it out. Then he sat back, and they appraised each other. It felt like it could go either way. She could clear her throat and pull on her clothes and announce that they should probably head back out and they could remain friends—good friends, best friends, maybe—for the remainder of the summer.

Or she could reach her hand up to his face and kiss him back, harder this time, with their mouths open, and she could press her body up to his and steal his warmth and rip that Slowdive T-shirt up over his head and roll around on the shores of Shangri-La with the waves lapping at their feet like they were the romantic leads in a black-and-white movie, and they could spend the rest of the summer falling in desperate love with each other, making out under waterfalls and having sex in open fields of wildflowers.

"Say my name," she said.

He hadn't said her name all day, she realized. Or maybe ever. She had introduced herself on that first day. It was possible that he had forgotten it, the way people do. Amy herself never forgot a name. The trick was to make note of it in the first place. It wasn't that people *forgot* names—they just never took the trouble to learn them in the first place. It was easy to just not know someone's name. Years could go by. You could get away with it. This would explain a lot. It would explain why Cory was so happy to keep her talking as they stood side by side, washing dishes. Maybe he was trying to get her to say it.

Right then, at the lake's edge, he looked startled by her question, then nervous. He didn't know it.

God, Amy thought, was it really so much to ask? For someone to know her name?

He swallowed, and she could see his Adam's apple dip up and down. His silver eyes looked straight into hers, and he said it. "Amy," he said. "Amy Linden." And that was it. They were in love. She loved him.

She raised her hand to his face and drew him toward her.

CHAPTER 11

RAMONA

"So where is he? Cory? If he's my father?" I asked Amy. She had paused her narration, leaving her hand outstretched, as if she were still feeling her hand on Cory's cheek. I wanted to get caught up in this story, this new version of how it all began, how *I* began. I wanted to, but I knew better now. It was hard getting invested in it, this whole new character. Silver eyes? Seriously?

The boat bobbed up and down on the water, and Amy squinted at me, shielding her eyes from the sun with her hand. "Let's go back to shore," she said. "I'm feeling a migraine coming on." They happened like this sometimes, she told me. They could come on suddenly. The boat, the sun. It was all too much, she said. She could feel the nausea overtaking her. "I'm going to get seasick," she said.

The boat was barely moving. Drifting softly along the water, but very slowly. Jonathan and Gabe were still close to the shore, pedaling around in their blue plastic boat.

"Not yet." I didn't want to go back to shore. I didn't know when I would be able to get her alone like this again. She could just avoid me, and then I'd go back home, and then what?

"Ramona, I'm serious—" Amy squinted again, like she was auditioning for a headache commercial, and pressed her palm against her forehead.

I held on to the oars. "Tell me about Freddy, at least."

"What about him?"

"How did he fit into all this? You were in love with Cory—my dad—but then you're in New York with Freddy. And then—"

"It's a long story."

"I have time. And nowhere to go."

Amy let out a pitiful little whimper.

"Tell me and I'll row you to shore," I said. "I promise."

~

After that first time Charlotte visited Amy, she came by all the time, usually unannounced. Flinging open windows, wiping down counters, plucking stray pieces of laundry from the floor or the couch and throwing them into the hamper. She was no-nonsense and polite, but also, Amy thought, kind, if only in that ice princess way of hers.

Amy made the foolish decision to confide in Charlotte. She told her, one day, that she worried it had been a mistake—having a baby, moving to New York, missing her own father's funeral, everything. She couldn't escape the dreams, the dreams of the baby in the water, her hands pushing her down, the dreams that made her terrified to go to sleep and terrified to be awake, too, in case they were prophetic. In case they came true. She didn't tell Charlotte all that, of course. She used more general terms: "I don't think I can do this." Charlotte would listen and then dismiss her worries. Of course you can, she might say. Or just take it day by day. That's all anyone can do. Just take it day by day.

One evening, Freddy announced he wouldn't be eating dinner at home. His parents wanted him to go over to their place. "What about me?" Amy asked. "What about the baby?"

"My mom says she wants to talk to me privately," he said. "She has something to tell me. Something important."

The two of them speculated about that. What could it be? After everything that had happened with her dad, she imagined it was something health-related. An illness that they—that all of them—would have to deal with. Appointments and diets and hospital visits. She sympathized, but she was annoyed. Annoyed that they would pull Freddy away from her, away from her and away from me, the baby. Charlotte knew that she was struggling, how she waited, every day, for Freddy to return home from his classes. The hours passed by so slowly, taking care of an infant. Staying cooped up in the apartment all day was mind-numbing, but gathering everything they might need for an outing and getting out the door was exhausting, too, a project almost insurmountable in scope.

It was so boring, taking care of a baby on her own, but at the same time, terrifying. Anything could go wrong, and if it did, it would be her fault. She wasn't herself, not yet. Deep down, she still felt like she shouldn't be trusted with me. Her dreams still haunted her. So every evening, the moment Freddy stepped inside that door, she almost melted with relief. They made it through another day.

Part of her wondered if Charlotte had called Freddy away on purpose, to test her. She knew Amy was hanging on by a thread.

Freddy came home late, later than expected. She was waiting up for him in their living room, trying to pass the time. Flipping through channels on the television, opening up a book and staring at the words but unable to read, mindlessly turning the pages of a magazine. She knew as soon as he entered that something was wrong, something terrible had happened. She could see it in his posture. Even after a full day of classes, he had a light, almost bouncy way of entering a room, but on that night, his movements were slow and sloppy, as if someone had pricked him and half the air had leaked out of him. "Freddy?" she called out. She was afraid, then. Afraid of what he was about to tell her.

He went straight to the baby. To me. I was asleep in my Moses basket next to Amy.

"She's asleep," Amy whispered.

It was as though he couldn't hear her. He lifted me up, and Amy sat up straight on the couch, wary. Never wake a sleeping baby. Of all the rules and tips she had gleaned from the dozens of baby books Charlotte had left for her, this was one that seemed the most valuable. A baby could cry for hours at a time, at the top of her lungs, her face beet red and wet with tears, no end in sight. You could feed her, change her, burp her, bounce her, and nothing would cause so much as a one-minute reprieve from the wailing. What is going on in there, Amy wanted to ask me as I wailed. Just tell me what's wrong and I'll fix it. I promise I will do anything to make it stop, anything, anything.

All this to say—when I was asleep, Amy did anything to keep it that way, to guarantee the silence. And she wasn't just doing it for her own sake, her own selfish need for peace and quiet. She was doing it for me. If infants didn't get enough sleep (the baby books warned), it could cause permanent damage. I could lose precious brain cells.

Freddy lifted me gently. So gently that I twitched and stretched but didn't wake. I settled into his arms and gave a satisfied little snoring sound. Amy relaxed.

He paced around the room a little, bouncing me, murmuring something to me, and then he made his way back to Amy, and in the lamplight she could see his eyes were raw and bloodshot. He had been crying.

She didn't say anything. She didn't ask him what his parents had told him.

Freddy told her. He said, "She's not mine," and his eyes glistened. His mother had done a paternity test. It proved it.

"What?" Amy sputtered. She was shocked. Well, she wasn't shocked that I wasn't Freddy's. She knew that. Or at least, she knew it was a strong possibility. She was shocked that his parents had done that behind her back.

She cried. She told him how sorry she was. "I never cheated on you," she said, and that was the truth. "There was someone else—before I met you."

There had been someone else—no, it wasn't important who it was, no one Freddy knew, of course not, he was completely out of the picture—and then Freddy and Amy had that drunken night at the bonfire. She had felt so guilty. Remember that, Freddy? How guilty she had felt? Of course he remembered. She wouldn't have sex with him again, not until later, the end of summer.

"I guess deep down, I knew it might not be yours," she said gently. At this point they were both sitting on the couch, her on one side, Freddy on the other. He was listening, though. He wanted to believe her, to trust her. "It's just—I wanted it to be true. And it could have been true, you know?"

Freddy and Amy talked for hours. They drifted off to sleep and woke up in the morning, the first rays of dawn coming in through the window, Amy slumped over on the couch, Freddy half on the floor, half draped over the couch, his arm across her legs. She had asked him if he could ever forgive her, and he said yes. He loved her. He loved me, the baby. "Our baby," Amy said.

And so that was that—or so Amy thought. Charlotte came to pay her one of her visits a couple days later. Amy didn't want to let her in. She stood in the doorway and said it wasn't a good time. Not today. Charlotte insisted. She practically pushed the door open and started on her usual bit, the tidying. "Stop that, Charlotte," Amy said. Amy knew Charlotte hated it when she called her by her first name, and usually she did remember the honorific, she tried to do what she asked, but this time she didn't. She couldn't believe what Charlotte had done! Going behind her back like that, trying to tear her family apart. How dare she, really.

Charlotte assessed Amy coldly. "Freddy is not the father of that child," she said. "He's too young—too young to be saddled with you, with another man's child."

"It's his choice," Amy said. They had made plans. He would graduate in a couple months. He could get a job. She could go back to work. They would make a life for themselves.

"What would it take to make you change your mind?" Charlotte said.

"Change my mind about what?"

"We'll offer you ten thousand dollars," Charlotte said.

Amy almost laughed. "For what?"

"To leave Freddy. Leave New York."

"Ten thousand dollars?" Amy was incredulous. Seriously? If she was going to try to pay her off, you would think she would at least offer her enough to get back on her feet. Maybe even start a new life somewhere.

"How much do you want?" she said. "Name your price."

"I'm not going to be paid off."

Charlotte kept insisting. Twenty thousand, thirty.

"You can go up to a million," she said. "I won't take it."

"And what about Freddy?"

"I love him," Amy said. "And he loves me. He loves us. He wouldn't just let us go, not without a fight." She wasn't sure this was true, not exactly, but she said it with conviction.

"I'll cut him off," Charlotte said.

"What?"

"If you stay with him, you'll get nothing," she said. "And neither will he." She cast her eyes around the apartment. "You'll have to find someplace else to live. Freddy will need a job—a good job. You could go back to the Hedgewick, I suppose. What are we paying you there?"

"Not enough."

"It will be difficult," Charlotte said. "He'll grow to resent you. He'll resent the baby."

"I can't raise a baby like that." Inside the apartment, it was warm, the radiators constantly pumping out heat, but she had gone completely cold, almost numb. If she stayed with Freddy, they would be poor, living in some tenement building, barely scraping by. She would be worse off than ever. But if she left, she would be a single mom with $10,000. Or, okay, $30,000. Both options were horrible.

Charlotte said she would give her twenty-four hours to think about it. That was how she must run things on the board of the hotel group, delivering ultimatums in those perfectly tailored pantsuits, that meticulously coiffed pixie haircut, those oval fingernails buffed to a high shine.

When Freddy came home, they had dinner. When he heard the baby—me—fussing, he picked me up and bounced me up and down, singing little songs at a low volume, so low that Amy couldn't make out the tune.

When he put me down in my Moses basket, sound asleep, Amy went to him and put her arms around him. He kissed her, and she led him to their bedroom. He worried it was too soon—too soon after the baby's birth. They hadn't had sex for months, since before Amy's father had died, before everything. But no, she assured him. The six-week mark had come and gone. They were overdue. It felt different, then. Her breasts were hard with milk, large and swollen, and all the books had warned her about how painful it might be, that first time after childbirth—"Your body has undergone extensive trauma," as one book put it—but she wanted him, desperately, and she pulled off his clothes. It was like that first time, the time in the laundry room, both of them drunk, their teeth crashing against each other when they kissed, both of them out of their minds and existing just in their bodies, two bodies reaching for each other in the dark.

When Charlotte came over the next day, Amy was prepared. The entire apartment was spick-and-span. No clothes for her to pluck off stray surfaces, no dirty dishes in the sink for her to wash. I was fed and changed and bathed and dressed in a clean onesie. On the kitchen table, Amy had set out a pot of tea and a plate with an assortment of little cookies, the kind that came in a collectible tin. She sat Charlotte down and poured her a cup of tea. Charlotte said she needed to know Amy's answer: Would she take the money and leave her son alone? Or did she insist on staying with her son, allowing him to raise another man's baby in poverty and misery, surely ruining all their lives in the process? She didn't put it quite like that, of course, but that was the gist of it.

"I don't want your money, *Charlotte*," Amy said, overenunciating her name. She opened her mouth to respond, but Amy held a finger up. "What I want," she said, "is a job."

That did surprise her. Her teacup went clattering down with a little too much force, spilling liquid into the saucer. A tiny drop hit her pale-blue silk blouse, a little dark dot just below her left breast, and this imbued Amy with the confidence she required to lay out her terms. The first time she had seen Charlotte in real life, she was striding through that grand old lobby of the Seven Glacier Hotel. Amy was sitting at the hearth of the central fireplace, playing cards. With Cory. She remembered it cinematically, almost. Charlotte walking by, Amy stopping whatever she was doing, freezing midair like a child playing Statues. Do you know who that is, she had said to Cory. That's Charlotte Bennison. He had laughed. He hadn't recognized her. Why would he? He had grown up in a rundown plains town forty miles outside the park. He worked at Seven Glacier for his photography, not because he wanted a toehold in the hospitality industry. No one worked for minimum wage as a seasonal worker in a remote mountain lodge because they thought it was some sort of career move. Of course not. That would be foolish.

Seeing Charlotte back then affected Amy. She admired her. She wanted Charlotte to take Amy under her wing, teach her everything she knew. And then, one day, she could be her. A version of her.

"I have experience," she said to Charlotte now, trying not to fixate on the dark little dot of tea staining her blouse. She looked her straight in the eye.

"Working the front desk at the Hedgewick." Charlotte had regained her composure and said the words with almost no intonation.

"At the Hedgewick and at Seven Glacier. I've worked in the kitchen, too, and when we ran the residency—back when my parents ran the artists' residency on Elena Dodge's estate—I ordered supplies and helped out with events. I'm ready."

"Ready for what, exactly?"

"I want to run a hotel," Amy said. "I want to do what you do."

Charlotte gave her a patronizing smile that said, Oh, honey, you'll never get there.

Amy pressed on. "It's not as if I'm asking for a seat on the board or something." (Not *yet*.)

"What are you asking for?"

"Hotel manager. Someplace small—somewhere like the Hedgewick. You have hotels all over the world. Send me wherever you want. Back to Oregon. Kathmandu. I promise, if you do this for me, you'll never hear from me again. And neither will Freddy."

"What makes you think you could manage a hotel?"

"I know I can. I watched Jacob do it at Seven Glacier, and he's an idiot."

Charlotte scoffed at this. Amy felt temporarily guilty for throwing Jacob under the bus like that—he was actually a very competent manager. Charlotte hadn't been there at all last summer, so it wasn't as if she would know.

"Anywhere in the world? What about the baby?"

"I'll take her with me."

~

Freddy didn't come home that night, or the night after that. Amy assumed his mother told him—told him she was leaving him, that she had successfully paid her off. She kept thinking he would come by, that last week she spent in New York. Wouldn't he want to yell at her, to beg her to stay, or maybe just to tell her off, tell her how horrible she was being, how unfair? He was willing to raise another man's child with her, and this is what she did in response? Or maybe he would accuse her of using him, of planning this all along from the very beginning, tricking him into being with her so she could skip a few rungs on the career ladder. Maybe he did believe that, but that wouldn't be accurate. What kind of plan would that be, anyway? Or maybe, she thought, he would stop by to say goodbye to me, Ramona, the little baby with a head full of dark curls, the baby who was almost his. Almost.

∼

The last week in New York, alone in the apartment with a new baby, was the worst week of her life, ranking up there ahead of the week she found out her father died, or the week she gave birth in a stupor. Her visions of harming the baby intensified, and anything seemed to set them off, not just the errant drip from a faucet or the gentle lap of water in a sinkful of dishes. She couldn't open the oven door without picturing her loading the baby into it like a casserole. If she looked out the window, she had a vision of me falling. Every time it happened, she startled, jumped the way you do in a movie theater when the psycho killer comes out from nowhere with an axe. Her heart would speed up and she would have to sit down, wherever she was, on the floor of the bathroom or the kitchen, and screw her eyes shut and press her hands over her ears to block out the sound of me screaming.

She was afraid to pick me up. Afraid to feed me. Afraid to touch me. What was wrong with her? They had done this study on orphans sometime in the Victorian era. She remembered reading about that somewhere, maybe in one of her baby books. The attendants fed a group of babies, changed their diapers and clothes, but otherwise ignored them. No one held them or talked to them. The babies cried themselves to sleep at first and then, quickly, within days, went silent. And then they died. All of them.

Amy looked at me, her baby, and could see how beautiful I was. Anyone could see that! It hit her intellectually, as if it were an indisputable fact, but she couldn't feel it. If things continued like this . . . Amy couldn't complete that thought. It was too dire to contemplate.

∼

She chose the perfect family for me. A married couple in their thirties, a good fifteen years older than Amy. She pored over pictures of them living their carefree lives, in their big house in Saint Louis, a beautiful old brick house, an honest-to-god Victorian mansion with a mansard roof and a turret. They volunteered as ushers at the Fox Theatre, and they took trips. Not the usual boring trips to tropical islands. They went hiking in the Alps alongside long-haired cows and trekking from village to village on the coast of Italy. They camped along rushing rivers and skied down snowy slopes in color-coordinated ski suits. They were laughing in all the pictures, their mouths wide open. They had steady jobs. They "valued education." This was who would raise me, who would give me the childhood that I deserved, the one Amy couldn't give me.

Charlotte Bennison made good on her word. Amy managed a hotel in Seattle. She wanted Portland, to be closer to her mom, but they didn't have any hotels there. Her mom was doing okay on her own, no thanks to Amy. She had moved back to Ashland and started teaching at a small studio. She helped her friend run a gallery. In many ways, she was back to her old life, the one they had before Elena Dodge died, before her dad got sick. So all of this—them losing their caretaking gig, her dad dying, Amy heading out to Seven Glacier and New York and having a baby and putting her up for adoption—all of it was just a blip. None of it had meant anything, or made one bit of difference. She hadn't swooped in and saved her family from ruin the way she had dreamed about. She had barely saved herself.

~

Amy studied me from across the boat. "As soon as your new parents took you, I was fine," she said. "I never had those dreams again."

I wasn't sure what kind of expression I was making, but I was going for blank. It was strange, sitting there, listening to this story that was about me but that—at the same time—seemed to have nothing to do with me. That baby Freddy cradled in his arms was *me*. The parents Amy had chosen were my parents.

"You can see why I didn't want to tell you any of this," Amy said.

"Amy—" I started. I was starting to feel guilty. She invited me here. She wanted to show me this place that meant so much to her, and here I was, hounding her for information, dredging up all her painful memories.

"And what was the point of any of it?" Amy was saying. "Everything that happened? My dad was already dead. I picked the perfect family for you, and they sucked. You come here wanting to know all about Freddy, and he's not your father, and now you want to know all about him, about Cory, and I get that, but I don't know what to tell you. I can't tell you!" She was crying by the end of this, burying her face in her hands.

"Can't tell me what?" I asked gently.

"What really happened."

"Why not?" I kept my voice very soft. Very calm. The way you might coax a cat to climb down from a tree limb. "You can tell me," I said. "It will be okay. It might be better, you know. To talk about it."

She lifted her face from her hands and peered through her fingers like a child watching a horror movie, as if viewing the gore and guts and mayhem through the slats of her fingers shielded her from it somehow, made it more tolerable. "I'm having trouble remembering," she said in a tiny voice.

I wanted to roll my eyes at that, but I did my best to restrain myself. My mind sifted through a variety of responses, finally landing on, "Like you blocked it out? That can happen sometimes with traumatic experiences. Selective amnesia."

"It's just that—you being here—it's messing with my head. Everything is just sort of rushing up to the surface. You coming to Seven Glacier, where it all began—I wanted you to come here, to see it for yourself! But I don't know." She gave me a desperate, pleading look. "Maybe it was a mistake."

"A mistake?"

"If you knew . . ." Amy started ominously.

What? If I knew *what*? I wished I could reach over and shake the truth out of Amy. However, I kept my cool. Lure it out of her. That was the way. "Can I ask you something?" I said. "One more thing. One more question. Then I'll row us back to shore."

Amy nodded.

"Why do you come back here, to Seven Glacier? You and Jonathan, you bid for the contract to run these hotels, right? You come back here all the time. You were here all summer. You spend your vacations here. I mean, if it's so triggering to be here, to see me here, then—"

"Oh no, Ramona!" Amy interrupted. "I have to come back here. There's just something about this place. As soon as I came here, that first year, I knew. I belong here. Everything started here—my whole life. My whole life revolves around this place. I can leave, I can try to escape it, but it would just pull me back, over and over again. I need to be here. It sounds crazy, but it's like I need to—keep an eye on it."

That does sound crazy, I didn't say.

"I love it here!" Amy said, and it was like she had forgotten our entire conversation. The migraine—or the fake migraine—the outburst about not being able to tell me what really happened, or not being able to remember. She smiled at me then. "Why wouldn't I want to come back?"

CHAPTER 12

—

AMY

I was awakened by the sound of knocking on my door. It was barely light outside, the crack of dawn. I covered my head with my pillow and tried to ignore it, but the knocks only got louder. "Okay, okay," I mumbled, and I flung back the covers, leaving Jonathan asleep on the bed. He could sleep through anything.

I opened the door and there was Ramona. "Hey!" she said. "Can I come in?"

"It's the middle of the night," I grumbled, but I led her into the cabin and pulled out a chair for her at the kitchen table. She didn't sit down.

"How's your head?"

I put my hand to my head. It felt fine. "Good," I said. "Much better."

"Perfect. I wanted to get an early start. You can get dressed. I'll wait."

"Early start to what?"

Ramona's eyes shone. "I want to go to Shangri-La."

"What are we going to do up there?"

"It's where it all began," Ramona said. "You told me that."

"Did I?" Of course I did. I was always doing this, it seemed. Talking myself right into a corner. Why did I tell her about Shangri-La? I wanted to tell her, I reminded myself. I wanted to tell Ramona the right story, exactly what she needed to make her feel whole. She deserved that. But still, going back to Shangri-La after all these years—

"It's not a good idea," I said. "It's dangerous."

Ramona opened my refrigerator and peered in. "We can make lunch here or get one from the restaurant. It opens at six thirty."

"I know when it opens."

"So you'll take me there? To Shangri-La?" Ramona seemed jittery, pumped up, as if she had already stayed up all night and then taken about five shots of espresso.

"I doubt it's even there anymore," I said. "It's been years."

"Nice try," Ramona said.

"I just mean, it's not even a real trail. It's a secret trail, handed down from generations of employees. You thought Ridgeline Loop was sketchy—this is way worse. All these brambles you have to bushwhack through, cliff ledges you have to crawl along—"

"Yeah, you told me all this yesterday."

I made one last-ditch effort to avoid going back to Shangri-La: "We can't drive up to the trailhead because you go down a different way than you go up, and we can't hitchhike there. It's not the '90s anymore."

"Evan has a car. She said she'd take us."

"*Evangeline?* From the front desk?"

Ramona blushed and pulled a folded piece of paper from the pocket of her shorts. "She gave me directions, too," she said. "In case you forgot the way."

~

Evan dropped us off at the mile-marker sign. We stood on the shoulder of the road and watched as she maneuvered her car around so she could head back to Seven Glacier. "Have fun!" she called out her open window as she drove away.

"She's cute," I said. Short platinum-blond hair with dark roots. Large round eyes rimmed in messy black eyeliner, and multiple piercings in both ears.

Ramona didn't respond to that. She had her little piece of paper open, the map Evan had drawn for her. She folded it back up again and put it in her pocket. "This way." Ramona started marching up the mountain toward the tangle of brush. All business.

I followed her. "I *know*."

When we reached the brush, we stopped. Ramona took off her pack and reached for her water bottle. I did the same. In the car, Ramona had sat up front with Evan and I had sat in the back, taking in the scenery. It never got old, this place. I would never get tired of looking at it. The two of them chattered and laughed—they were really hitting it off. On the hike, after Evan had driven away, Ramona and I hadn't exchanged more than a few words, none of them amounting to anything. She was still angry with me from yesterday. I could feel it, the anger, the way she held it inside her. I didn't blame her.

"Can't go under it," I said, looking into the branches that blocked our path forward. "Can't go over it. Gotta go through it."

Ramona gave me a blank look.

"'Going on a Bear Hunt'? You know that song? Or—it's not exactly a song. More of a chant."

"Everyone knows it."

"Right."

We didn't talk as we made our way through the brambles. It was a mistake to come here, to come here with Ramona. She wanted me to remember, to bring it all back, to let the memories trickle up and out of me until I was spilling everything. It wasn't as if I had forgotten what happened all those years ago. It wasn't as if I was lying to her. It wasn't selective amnesia, either, as Ramona had suggested. It was just easier not to remember. Memories haunted us because we let them, but that was the thing—we didn't have to let them. We could skip over them, jump ahead to the next part, the better part. Like watching a movie and fast-forwarding through the boring parts, and the scary parts. The highlight reel.

It was harder to do here, though, on our way through the thicket of brush to Shangri-La. Ramona had been counting on that, surely. Soon, though, it became so difficult to make our way through that my mind focused only on that, on inching forward, pushing through branches and making my way out, to the other side.

Finally we emerged from the tangle of branches, and I laughed in relief. Ramona was a mess. A determined mess. Leaves in her hair, scratches across her arms and legs. Her face red and damp with sweat. "We made it," I said, and I pointed up to the cliffs in the distance. "This is the easy part."

She exhaled loudly and chugged more water.

"Breathe," I said. "Take your time."

"I'm ready," she announced a few minutes later, and we set off toward the rocks.

"Okay. This is the part we have to climb up," I explained unnecessarily. I pointed to the ridge we would have to crawl along. Ramona had already flung off her pack and flopped down on a rock.

I sat down beside her, and we looked down at the hill we had just trudged up. The tangle of trees we had bushwhacked through looked far away. I dug through my pack in search of snacks. Trail mix; salted almonds; string cheese, a bit too warm in its plastic sleeve; a couple oranges. I took out an orange and handed it to Ramona, who seemed to be one of those people who could peel the fruit easily, tearing off large sections of the peel in three or four pieces, revealing the perfect globe underneath. She was already breaking it off into sections and biting into it while I was still struggling to dig my fingers through the skin. My fingers were already stained, my nails dirty with orange peel and pith.

"Give it to me," she said, and I handed it over. She handed the denuded orange back to me and arranged the pieces of the peel together in a neat stack.

"How did you do that?" I marveled. "It can't be genetics."

"Maybe it's from my father's side," she said.

"Maybe," I said.

Even after we packed up the neat pile of peels and continued up the hill, the oranges' sharp, citrus smell still lingered in the air and on my fingertips.

"It's steep but it's not, you know, technical rock climbing," I said as we looked up at the cliff face.

"I know that."

"We'll take it slow. I've done this before. I did this pregnant. With you."

"That was probably a stupid idea."

"Yeah. It definitely was."

At the top of the cliffs, looking down at Shangri-La, the secret lake nestled down in the valley, it was just like it was before, so beautiful but also weird and lonely, away from everything. There were no trees, just scrubby brush and grass growing from hard earth. It was so strange and otherworldly, like landing on a distant planet. We were high up in the air over here, everything quiet and still. It was cold, too.

"Look at that," I said to Ramona as we stood side by side, looking down at the lake below, mirror-still, reflecting the sky. I still found beauty in it, despite everything.

"You're never going to tell me the story, are you? The whole story—whatever it is you don't want to tell me. I promise you, Amy, I can handle it. That's why I came here. I'm ready. Whatever it is—you can tell me."

"When we get there, I'll tell you, okay?"

"Promise?"

"I'll tell you everything."

CHAPTER 13

—

Amy

By the time Ramona and I reached the shore, the weather had shifted. Clouds crowded over each other, obscuring the sun, and wind whipped up the surface of the lake. We sat down on the shore's pebbled surface and rooted through our packs for extra layers. "We shouldn't have come here," I said. "Not this late in the season."

I could hear the waves now, the sloshing of the water. When I looked out it almost seemed like it was breathing, the dark water rising and falling, churning, frothing up. I closed my eyes and placed my hands over my ears, trying to block out the sound.

"Amy?" Ramona was saying. "What's wrong?"

"This was a mistake. It's not fixing anything." I looked over at Ramona to see if she saw it, too, the way the lake was tilting, shifting. I opened my eyes wide, trying to—I don't know—comfort her, maybe. Tell her it would be all right. The world might be ending, the lake might swallow us whole, but we would be together. At least we had found each other, in the end. Right?

She said my name again and shook me, gently, and I blinked my eyes. When I looked back at the lake, it looked normal again. I tried to laugh it off, but it came out forced.

Ramona handed me her water bottle and urged me to drink. "You're probably dehydrated."

I took the bottle from her and drank until it was empty. "It's weird being back here," I said when I finished. I handed the bottle back to her.

"What happened here?" she whispered. "Is it about my dad?"

I nodded but couldn't seem to say anything.

"What happened?" she said, and her voice was hushed and urgent.

"I think my blood sugar is low," I said. "Do we have any candy—a granola bar or something?"

Ramona riffled through her pack and produced a granola bar.

I unwrapped it and bit into it. It was sweet and dry, but I gnawed at it until it was gone. "Well, this is where we fell in love," I said to Ramona, and she didn't move a muscle. She just sat, completely still, frozen, as if the slightest movement would break the spell and we would both turn to dust. I gestured to the lake before us and up at the mountains surrounding us. Millions of years ago, glaciers carved them out into this wide bowl. I patted the ground beneath me with my palms. "Right here."

I swiveled to Ramona, who was regarding me cautiously, as if she was afraid of what I might do next. I was scaring her. I tried to smile. "Why did everything have to change?" I said. "Everything was so perfect, that first summer. If everything had just stayed the way it was . . ." I trailed off, realizing what I was implying: Everything was perfect until I got pregnant. Until I had you. I squeezed my eyes shut, trying to think, and then I opened them again, staring straight at Ramona, my daughter. "I just mean it was so idyllic back then, that first summer. I decided—right here!—that I was going to do it."

"Do what?" Ramona asked.

"Fall in love with Cory Duncan."

He was so *cool*, I explained to Ramona. I realized that, once we got to Shangri-La. I was shocked I hadn't seen it immediately. He was also handsome in the way that rock stars are handsome. Too thin, clothes holey, eyes sunken, hair scraggly. He wasn't on heroin or anything like that—he just cultivated the look. It was the 1990s. I liked him. I liked the way he listened to me when I talked. He watched me, eyebrows lowered, like he was really concentrating.

And he liked me. He seemed impressed by me. I would talk while we did the dishes, and he would smirk at all the right spots. He found me funny. From all my magazines, I had learned that both men and women valued a sense of humor. But what men meant by this is that women should laugh at all their jokes. This explained a lot.

I made Cory laugh. He wasn't threatened by it. He liked me to be in the spotlight. He was content to stay behind the camera, taking pictures. Usually he had that lens pointed at something wild, something in nature, but sometimes I would find him watching me, a thoughtful look on his face, and he would raise his camera up and snap a picture of me. That was all I ever wanted. To be seen.

I didn't think so much about a future with him, the way I used to with my high school crush, daydreaming about love and marriage. It was more how I felt in the moment, when he looked at me.

We spent that whole summer together, the two of us. We had no other friends. Just a blur of washing dishes, hiking up to waterfalls, borrowing a car and driving across the border to Canada just to watch a movie, blasting that haunting music that Cory was into, reverberating guitars and echoing vocals.

We had so much in common! Our childhoods had been different, but that summer, we were both poor, working as dishwashers. We came from nothing. Didn't they like to say that, about successful people? That they had come from nothing, but look at them now. If I did picture us in the future, it was only vaguely. I was more invested in the now. How it felt to have someone look at me the way he did. Touch me the way he touched me. See me the way he saw me, with those eyes of his, those silver eyes. They were like mirrors.

I had been staring out at the lake as I talked, lost in my memories, but I turned to look at Ramona then. "You have those same eyes, you know."

"What?" Ramona laughed. "My eyes aren't silver. They're gray. Just ordinary gray."

I looked into Ramona's eyes, really focused on them. "They have that same limbal ring," I said. "They're not silver—but they're not ordinary, either. They're like storm clouds."

We both blinked at the same time, suddenly awkward, and each of us turned back to watch the waves lap up on the shore. I folded myself up, wrapping my arms around my knees. "It was the perfect summer," I said. "But it had to end."

Cory and I hadn't discussed it very much, the end. We hadn't discussed it because there was nothing to discuss. I had to get back to Medford to take care of my dad once my brother started school again. Cory lived at home with his mother in Greatfork and commuted twenty miles to the community college. We wanted to be together, but it seemed impossible to work out.

And then it was my last day. Cory would be staying on a couple more weeks, until the end of the season. We were standing side by side, washing dishes, not talking much because we knew it was the last time.

Another cart of dishes rolled up and another, and everything was just dirty dishes and the clanking sounds of the machines and the carts and the dishes clattering everywhere and scraps of food and suds and steam and cooks yelling and waiters swishing in and out of doors. I couldn't stand another minute of it. This was it for us, and we were washing *dishes*? We were wasting precious time! I untied my apron and ripped my bandanna from my head. "Let's go," I said to Cory.

He looked up from the rubble, surprised. "Now?"

I nodded, smiling. I laughed. "What are they going to do, fire us?"

I placed my hand to his face and pressed myself against him, my damp and rumpled body to his. He kissed me, and when his mouth was on mine, I laughed a little bit, and then we were really kissing, the dishes forgotten. My hands untied his apron and he pulled it over his head and then we ran out of the kitchen, laughing, like we had just robbed a convenience store at gunpoint and had gotten away with it, our fists full of cash.

"Come on!" I grabbed his hand, and we ran across a short path to the women's dorms.

I fumbled for my keys at the door, and Cory took my hand and held it against the door and kissed me again, and we murmured to each other how much we wanted this, to be together one last time. We would stay up all night, entwined in each other's arms, and then I would leave and he could send me off at the train station and it would all be so beautiful and sad and romantic and we would write and visit and promise to return here next summer. We promised, we promised!

Finally I turned the key in the lock and we stumbled inside, but then we stopped short. My roommate, a nineteen-year-old girl from Slovakia, with high Slavic cheekbones and thick ash-blond hair she wore in a no-nonsense ponytail, was sitting on top of her bed, hugging her knees to her chest, crying her eyes out.

"Radka?" I crept into the room, pulling Cory in with me by the hand.

Cory and I sat side by side on my bed. I wondered briefly if I should go to Radka, sit next to her, put my arm around her, offer her a Kleenex, but we didn't have that type of relationship. I spent all my free time with Cory, and she hung out with a group of other international workers, an Austrian named Birgit and a few others I never learned the names of. On her days off, she would put on a rust-colored string bikini, slather herself in SPF 4 sunscreen, and lie on a towel behind the employee dorms blasting "Sweet Surrender" on her portable CD player. Just that same Sarah McLachlan song, over and over, while her skin toasted.

But now Radka was hunched over on her bed. She let out a long, shuddering sigh and reached for a tissue. She dabbed at her face and blew her nose.

"Lay-dee-dee-dide," she said at last, a series of syllables that made no sense to me at all.

"What?"

157

She said it again, this time with more emphasis: "Lay-dee-DEE-dide!"

Cory and I exchanged glances.

"I don't know what you're saying," I said at last.

"Lady Dee. She was in car crash, in tunnel in Paris. They were taking pictures—"

"Lady Dee?"

It was only when she said something about the poor little princes, about William and Harry, that it clicked. "Princess *Diana*?" I asked.

"She's dead!" Radka almost yelled.

"But I just saw her" was all I could think to say. Only days before, it seemed, on the cover of all the magazines. Princess Diana was on a yacht somewhere, perched on the edge of a diving board in an aqua one-piece bathing suit. She had a new boyfriend, the tabloids said.

"He's dead, too," Radka said grimly.

I didn't cry, not like my roommate, but it rattled me, this news. It made me want to rewind everything, go backward in time to the moment before I knew. Maybe, maybe if we hadn't left work, maybe if we had worked through the shift, we wouldn't have run into my roommate, she wouldn't have told us the news. Maybe, somehow, I'd never have to hear it. I'd live my life not knowing, and everything would just stay the way it was, Cory and I in love and Princess Di perched on the edge of a diving board in an aquamarine bathing suit.

~

Eight months later, I found myself right back where I had been the last season, washing dishes at the Seven Glacier Hotel. Except this time, I was all alone. It was the very first day and it wasn't supposed to be hectic, not yet, but the dishes kept coming, and I was struggling to keep up. I worked quickly, scraping dishes, filing them into the racks, but I was sloppy, my movements jerky. How had I managed to wind up here, in the back of the kitchen again? With my experience, my background!

Just then Stuart wandered back to check on me. "Let's speed it up, Linden," he said, his eyes twinkling. Stuart with his stupid shiny black shag haircut.

I whirled to face him, jabbing a gloved finger at his smirking face. "How dare you!" I burst out.

Stuart stepped back, holding up his hands in a mock "surrender" gesture. "What did I do?"

"The guy in human resources said you requested me back here."

"You're *welcome*." Stuart didn't seem particularly bothered by my anger. If anything, he looked slightly amused, the way he always looked. Nothing ever got to Stuart.

"I don't *want* to work back here. And what about Cory?"

"What about him?"

I made a show of looking to my left and right. "He's not here. He got assigned to Lake McArthur!"

After writing and emailing for eight long months, we had our reunion all planned out: we would meet in the hotel lobby on the very first day of the season. I imagined us spotting each other from across the room, running toward each other, twirling around—the works. But when I got there, he was nowhere to be found. It was the human resources guy who told me he had been assigned to a different location, an hour away.

Stuart shrugged. "Sorry."

"I was *supposed* to be working at the front desk." I could feel a pressure behind my sinuses, tears welling up behind my eyes.

"Listen, Linden, it's a summer job. You're supposed to be having fun. That's what it's all about, man!" I suppose that was what it was all about for Stuart. On his days off, he could be seen strutting around in heavy metal band T-shirts with the sleeves cut, a comb in the back of one jean pocket, a set of drumsticks in the other.

"Not for me," I said, but Stuart had already turned to leave.

I returned to the dishes, still fuming. The bussers filled the rubber bins too high, as if they had taken it as some sort of engineering challenge, piling as much in as they could, cups in stacks of twenty, plates teetering like the Leaning Tower of Pisa with forks sticking out from the turrets, bowls still half full of soup sloshing in the corners, a pot of murky steaming liquid—pasta water?

I could barely transfer one of these bins from the cart to the counter, which I needed to do in order to free the cart for some harried busboy, trying to be a diligent and good worker, despite everything, despite the fact that this had done me more harm than good. My great work ethic was what had landed me here, back in the kitchen, and how was that fair? I had walked by the front desk, just to see my competition, those lucky girls who got to stand there in their clean black pants and perfectly pressed white blouses and smile at guests all day long, and I didn't get it. I didn't get why they got those jobs over me. What did they have that I didn't?

That was what I was thinking as I attempted to hoist that over-packed rubber bin from the cart to the counter. And besides that, how, after eight months of letter-writing and emailing, had Cory and I ended up together but apart, separated for the entire summer? It just wasn't fair. It just didn't seem right. Didn't I deserve a break? One more perfect summer, that was all I asked, really.

And that was when it happened. The bin slipped straight out from under me. It just fell—crashed—down, right on my feet. Hot water splashed up from that pot and soaked onto my pants, slapping the skin underneath. The plates in their tower slid off each other and onto the floor. Glasses shattered and I yelped, and then, an instant later, burst into tears, out of pain or humiliation or just exasperation, or maybe all of those things at once.

"You okay, Linden?" Stuart had appeared at my side immediately after the commotion, mop in hand. The busboy, too, had appeared by my side, and both of them were already busy picking up the mess.

"I'm sorry," I muttered, and bent down to help out.

"Take five—we'll clean up around here." Stuart didn't seem angry, but then again, I was his only dishwasher.

Without saying anything, I exited the kitchen through the back doors. My face was still wet from tears, but I was no longer crying. Outside the building, I paced back and forth, trying to calm myself down. When that didn't work, I kicked my sensible, close-toed shoes into the dirt. A cloud of dust bloomed up and settled onto the wet spots on my pants. It would serve Stuart right if I just quit. *Kick!* Take five? I'll just take the rest of my life! *Kick!*

"Whoa, whoa, whoa!" said a voice, a young man's voice. "What happened *here?*"

I looked up, and there he was, my hero in lederhosen, smiling down at me with his endearing mess of curls and perfect smile. Freddy Bennison.

~

Ramona and I sat on the shores of Shangri-La, shivering. I wrapped my arms around my legs. "We should get going." Hard drops of rain fell, but sporadically, like a leaky faucet that had been shut off but still produced a trickle.

Ramona held her face up to the sky, her eyes closed. She breathed in, smiling slightly, like a woman undergoing a religious experience.

I breathed in, too, mirroring her. The rain unlocked the smell of the earth along with the deep green scent of the lake.

"Not yet." She placed her palms up to feel the drops on her skin. "The drops are far apart."

Sure enough, the clouds overhead shifted over, and the rain stopped.

Ramona looked over to me, a triumphant smile on her face, as if to say, See! No more rain.

"I heard there used to be a boat up here," Ramona said.

"Who told you that?"

"Evan. She thought it might just be an old legend, though. Like when the seniors try to convince the freshmen that there's a pool on the roof of the high school."

"Ha!" I said. "I forgot about that."

"About the boat?"

"About the pool on the roof. The seniors even tried selling tickets at my high school. One of my friends fell for it and lost ten dollars."

"But what about the boat? Was there one?"

"How would you even get a boat up here?"

"Good point." Ramona sat up straight. "All right," she said. "I'm ready."

I twisted around to pick up my pack, gather up my things, but Ramona stopped me.

"For the end of the story. You said this is where it all began." She patted the ground the way I had done earlier. "You said it started right here, and it ended here, too."

"We can talk about it on our way down," I said.

"Or we can talk about it right here."

"I don't know what you're expecting to hear, but it's not going to bring you any closer to figuring out—anything."

"Okay, Amy," Ramona said. "If it isn't that interesting, then why didn't you just tell me in the first place? Why were you wasting my time with this decoy story, just to throw me off the scent—"

"You're being ridiculous."

"So you and Freddy had that one-night stand, right? But you were together—you were supposed to be together—with Cory. My dad. Did he ever find out?"

"Eventually. Yes."

"So that summer, you were with both of them. Cheating on Cory with Freddy. Is that how it went?"

"The one-night stand was a mistake. I think I made that pretty clear. I regretted it!" The look on Ramona's face indicated that she was having trouble believing me. "I loved Cory! And then I had to go and ruin it. I was out of my mind after that whole thing with Freddy. How could I have done that? With Cory it was—it was true love. True love means you don't even look in anyone else's direction, right? It's all-consuming. So how could I have done that?" Ramona tried to interrupt, but this time I wouldn't let her. "Freddy and I, we had our—you know, what happened in the laundry room. The next morning, I was walking home, and I had the near-death experience with that bear, and I vowed to never do anything like that again, to turn my life around, live the straight and narrow and everything—"

"Give me a break," muttered Ramona.

"And that day, I went over to McArthur Lodge to see Cory. It was Friday. We got the same days off, Friday and Saturday. And when I saw him—I was just so happy to see him, after all those months. And I *wanted* to tell him; I had planned on telling him. It's a long shuttle bus ride from Seven Glacier to McArthur, almost an hour. I was going to tell him I had made a mistake, a huge mistake, and you know what? If I had, everything would have been different. He would have been upset, but he would have forgiven me. He was like that. But I didn't. I couldn't. I chickened out."

I had worked myself up, telling this story, talking faster and faster. Ramona was quiet now, watching me, waiting for me to continue. "And I didn't cheat on him, not after that one time, when I was drunk." Ramona gave me a doubtful look and so I amended my statement: "I fooled around with Freddy, yes. But I didn't *sleep* with him again. I mean, not until after—after it was over with Cory. I mean—not that that's okay. I was twenty-one years old. My brain wasn't even fully developed at that point."

"I'm twenty now."

"Okay, well, you're a lot smarter than I was back then. That summer—it was a weird time."

"And then what?"

"You know what. I found out I was pregnant. It was the end of the season at that point. Around this time of year. Early September. That's when I realized how far along I was, already eighteen weeks or something—I told you this part."

"Right." Ramona leaned in, her eyes focused.

"Well," I started. I was trying to choose my words carefully. Trying to figure out the words to explain everything in a way that would make sense to Ramona, would give her what she wanted. "I told Cory over the phone. I told him I was pregnant. He flipped out."

"Flipped out? Like—what?"

"I mean he was freaked out. I told him I was already four months along, practically, that it must have happened at the beginning of the summer. He wasn't ready to be a father, he said. He had dreams. He wanted to be a wildlife photographer. Did I tell you that? He loved photography, just like you."

"You told me."

"Right. He said he needed time to think. I couldn't believe it. I thought he loved me. I thought he would do anything for me. I was crying my eyes out. A few hours later I got a message from him. He left a message for me at the front desk, and one of my coworkers delivered it to me in my dorm: 'Meet me at Shangri-La, noon tomorrow.' It gave me hope, that message. Shangri-La! That was where we fell in love. That was where—where it all began."

"He wanted you to go on this crazy hike through the bushes and up a cliff when you were pregnant?"

"We had just done the Ridgeline Loop the week before—I don't know, it didn't strike me as odd at the time. It seemed romantic, maybe. Also, Shangri-La was halfway between Seven Glacier and McArthur—so it made sense, to meet me in the middle. That was what I was thinking."

"Still," Ramona said.

"The next day I hitched a ride to that mile-marker sign. I got there in the morning. He'd said to meet him at noon, but not when to show up at the trailhead. I waited there for a while and then I figured he meant to meet at the lake at noon, so I got going. I did that whole thing on my own."

"Eighteen weeks pregnant."

"Yes."

"What was he thinking?"

"I don't know. I thought he wanted us to make it work. I thought that was why he wanted to meet up here." I lifted up my arms to the sky and right then, as if I had conjured it, the breeze lifted up, whipping our hair. From the cold, pebbly shore, we surveyed our surroundings: the glacier-hewn mountain walls, the lake, the sky. I wrapped my hands back around my knees, staring out at the water. "It was different that first time. Warmer. The lake was like a mirror, so calm. Maybe he wanted that again, to go back to that time, back before everything got so screwed up, back when it was perfect, just the two of us."

I let out a whoosh of air, halfway between a sigh and a laugh. "Anyway. I managed to make it up here, expecting the whole time to run into him. I kept looking ahead of me and behind me, figuring he must be on his way, too. Then I started thinking maybe he had set out early. Maybe he was waiting for me there. But when I got over the cliffs and looked down, he wasn't here. That was obvious. I could see for miles and miles, and he wasn't anywhere. So I went to the shore"—once again, I patted the ground beneath us—"right here. I just sat down right here and waited."

"He never showed up?"

"I waited for hours. I waited until the sun started to disappear behind the mountains and I knew I had to leave before it got dark. I made it back down without breaking my leg or getting torn apart by a wild animal. I went straight to McArthur Lodge to find him. I pictured him waiting there on his bed or in the gift shop, contrite, apologizing maybe, telling me he just couldn't do it, he just couldn't be a father. But he wasn't there. His room was empty. He was just—gone."

CHAPTER 14

A MY

To leave Shangri-La, you don't go back down the same way you come up. What you do is you walk around the lake. You walk over the ridge, and another valley spreads out before you. To get to it, you have to slide down some scree until you land, laughing and choking on sand and dust, at the base of the hill. After that it's easy. You're on the valley floor. You follow a river all the way to the main road and hitch a ride back to civilization.

Ramona and I started back, following along the edge of the lake. We marched along in silence for a bit, and then Ramona started asking me questions. "Why didn't you just tell me all this in the first place?"

"It just seemed easier," I said.

Ramona clomped along beside me. I had to hand it to her—she kept up, no complaints. "It makes no *sense*," she was saying. "I mean, I ask about my father, can't you just say, it was this guy Cory and he split when he found out I was pregnant? It's hardly an unusual story. It's, like, the oldest story in the book."

"You didn't ask about your father," I reminded her. "You asked me about Freddy."

Although I wasn't looking at Ramona as we walked, I could almost feel her eyes rolling. "Not that again."

"I should have told you," I said. "I know that."

"I wanted to know who I am. Where I come from."

"It's just that—when you asked me about Freddy—I don't know. I liked the idea of it. Freddy wanted to be your father. He *was* your father, for just a bit. Maybe he even still would be if his mom hadn't come in and screwed it all up."

"Don't blame this on her."

"Fine. It wasn't her fault. I know that."

"Do you?"

"It seemed better than the truth, which is that your father left us. That he would rather take off and run."

We reached the part of our descent that required us to shimmy down a steep pile of crushed rocks. "This is the scree I was telling you about."

She frowned as she looked down at it.

"It's not that bad," I assured her. "You sort of—scrabble down." I sat down and pushed myself off with my hands, doing a little crab walk. Ramona took off a moment later, and before we knew it, we were down at the bottom, coughing in a cloud of dust.

We cleaned ourselves off as well as we could, slapping at the backs of our legs with our hands. "We can rinse our hands once we get to the river," I said.

"I got it!" Ramona exclaimed out of nowhere five minutes later. "I figured it out!"

"What?" I was walking ahead of Ramona, leading the way. I turned around to face her, and we both stopped.

"Someone could have gone to Shangri-La from this side with a boat and waited at the bottom of that hill we just slid down, right? And then someone else could go up the normal way with a rope. All they'd have to do is throw the rope down the hill and pull up the boat, right?"

I turned back around and continued tromping toward the river. I could hear it now, that sound of water rushing over rocks. "I guess," I said.

"That's got to be it!" Ramona seemed very pleased with herself.

"If there even was a boat," I said.

Once we reached the river, we were on the home stretch. We met up with an actual maintained hiking trail and would follow that for a couple miles until it led us to a small parking lot not far from the main road. The path was shaded, lined with ferns and late-blooming wildflowers. The water was low in the river now, at the end of the summer. Clear, cold water over smooth, round rocks.

I tried to remember walking back those other times, before. I couldn't. I remembered walking up, almost every detail. The bushwhacking, the cliff climbing, crawling along that ledge, that first glimpse down into the valley at the lake below, glinting in the sun, reflecting the sky. But coming down, walking along this very path—it was a blank.

"So you never went looking for him?" Ramona asked me. She was in the lead now that we were on an official path. She turned her head back to talk to me.

"Why would I? He left."

"But didn't you want to—"

"I was with Freddy, remember? I moved to New York. Freddy wanted to be with me. With us."

"So you just—let it go?"

"For all I knew, Freddy *was* your father. We had had unprotected sex. The timing added up. It wasn't like I was tricking him."

"Not exactly."

"Did I tell Freddy about Cory? No. But I didn't know he *wasn't* the father. Not until later. Not until Charlotte had to go and get some paternity test like we were on *The Jerry Springer Show* or something." I wondered if Ramona would even get that reference. "Or maybe I'm thinking of the Maury show. There were these daytime talk shows where—"

"So Cory—my dad—could actually still live around here," Ramona said over me. "What town did you say he was from—some plains town, right?"

"I doubt it."

"Someone might still be there—he lived with his mom, right? What was her name?"

"I don't know," I said. "I don't remember."

Ramona picked up the pace. She was practically skipping down that path. "Oh man, she could still be there. She's my grandmother! My biological grandmother! I never had a grandmother. My mom's mother died when I was young, and my dad's mom lived in Florida and I hardly ever saw her. She sent me birthday cards with money inside, one dollar for every year of my age. But then my brother and sister? Her real grandkids? They got checks on their birthdays. Fifty dollars a pop. Can you believe that?"

"My mom's still alive. She would love to meet you. We should plan on it. Maybe this Christmas or—"

"That would be great," Ramona said. "What was the name of that town again?"

"What town?"

"The town where Cory grew up—you said it was forty miles from here, forty miles east. I can just look it up, you know."

"Greatfork," I said.

"Greatfork." Ramona clapped her hands and laughed. "Greatfork!"

"Look, Ramona, I'm not saying don't go looking for her. I'm just saying"—what was I saying?—"I'm worried about you, is all. He left us. He didn't want to be a father. For all I know, that hasn't changed."

"I've been rejected by my father my whole life." Her voice was still light, as if this was just a simple fact, one she had accepted long ago and now found almost amusing. "What's one more?"

~

At nine o'clock the next morning, Gabe knocked on Ramona's door. I was standing behind a large lodgepole, out of Ramona's line of vision. She answered in her pajamas, a matching summer set, short-sleeve green plaid top and drawstring bottoms. "Hey, little brother," she said.

"Ready for your next lesson?" he asked her.

"What time is it?"

"It's never too early to learn." Gabe smiled his gap-toothed smile. He was missing about half his teeth at this point, and he hadn't had a haircut since the end of spring. That chunk of hair in the back had matted up into such a huge tangle I would have to probably cut it out with scissors if we didn't get to it soon. He was also wearing mismatched socks. He looked unkempt and adorable, like some scrappy kid in a postapocalyptic movie who goes around hunting with a slingshot.

"Sorry, buddy," Ramona said. "Maybe later this evening, okay? Or tomorrow?"

"Why not now?" Gabe insisted.

"Isn't it supposed to rain?"

"It's not raining right this *minute*."

"I have some things I need to do."

"Things like what?"

"Oh, nothing that exciting."

"I can come with you," Gabe said. "We can talk." Gabe clasped his hands behind his back and bounced up and down on his heels. He was really selling it, I would give him that.

Ramona poked her head out the door and looked up and down the hall. "Amy, I know you're out there!" she yelled. Then, to Gabe: "Your mom put you up to this, didn't she?"

"Don't be silly," he said. I couldn't see his face, but I could imagine it: his serious eyes with their long dark lashes, blinking up at her, the picture of innocence.

Ramona tousled his hair and said, "See you later, okay, Gabe?" Then she yelled out into the hall again, "Nice try, Amy!"

Gabe came up to me and said, "I tried."

"No, that was good. A very convincing performance."

"I don't think she fell for it, though."

"*I* would have taken you up on it. You're an excellent teacher."

"I know." Gabe heaved a huge sigh, shaking his head sadly.

I took his hand and walked briskly through the halls of the lodge. "Listen, Gabe, are you okay hanging out with Dad one more day? I have to go somewhere."

"Where?"

"Tell Dad I'm with Ramona again."

"But you're not."

"I'm going to be—I'm going to join her. Okay?"

We exited the lodge and practically jogged along the paths to our cabin, hand in hand. Overhead, clouds gathered in the sky and the air felt cool, the way it did here at Seven Glacier this time of year. It surprised me every year, how suddenly it could happen, the way the season changed in an instant, as if someone had flipped a switch. "Dad will be back by ten, I think he said." Jonathan was off mountain biking on some trails—either that or jogging around one of the lakes. I was only half listening when he left earlier, though he did say he would be back by ten. I was pretty sure about that. Anyway, that was usually around the time he returned from his morning outings. "If he doesn't come back, you can always go into the lobby, right? The girls love it when you help out at the front desk."

"Maybe I'll come with you," Gabe said.

"Not today, sweetie."

"I think I want to," he said. "I need to talk to Ramona."

"Later this evening—isn't that what she told you?"

"We have a lot to talk about," said Gabe.

"I think Johnny might be coming in today," I told him. By then we were back in the cabin. I was rushing around, getting my things together. Sunglasses, granola bars, keys—I threw them all into a shoulder bag. Johnny was a little kid Gabe's age, the son of one of the cooks who lived in St. Anne. His girlfriend dropped Johnny off some days, and he would spend all day running around the lodge, tripping the servers in the kitchen, until his dad would yell at him to play outside. Gabe loved him. After they spent time together, Gabe would come home with all sorts of questions about boobs and blow jobs, or he would report to us, virtuously, that Johnny had wanted to set off firecrackers from the boat dock but that he, Gabe, had refused, because "they are illegal and they are a FIRE HAZARD."

So I didn't really want Gabe to run around with Johnny, but the likelihood that Johnny would show up today was pretty low anyway. He might even be back in school by now, with any luck.

"Why don't you go look for him?" was the last thing I said to my son before I slipped out the door.

Outside, I scanned my surroundings. The back side of the lodge, the paths from the lodge to the parking lots. I didn't have a good view of the parking lot itself, but I figured that was where Ramona would be heading. I just hoped I hadn't missed her.

I ran up the stone steps to the parking lot and stood up on the little wall at the top of the stairs. From there, I had a great view of the back of the lodge and most of the parking lot. She wasn't there. Either she hadn't come out yet or she had already left. It was more likely she hadn't come out yet. She wasn't even dressed when I made Gabe knock on her door, and that couldn't have been more than ten minutes ago. Gabe hadn't convinced her to stay here today—and I didn't blame him, not in the least; he had done a great job, just the way I had coached him—so she knew I was onto her, or at least suspected. That meant—

There! I spotted her striding out the main doors of the lodge. She looked to her left and her right. I jumped down from the ledge and hunkered behind a car. She hadn't spotted me. It probably hadn't occurred to her that her mother, her biological mother, would be stalking her, standing on a stone ledge and spying on her from above. Well, maybe "stalking" was overstating it. I did ask myself, in that moment, what, exactly, I was hoping to accomplish by following Ramona out of the parking lot. I knew where she was going, and I knew what she was going to find. So what was the point of watching it all happen? Instead of following her, maybe I should have been running in the other direction. Gathering up Jonathan and Gabe, packing our bags, and heading out. How about Thailand, I could suggest to Jonathan, and he would probably jump at the chance.

But no. I couldn't do that. I couldn't abandon Ramona, not again. I had to see this through, and I would. I would see this through. She walked out of my line of sight, and I had to sneak behind her, ducking behind other cars in case she turned around and saw me. Then I watched as she got into a car—Evan's car, the same car from yesterday—and headed out of the parking lot.

As soon as her car exited the lot, I darted to my own car and jumped in, throwing my bag down on the passenger seat. I felt a bit crazed, but also excited, like I was a character in a TV show, a cop about to pursue a criminal in a high-speed car chase. I'd never tailed anyone before. The road that led away from Seven Glacier Hotel to the main highway was only partially paved, usually in disrepair from the harsh winters, so driving down it was slow. It was easy keeping an eye on her while also staying a safe distance back.

"Call Jonathan," I said out loud, and my phone dialed my husband. The call went straight to his voicemail, as I had expected. I left a quick message explaining that I had to run an emergency errand and that Gabe was fine, either fending for himself at home or possibly in the lobby or possibly somewhere else, looking for Johnny. "Actually, I'd rather him not play with Johnny, so if he's not in the cabin, could you try to find him?" I concluded.

You know what, I was a terrible mother. That probably had occurred to Ramona several times on this trip. Well, maybe that was for the best. Maybe that would give Ramona what she needed—the sense that she had led the right life after all, that the mother who had raised her had done a much better job than I ever could have. Ramona had shown me her school pictures, that first time we met. Kindergarten with her hair in pink barrettes, first grade her hair in two thick braids and a pinafore dress, and on and on until senior year, braces off, smiling a radiant smile, her curls dark and glossy. Her mom, the woman who raised her, definitely never let her out of the house in mismatched socks. Her mom wouldn't have let her curls tangle up into knots she would have to hack away at with scissors at the end of the summer. Her mom would under no circumstances let her go running around with a hooligan who literally played with matches.

Ramona put her blinker on. She was turning right onto the highway. I slowed down and waited until she turned before I followed her. I knew where she was going. I had known from the beginning.

I trailed Ramona all the way to Greatfork. It was easy, the perfect amount of traffic for surreptitiously following someone. Not so much that you lose sight of them, not too little so it starts getting obvious, they start wondering why the same forest-green Volvo has been popping up in their rearview mirror for the last forty miles or so. Overhead, storm clouds gathered, piled on top of each other, obscuring the sun. The grasses on the plains glowed eerily in this light.

Greatfork was a depressing little town, just as Cory had described it to me. Everything felt spread out. Operational gas station, abandoned gas station, little windowless brick post office, a park with desiccated grass and old playground equipment that hadn't been updated in the last half century. Ramona pulled off onto a road lined with houses, all in some state of disrepair. No one was around—whether they were hunkering down inside or gone somewhere, I couldn't say.

Easing off the gas, I widened the distance between our cars. I hadn't followed her this far only to get caught now. Ramona parked at the curb, and I pulled over to the side of the road, idling the engine as she got out of the car and walked up to the front door. Only once she had stepped inside did I drive up and park on the other side of the street under a large, half-dead cottonwood tree, one of the only trees on the block.

The house Ramona had walked into was probably the nicest house in the neighborhood, which cheered me somewhat. However, that was not saying much. It was old, and it needed a fresh coat of paint and a new roof, but baskets of petunias hung along the front porch.

I sat crouched down in the front seat of my car for three hours. An hour in, it started to rain. Drops splattered on the windshield, sporadically at first, and then all at once, a loud, syncopated sound, like machine-gun fire. The wait gave me a lot of time to think—about Cory's mother, what she looked like, what her life was like, what she was saying to Ramona, what Ramona was saying to her, how Ramona was taking the news, how Cory's mom was taking the news, what Ramona would do when she finally emerged, how she would look. She would be devastated, obviously. She would have questions. The rain slowed down again, and then it stopped altogether, leaving the asphalt streets shiny, with clouds of steam evaporating off them.

Finally that front door opened. That was what I saw first, just the door yawning open. Ramona stepped out onto the porch. She was still talking to the person inside. "Stay inside," I muttered. I didn't want to see her, Cory's mom. I couldn't take it. She would be withered and gray, hunched over from weak bones, wearing a sad cotton housedress, white with pink flowers, perhaps, faded from years of washing and drying on the clothesline out back.

A woman stepped onto the porch, and she and Ramona hugged tightly. I readjusted my mental image of his mother. She was not old and gray. She was barely even old. Of course she wasn't. She would be in her early sixties, her hair still dark, straight with loose bangs. She was wearing a tank top and denim shorts and she was very pretty—even from my vantage point, hunching down in the front seat of my car across the street, I could see that. Her petite build, her delicate features, her tanned limbs, her bare feet.

"Oh my god," I said out loud. "Oh no."

Of course I knew. I knew exactly what Ramona would find out when she met with Cory's mother. I just kept thinking I could control it, control the way the story was told. Tell it in a way that would make sense, would make it better somehow. I hadn't prepared myself to hear it told another way, from another angle. Like lifting a smooth stone and seeing the hidden underside, slithering dark-dwelling bugs, earwigs, and centipedes writhing underneath. Better before you knew. When it was just a nice smooth rock decorating the garden bed.

Cory's mother went back inside the house, and Ramona walked down the front path to her car.

I flung my car door open. "Ramona!" I shouted, running toward her. "Ramona!"

She whirled around to see me standing there, right next to her. I begged her with my expression: Please, Ramona, please. Let me explain. I can explain everything.

"Get away from me!" Ramona said, but she didn't get in the car.

I said her name again.

"You knew. This whole time, you knew." Her face crumpled up and her eyes, already tired and red, filled with tears. She blinked and they fell down her face, all at once.

I nodded helplessly. I reached for her, raised my hands to bring her to me, but she flinched, avoiding my touch.

She threw herself into the car and slammed the door shut behind her.

CHAPTER 15

RAMONA

I turned my key in the ignition and revved the engine, but before I could drive away, Amy ran in front of the car, slapping her hands on the hood. I slammed on the brakes and stared at Amy through the windshield. Had she *followed* me here, all the way from Seven Glacier? She had this desperate, beseeching look on her face that made me want to stomp my foot on the gas and run her over. I unrolled my window. "I'll run over you, Amy! I swear I will!" I yelled out.

"Ride back with me!" she yelled. "I'll explain everything. I promise."

"I'm not going anywhere with you."

"I can send someone to pick up Evan's car. Or you can drive, it doesn't matter. I just want to explain—"

I put the car into reverse and backed away from Amy, spinning the tires on the ground. Then I drove toward her again, gaining speed. I swerved around her and drove off. My vision blurred with tears. I drove faster and faster, away from that town, back on the highway. It was raining, really coming down. I pressed my foot down on the gas and kept going, windshield wipers flapping back and forth, back and forth. Amy was following me, she had stalked me, driven all the way over to Cory's mother's house, Cory's childhood home, and—what? She must have been sitting out there in the car for hours, and—

My heart was beating very fast, a million times a minute, and I couldn't breathe. Just drive. That was all I could do, just whip down the highway as fast as I could. I would drive back to the lodge, grab my bags, check out. That was it—I was done.

When I got back to the lodge, I was still caught up in everything that had happened, my pulse racing, my eyes stinging. I ran inside and ran straight into Jonathan. I mean, I literally ran into him, crashed right into his chest in the lobby by the front desk. "Whoa, there!" he said in his jocular voice. Then he must have seen the wild look in my eyes because he guided me to a quiet corner, away from the desk, the tourists sitting on armchairs reading books or relaxing over glasses of wine from the bar. "What's going on?"

I wondered, then, if he was in on it. Amy might have told him everything, the whole story. He certainly hadn't seemed shocked when she introduced me to him, as if this was just par for the course for him, a day in the life married to my biological mother, Amy Linden. "My father," I said.

Jonathan was studying my face carefully, as if he was trying to figure out what to say next. He lifted up a hand—maybe to place on my shoulder, maybe to pat my arm—but appeared to think better of it and let it drop back down to his side. "Your father?" he repeated carefully.

"What do you know about him? What did she tell you?"

"Are you talking about Frederick Bennison? He—"

She had kept him in the dark. In a way, it made me feel better. It wasn't just me. She did this to everyone. "No!" I snapped, impatient. I wanted him to understand. I wanted him to catch up. "It wasn't him."

Jonathan's expression didn't change. If anything, his face just froze for a few seconds. Then something appeared to come over him, and his features relaxed—eyebrows slightly lifted, a small smile. "That's Amy's business," he said. "What happened back then—"

God, this was infuriating. I wanted to grab him by the arms and shake him. So I did.

"Jonathan, wake up!" Suddenly I saw myself the way everyone else must see me. Screeching into the parking lot, running into the lodge, crashing into Jonathan, grabbing him by the arms. I looked back at the front desk and, for a split second, Evan caught my eye. She lifted her eyebrows slightly and then looked down. The girl standing beside her—Georgia?—picked up the telephone and began speaking into it.

To his credit, Jonathan didn't seem to care that I was making a scene in the middle of his hotel, that my hands were clenched around his biceps. He was observing me, concerned. Calm, very calm. Maybe this was what it took, to stay married to Amy all these years. Extreme equanimity.

I lowered my voice. My hands were still wrapped around his arms, but I loosened my grip. "It wasn't Freddy. She *thought* it was Freddy, or could be Freddy, but it wasn't. It was someone else. Cory. Cory Duncan," I explained. Very softly, so only he could hear it. I gave Jonathan a piercing stare and he swallowed once, as if he knew what I was going to say next. "He's dead," I said. "He's been dead all along."

I left him there and headed up to my room, but once I got there, I knew I couldn't leave, not before I heard whatever it was Amy would have to say to explain what I had learned earlier that day. Would she tell me the truth? Probably not. But she knew what really happened, and I would try to force it out of her if I had to before I was going to leave. Still, I didn't want to wait around for her to show up to my room. I needed to calm down, to get my head on straight first.

I spent the rest of the afternoon walking around the lake. The rain had stopped by then, but the sun was still obscured by banks of clouds. The air smelled clean, rinsed out, and although it was chilly and I wasn't wearing the proper clothes, I stayed out for a long time, meandering away from the lake and down a footpath I hadn't explored yet. This is where I'm from, I kept repeating to myself. Back at the lodge, I ordered dinner at the café and ate it by myself on an Adirondack chair on the balcony. By the time I went back inside, it was after ten. Dinner service was over. The dining room was dark and empty. I sat at a table by the window, looking out at the moon. That was where she found me.

She pulled the chair across from me out from the table very slowly, as if not to startle me with a sudden noise, and she sat down. I looked up at her but didn't say anything.

"Ramona," she started, "I want to explain—"

I held up a hand. "Don't," I said. "I won't believe a word you say."

She opened her mouth and then took stock of the situation and closed it again, nodding for me to continue.

"You told me his name. You told me he lived around here. I was excited—I mean, he left us, left me, or so you said, but still—it's twenty years later. I'm not going to ruin his life. Maybe he would want to meet me. Maybe he had been wondering all this time how I had turned out. So when we got back here, I looked him up. I didn't know how he spelled his name. With a *K* or a *C*, with a *-y* or an *-ey* or what. Or maybe even Cori with an *i*—even though they were all girls. All sorts of people popped up, but none of them seemed like they could have been him. But then when I looked up Duncans in Greatfork, there was only one. Meredith Duncan. She seemed like the right age to be his mom, and her number was listed. I called her and she picked up."

I couldn't look at Amy while I talked, so I gazed out at the moon reflecting off the lake.

"My heart was beating so fast. I just called her, not planning out what I was going to say or how she was going to even take the news, if she would want to talk to me. I just did it. I asked her if she was Cory Duncan's mother, and she hesitated a long time before answering. She said yes. And so then I asked her if he was there—could I talk to him— and she asked me what this was concerning, what was this all about, and I said, 'This may sound crazy, but I think he's my father, my biological father.' I asked if he worked at Seven Glacier Park the summers of '97 and '98, and she just took in this sharp breath and said I should come visit her.

"And—you know what happened next. I borrowed Evan's car, drove over there. You saw the town—so weird, being out there, like it was the middle of nowhere, just this run-down little town with one gas station and a bunch of weird shops. It was strange imagining anyone living there, especially my own father. Maybe he would be there, I was thinking. Maybe she would have called him, and I'd be able to meet him."

"Oh, Ramona."

"She hugged me when she saw me." Tears welled up in my eyes, but I took in a breath and didn't allow them to fall. "You saw her—she's small. Dark hair and dark eyes. We hugged for a long time. It seemed like she just believed me, or maybe she just wanted to believe me, you know? Like a part of him was there, showing up at her doorstep.

"She invited me in. She had already laid out a bunch of photos and albums. They were all arranged on the coffee table. She had them waiting for me, to show me. She asked me how I found out, or what I knew, and I told her about you. How I'd been adopted as an infant and that I found you, and you told me about Cory, that you'd just told me, and she just listened to me, a sort of stunned expression on her face, and she was like, 'I had no idea, I had no idea.'"

Meredith's house—Cory's house, the place he had grown up—felt very still. As if it had remained unchanged all those years, just sitting there, waiting for Cory to return. It was a creaky old place, built in the late 1800s, with slanted wood floors and heavy wooden furniture. Meredith handed me a glass of lemonade, and we sat on her dusty old couch together, poring over the photographs. Cory as a baby, with a shock of black hair and a grumpy old man expression. Cory in first grade, smiling into the camera, holding up some sort of award he had won in school. He was wearing brown corduroy pants and a red-and-blue velour shirt, and he looked so awkward and adorable that it sent a pang through me, like I wanted to protect him, protect this kid from whatever happened to him later.

Even while I was talking to her, my grandmother, I kept hoping Cory would wander out from one of the bedrooms or walk in through the kitchen door at the back of the house. It was possible, I reasoned. He might have freaked out when Amy told him she was pregnant. He might have disappeared, just like she said. But it wasn't as if he would stay away forever. He would travel around a bit, get a job in some distant town, and then he would come back. He wouldn't just disappear off the face of the earth. Right?

And so I asked her where he was now, what he was doing. And her face fell. Honey, he died, she said.

I knew it even before she said it, really. As we flipped through the pages of the photo albums, the pictures of Cory got sparser as the years went on. And they ended when he was eighteen, a senior in high school. It was the generic studio photo with the mottled blue background. He was wearing that fake tux every boy wore for those pictures, with the jaunty black bow tie. He was smiling, revealing teeth that overlapped a bit. I had those teeth, just like that, before I got braces.

Amy shut her eyes, and I wanted to reach out and shake her, force her to look at me, but then, as if she sensed it, she opened them again and nodded once: continue.

"He disappeared at the end of the summer, in 1998, just like you said," I said. "She didn't hear from him for a while, and when he never called, didn't come home at the end of the season, she called the hotel where he worked and they said he had packed up all his things and left without a word a couple weeks earlier. This made no sense—he wouldn't just pick up and leave like that, not without telling her, his own mother. She tried calling the police, and they refused to help her. He left on his own accord, they told her. She went crazy, then, looking for him, wondering what happened to him. But he was gone. The season had ended, and almost everyone had left by then—there was no one to ask."

Amy put her hand to her mouth. "Oh my god," she whispered.

I leaned in. She needed to hear this next part. "I told her what you said—that he freaked out about the pregnancy. That he didn't want to be a father. She didn't buy it." A cloud passed over my grandmother's face when I told her that. He wouldn't do that, she said. Truly mystified by the mere suggestion of it.

"Ramona—" Amy tried to interrupt me, but I held up a hand.

"So for seventeen years, she just lives with it. Lives with the not knowing. That's the worst part of it—that's how it was for me, too. I told you this, how there's this mystery hovering over your whole life and—and anyway, seventeen years later, that's when they found a body at the bottom of a lake, right here in the park. You'd think this would be major news, right? But it was nothing. She showed me the clip from the paper, it was maybe three inches long, buried in the back somewhere. A body found at the bottom of a lake with a camera around its neck."

Meredith wished she could talk to Cory's girlfriend, Amy, but she had no way of tracking her down. She didn't even know her last name. Then in 2015, when his body was identified, they opened up the case in earnest, but by then it was too late to find any leads, follow any clues. The investigation fizzled out.

I told Amy this, my eyes trained on her the whole time. In the moonlight she looked eerie, the shadows of her face darker than usual. "I asked her what the name of the lake was." My voice went cold. "It was Shangri-La."

"There's another side to this," she said, and she tried to reach for my hands, the way she had earlier, back when I still believed her, believed she could tell me what I needed to know. "What happened that day— there's more to it. I can explain—"

"I'd love to hear it, Amy! I'd just love to hear how he wound up at the bottom of the lake, forty feet down, with a camera around his neck. He couldn't have *swum* out there. That's what his mom told me. He didn't know how to swim!" I was crying then, hot wet tears streaming down my cheeks.

I heard her sigh softly, and she leaned in and wiped my face with her hand, gently, the way I had seen her do with Gabe, the way a mother would, and I let her. I let her do it. "I want you to know something," she said, and I could barely make out her words I was crying so hard, sniffling and choking with sobs. "I want you to know that I loved him."

CHAPTER 16

RAMONA

After Amy woke up in the top bunk with Freddy's arm slung over her, after the walk of shame back to the lodge, after the near-death experience with the grizzly, she went into the lodge and called home. That's what she told me, as we sat in the dark dining room. After waking up her little brother and chatting with her dad, she headed back to her room. By then it was almost eight o'clock. Her roommate, Brooke, sat up when she opened the door. "Good morning!" Amy trilled.

Brooke squinted up at Amy from her bed. "Were you out all night?" she asked groggily.

"I got up early," Amy said, which was true. "I went to the lodge to call home," she added, which was also true.

Brooke laid her head back on the pillow, one arm flung over her eyes. In a flash, Amy undressed, pulling on her bathrobe and gathering what she needed for the shower. "Want to go down for breakfast?" she asked Brooke on her way out.

After the shower and breakfast with Brooke in the employee dining room, she felt better. Brooke had to start her shift, and Amy had her weekend ahead of her, Friday and Saturday. The shuttle to McArthur Lodge left at ten o'clock, and she planned to be on it. She told Brooke she was going on a backpacking trip "with friends," which was not true, but for some reason she hadn't told her about Cory. She didn't think Brooke would understand.

~

The shuttle ride from Seven Glacier Hotel to the McArthur Lodge took almost an hour, a scenic drive over mountain passes, along rivers and meadows, mountain goats teetering on cliff sides, etc., etc. All that passed outside her window like a movie she was only half watching. As soon as she stepped off that shuttle, she was going to launch right into it with Cory. No hello, no hug, definitely no kiss—not until she had unburdened herself. In her head, she went through several versions. The soft entry: I have something to tell you. The warning shot: I have a confession to make. The desperate plea for forgiveness: you said no matter what, you would always love me. She considered these all, and one more, the direct shot: I cheated on you. I cheated on you. I cheated on you.

Until she confessed, she could never, in good conscience, move forward with Cory, with her entire life.

Then she saw him standing there at the entrance of McArthur Lodge, waiting for her. He was leaning against a pole and talking to a bellhop, some blond kid in lederhosen. He laughed at something the bellhop said, and his hair flopped in front of his face. He swooped it back with one hand, and that was when he saw her—or rather, the shuttle—coming toward him. He had those same fake Ray-Bans on, the ones with the safety pin holding up one arm, and a white T-shirt, or at least a formerly white T-shirt, and jeans. At the sight of him, so incongruous among the Mormons in their bright, clean summer clothes and the climbers in their technical gear and the employees in their imitation Swiss uniforms, a lump formed in her throat and their entire relationship flashed before her eyes, from that first week in the kitchen, to Shangri-La where they had first kissed, where it had all begun, to all those months emailing each other, promising to meet back here, back at Seven Glacier Park.

The shuttle lurched to a stop, and she grabbed her bag and stood up, pushing past the guests onboard, not employees but tourists either visiting this side of the park for a day or transferring hotels. Amy jumped out of the shuttle and into Cory's arms, burying her face in his neck and holding on to him.

"Hey," he said, and he squeezed her back.

"I'm so sorry," she sobbed. "I'm so sorry." But when he asked her what she had to be sorry for, she wiped the tears from her face and regarded him, removing his sunglasses so she could look into his eyes. He leaned in to kiss her and she kissed him back, and when they broke apart they were both laughing. Finally together again, after all those months.

"Let's go to your room." She was insistent. She needed him, needed to be with him, to erase what happened with Freddy. Maybe it was as simple as that, like a videotape with an old show you had already watched. You could just tape right over it, and the old show was gone, a new one in its place. They could start over.

All they cared about was being together, was being alone together, but they couldn't go back to his room, not until later, not until his roommate left. Cory said he knew a place, he had figured it out, and he took her hand in his and led her down a shaded trail through the woods. At first it followed down Lake McArthur—a small, dark-blue jewel of a lake surrounded by old growth conifers—but instead of following the loop all the way around the lake and back to the lodge, they veered off on another path, a quiet, damp trail winding past the giant trunks of trees and ferns that arched up to their shoulders.

"Where are you taking us?" she whispered, as if they were in church or some holy place requiring reverence and awe. Cory was still holding on to her hand and squeezed it. He looked back at her and smiled, revealing his imperfect teeth, the canines out of place, jutting out just a little in the wrong direction. Of course she thought then of Freddy, Freddy and his perfect teeth, as white and smooth as Chiclets, as tiles, and she felt a pang for Cory, who never had braces, who repaired his sunglasses with a safety pin, and she loved him for it, she did. And she knew she couldn't tell Cory about Freddy. It would be cruel to tell him, really, it would kill him, and there was no reason to tell him. He had never met Freddy, and Freddy never had to meet him. She would make sure of that. It was her duty to make sure of that, for Cory. To protect him.

They approached a giant rock, as large as a cabin, jutting out on the side of the path, and Cory pulled them both away from the trail, around the rock, where they could sit down on a little patch of soft green grass, away from the hikers, protected by the big rock and the trunks of trees and ferns. From his daypack he produced a large white sheet. "Borrowed this from housekeeping," he said. He unfurled the sheet, and it floated down onto the forest floor. Before it could settle down, Amy pushed Cory down onto it, falling on top of him, kissing him.

They kissed hard, making up for all that time they had spent apart, all those nights they had slept alone, and they pulled at each other's clothes. She kept thinking of that idea of her body, her life as a tape, a recording that could be taped over, re-recorded. She could erase the past, make it right, and that was what they did there, on the sheet, in the forest. They were desperate to be together again, desperate but giddy, laughing as she pulled his shirt over his head and then pulled off her own. He reached around to unclasp her bra and then looked at her as if he had never seen a woman topless before, let alone her, and she cupped his face with her hand and said she loved him. She loved him more than anything.

They slowed down. We have all afternoon, she said to him. We have all summer.

When they finished, she wrapped her arms and legs around him, gripping him tightly. "Don't leave me," she said. "Not yet."

He drew his head back and his hair hung down, brushing her forehead. He kissed her on the nose and then on the mouth. After another moment, he rolled off her. "Shit" she heard him say.

She sat up and placed a hand on his back. He was very thin. She ran her finger along his spine, along his bones. "What's wrong?"

"The condom," he said. "It's not there."

"What do you mean?" She stared at him in disbelief. Looked his naked body up and down, and then her own.

She had heard of the condom breaking. She hadn't heard of it disappearing.

"You put one on, right?" she asked him.

"You saw me do it."

"So where *is* it?" It took her far too long to understand the obvious, before she reached between her own legs, searching for it. "It's not there."

~

I had to stop her there. "Jesus, Amy! I don't need *quite* this level of detail."

"I just wanted you to know—it was an accident. I mean, I didn't just go around having unprotected sex all the time. With Freddy, I was drunk, but then with Cory, you know, it was this fluke thing—"

I cringed. "Did you ever . . . find it? You know what, don't answer that. I don't want to know."

"Obviously I got it out! Eventually. But of course by then it was too late."

"So all that stuff with Freddy later, fooling around with him, all those little rules about keeping your underwear on—"

"I was *trying* to resist him. I had a boyfriend!"

I shook my head.

"I was young," she went on. "I was stupid, okay? I loved Cory, I did. He was my first love. That first summer—it was so perfect. But when we got separated later, and then I met Freddy, and he was just so—he got me that job at the front desk, everyone loved him and he liked *me*, he picked me, and—I don't know. I guess I started . . . compartmentalizing. On Fridays and Saturdays, I was with Cory. When I was back at the main lodge, Freddy was there and it was like something separate, maybe."

"Like the Nazis," I said.

Amy had been gazing out the window, at the moon shining down over the lake, but she turned back to face me then. "What?"

"The Nazis did this. The most evil guards, the most sadistic, they would spend all day torturing the prisoners in the concentration camps, right? And you'd think they were the bullies, the guys who were punching the other kids on the playground when they were kids and smacking their wives around at home. But that wasn't it. They were just, like, normal guys. They would go home and play with their kids and play with their little dog, kiss their wife on the cheek, help their little Aryan kids with their homework. The perfect father."

"Okay, well—"

"I remember reading about this. It blew my mind. I was like, How could this happen? How can someone be so horrible, so monstrous, and then come home and act like nothing's wrong, go through the motions of a happy father, the perfect husband? It's compartmentalization, that's what it is. That's how they do it."

"Christ, Ramona, I'm not a Nazi."

I waved my hand in the space between us. "I know," I said. "I know. I'm just messing with you." I definitely didn't think Amy was evil. I was sure (mostly sure?) she had good intentions—even back then, with Freddy and Cory. I was sure she *believed* she loved Cory, and that she was doing her best to resist Freddy's charms. Still, I wished she would just own up to it. That was her whole problem, I decided. Not that she did what she did, but that she wanted to twist everything around, turn herself into some sort of innocent victim of fate instead of taking responsibility for her own choices.

"I did some stupid things! I was young. I made my share of mistakes, I know that—"

"No one is blaming you for sleeping around!" I snapped. "I'm blaming you for—for misrepresenting the truth. I can't believe a word that comes out of your mouth! You make Freddy think he's the father, you make me think that, and then you tell me Cory ran away when he didn't—something happened to him, something happened to him on that lake." I jabbed my finger up into the air, somewhere in the direction of Shangri-La. "Something happened to him, and you know what it is."

She sat back in her chair, chastened.

"They found the body in 2015," I told her. Cory's mom had shown me everything. The newspaper clippings. The police reports. "You worked here then—this was your hotel group. You knew. You must have known."

"I knew," she said softly, and I exhaled. I was so relieved to hear her say it, to admit it. "But it's not what you think," she continued.

"I don't know what to think! And whatever you say—I would have no way of knowing if you were telling me the truth. Can you do that, Amy? Tell the truth."

Her hands went to her head. "I'm *trying*. It was so long ago now."

"Come on, Amy," I insisted, but all the fury had drained out of my voice. I was just so tired.

"I want to tell you." Amy clenched her eyes shut, like a child trying to will away a nightmare, a monster under the bed. "But you'll never forgive me."

~

That first summer, Amy told me, everything was perfect, everything was great until right up to the end, when Princess Diana died and she had to go home to take care of her dad again. The second summer— well, I knew all about that already. After that one night in the laundry room, she didn't sleep with Freddy again. They kissed sometimes, but she wouldn't let him go further. Not at first, anyway. He thought she was chaste because she felt so guilty about sleeping with him, and she let him believe that. It was true: she did feel guilty for sleeping with him, but not because she was so pure like her Mormon roommate, but because she had a boyfriend. Freddy liked her. He respected her. And Amy was grateful to him because he got her that job, her dream job at the front desk of the Seven Glacier Hotel. She owed him.

Working at the front desk gave her a strange sense of power. She could see the trajectory of it—she could work her way up from there. She could imagine her future in the hotel, in the hotel industry.

She had Fridays and Saturdays off, just like Cory. When Freddy was singing and dancing in the cabaret—that was when she would go across the park to visit Cory. Freddy would look for her, seek her out in the audience. Or he would come by her room later, and she wouldn't be there. It would be bad luck for her to watch him perform, she would tell him. The more she pulled back, the more he wanted her. She was playing hard to get—that was what he thought. She was stringing him along. She knew that, even at the time. She should have let him go.

Every week she would see Cory. She kept him from visiting her at Seven Glacier Hotel. Her roommate was always around, she told him, and this was true. She was Mormon, she was very devout, she didn't even know Amy had a boyfriend because Amy couldn't stand the thought of Brooke judging her. Brooke hadn't even kissed a boy, she confided to Amy once. She wanted to save her first kiss for the man she married.

So usually, Amy would visit Cory at McArthur Lodge. If his roommate was gone, they could spend all weekend in his room. When that didn't work out, they would try to meet somewhere halfway between Seven Glacier Hotel and McArthur. They would hike around and have sex in the wilderness or in the back of his roommate's car, and Amy hated it. She hated that it had come to that, their beautiful romance had turned into something seedy and sad. Every week, she was getting closer to Freddy, and when she was with Cory, she could feel herself drifting. She didn't know what to do.

She couldn't explain it, how her feelings had shifted. That first summer, she and Cory had worked side by side, washing dishes. The next summer, they both had better jobs, and she would tell him about working at the front desk and it was like he didn't get it, why it was so important to her. To him, it was just another job, a step up from dish-washing for sure, but nothing beyond that.

And then it was almost over, the tail end of that second summer, the beginning of September. At Seven Glacier, summer crashed straight into winter, just like that. Most of the employees were gone by then, back to their colleges. Amy took the shuttle through the park as she had all summer, and Cory met her at the entrance of McArthur Lodge. He looked the way he always did, that casual lean against the lodgepole, those faded jeans and worn T-shirt and duct-taped boots. She stepped off the shuttle and he slung his arm around her, kissed her on the fore-head. "I have a surprise for you," he said, and he led her to the door of his room. "You ready?"

She nodded and he flung open the door. One half of the room was the same as before, with a neatly made bed covered in a vintage plaid fleece blanket, the kind with a satin edge. The other half had been cleared out, and all that remained was a bare mattress on a painted wooden bed frame. That was the surprise: Cory's roommate had left, and they had the room to themselves. That was part of the problem, that whole summer, not having anywhere to go, nowhere to be alone.

He pulled her into the room and they shut the door. She reached up to him and they kissed, tentatively at first, as if they had forgotten how to do this, how to be together when they had all the time in the world, when they weren't hunkering in the back of someone's car or listening for his roommate's footsteps outside the hall. "This is a surprise," she murmured into his neck.

He pulled her shirt over her head and unfastened her bra. He took his time, nudging the straps from her shoulders and then bending down to kiss each breast, letting the bra fall to the floor. She felt shy all of a sudden, standing there topless, in the middle of the day, and she said they should get under the covers, close the curtains. Cory kissed her again and said she was beautiful, he could look at her all day, and he would. That was what they should do—never leave this room.

"No one can see us up here," he said. The old wood-framed windows looked out at nothing but trees, a whole forest dense with firs and pines, their trunks wide and solid. It was like living in a treehouse, every shade of green visible through that window, like a piece of art, like stained glass, the sun glinting off every leaf and pine needle.

They fell onto the bed and relaxed into it, and Amy closed her eyes and tried to recapture the way it was at the beginning, how it felt to be in love with Cory, because she still wanted that—she wanted to feel the way she had before, last summer, before she had screwed everything up.

They hadn't talked much of what would come next, what they would do when the season ended. They could choose a city, Cory said, move there together. She would daydream with him. Yes, they could go anywhere! Portland or Austin or even, why not, London or Paris. The thing was, she had to go home. Her brother would be going back to school, and someone had to be around for her dad. She couldn't just move to another city with Cory—even if they had the money to do that, which they didn't.

Cory was busy unbuttoning her shorts, and she helped him push them down over her hips. Her underwear, too. He felt between her legs, and she covered her mouth with her hands to stifle the sounds she was making. "We don't have to be quiet," he said into her ear. "No one's around."

She moaned dramatically then, and that cracked them both up, and she kissed him hard on the mouth.

Cory raised himself up over her and stripped off his shirt, flinging it around a few times before letting it fly across the room. She helped him yank off his pants.

She instructed him to lie down on his back, and he obeyed.

He felt so familiar to her, but so different, out in the open, on top of the bed, in the middle of the day. We could be like this forever, she whispered to him, lowering herself onto him.

This was a turning point for them, she thought. She could feel it. They let themselves go, they made as much noise as they wanted. She cried out when she came, and then he turned them both over so he could finish, and he collapsed on top of her as she stroked the back of his head.

"Wow," she said, and for a while they just lay there, holding each other, catching their breath. The light shifted over their bodies, shadows of tree limbs and pine needles forming dark shapes on their skin, and she could feel Cory's eyes on her, on her body. His brow had furrowed in concentration, and he was just looking at her like she was a problem he couldn't quite figure out, and his hand reached out to touch her breast, absently, and then he let it drop down to her hip.

"What?" She found herself scrambling to cover herself with the sheet, though only minutes before she had been wild with abandon on top of him, her clothes scattered on the floor.

Cory looked up at her through the hair that had fallen over his eyes, and then he glanced back down. "Nothing."

"What is it? You were going to say something."

"Okay, this is going to sound weird," he said. "But . . ." He placed a hand on her breast. "They seem bigger."

She barked out a laugh. "What?"

His hand dropped and he glanced down, embarrassed. "Maybe it's been a while," he said. "Since I've seen them. Out in the broad daylight, I mean."

"I'm probably going to get my period soon," she said.

Both of them were silent for a few moments.

"When was the last time?" he said gently, watching her.

Her mind flashed back. She arrived here in May, mid-May. Now it was September. September. "Oh my god. I don't know."

"Think."

"I'm thinking. I know I had it on my birthday," she said. "Before I came here."

Cory ran a hand through his hair. "Last May?"

She nodded miserably. "Four months ago."

CHAPTER 17

RAMONA

The next morning, they stood outside the pharmacy at St. Anne, willing it to open. They had woken up early, too nervous to sleep, but they had a plan: borrow a car, drive to St. Anne, buy a pregnancy test.

"There's no point in worrying until we know for sure," Cory said. He had said it before. He said it last night. He said it in the car on the drive over. "There are a lot of reasons you could miss your period."

"I know," Amy said. They weren't looking at each other. They were leaning against the brick wall of the building, side by side.

"Stress," Cory said. "Exercise."

"I've been doing a lot of hiking," she said. "More hiking than usual." This was not true, not exactly, but she was trying it out. She liked this, as an answer to her problem. She was doing too much hiking! Surely when she was back home, away from here, this park, her hormones would level themselves out, her ovaries would get the message, pumping out eggs, shedding their lining—or whatever it was they did.

"It could be the elevation," Cory continued.

From behind the glass door of the pharmacy, a figure approached, flipping the CLOSED sign over to OPEN.

She took a basket by the door, and they wandered up and down the aisles. It was an old-school pharmacy, a place that hadn't gone under any major renovations since the early 1960s. Linoleum floors, numbered aisles, a pharmacy window at the back. It had a certain smell, a smell that was somehow familiar but hard to put a finger on. An old smell, a vintage smell, like school paste, like wood pulp and mint.

At the magazine stand she tried to focus on the headlines, but everything blurred together. Madonna celebrating her fortieth birthday, Bill Clinton confessing or denying something about Monica Lewinsky, *Titanic* finally coming out on video—she knew all that already. And it didn't matter anyway, did it? It was always the same, some new movie coming out or celebrities breaking up or getting back together—what was the point of everything just happening over and over again? What did it have to do with her, with her life? She just stood there, staring, having a sort of brief existential crisis, yearning to go back in time, to just a few weeks ago, when she cared about stuff like this, back when she had the luxury of wrapping herself in other people's problems, other people's lives.

"Hey," Cory said, and he tossed something into her empty basket. A pregnancy test.

She grabbed an issue of *People* from the rack and flung it in to cover up the test, even though no one else was even in the store, just the two of them and the pharmacist behind her little window at the back. They wandered up and down the aisles for ten more minutes before going up to the register. By then they had filled the basket with all sorts of things. Candy bars and a bag of Smartfood, Clif Bars, and a roll of film and a bottle of blue nail polish.

The pharmacist was old, or maybe just middle-aged with outdated hair, the kind achieved with hot rollers and hair spray. She wore big, plastic-framed glasses in clear tan, with the arms extending from the bottom of the lenses, a style popular only for a brief period in the 1980s. She wore a white pharmacist coat and didn't say anything when Amy approached with her basket. She just rang everything up, item by item, and dropped them into a plastic bag.

She announced the total, and Cory handed her the cash. She was placing the bills into the cash register when Amy asked her if there was a restroom she could use, and the woman said, "No public restroom. Try the diner across the street."

At the diner, she and Cory sat across from each other in a booth, studying the menu. Suddenly she was ravenous. She ordered a short stack, hash browns, and scrambled eggs. Cory got a coffee and a Denver omelet. She picked up the plastic bag and stood up. "Well," she said, "wish me luck."

Cory didn't say anything, but he nodded once as she made her way to the back of the restaurant.

By the time she returned, all their food had arrived. She sat down in front of her pancakes and reached for the syrup.

"Well?" Cory asked.

She poured the syrup on top, much more than she usually took, and slipped thick slices of butter between the pancakes and then another on top for good measure. "I'm starving," she said, and she took a big bite.

Cory hadn't touched his omelet, but he sat there patiently, his fork in one hand, knife in the other.

"We need to go back to the pharmacy," she said. "Get another test. Just to be sure."

"They can be wrong," Cory agreed.

This idea seemed to cheer them both, and they tucked in to their food. These tests weren't perfect. False positives happened all the time. Also, there was user error. She had never taken a pregnancy test before; she might not have done it right. It was complicated, reading all those instructions, she told herself as she chewed and swallowed each syrupy bite.

Except really, it wasn't so complicated. She peed on the end of a stick and a pink line appeared in a little window, the test line. That showed that the test was working. Everyone saw that line. Another line would appear next to it if she was pregnant. It might take up to fifteen minutes to appear, the instructions said. But it appeared right away, right along with the first line. It might be faint, the instructions said. Even a faint line meant you were pregnant. The line wasn't faint. It was dark pink, almost darker than the test line, as if it was very sure of itself, as if it wanted to not only announce the results but underline and bold them: **you are pregnant**.

Amy ate every bite of her breakfast and asked Cory if he would split an order of french toast with her, too. She asked if he could go across the street for another test. "They're twenty dollars," he said, but she gave him a desperate look and he said, "It's worth it."

He came back less than five minutes later with another plastic bag, a smaller one this time. He handed it to her, and she set it beside her on the booth. "I'll wait until after the french toast," she said.

Ten minutes later, she was back at that pharmacy, pleading with the woman behind the counter. How accurate are these things anyway, Amy asked her. The woman figured out the due date for her, using this little plastic wheel thing. February 5. She was still in shock. "I can't do it," Amy told her. She needed to consider her options.

"You're eighteen weeks along," the woman told her, and she didn't look sympathetic in the least. Nor did she look happy about it, as if she cherished this new life growing inside Amy. She was just grim and matter-of-fact: "Well into the second trimester, almost halfway through the pregnancy. Looks like you're having a baby."

~

"This can't be happening to me," she wailed to Cory on the car ride back to the park. "I can't believe this."

Cory said they could work it out. They had options.

"We don't have options!" she snapped. "It's too late!"

"You don't know that."

"I'm halfway through. That's what she said." Amy wanted to cry, or scream, but she was too panicked to do either. Well into the second trimester. How was this possible? She looked down at herself, her own body. Suddenly it was so obvious she was pregnant. The cups of her bra cut into her breasts. She had outgrown her favorite pair of shorts weeks ago and had been wearing a pair of cutoffs that fit lower down her waist. She knew she had gained a few pounds, sure, and every once in a while, standing at the front desk, a wave of nausea would wash over her, like a sudden bout of car sickness even though she was standing on solid ground, but she hadn't thrown up or anything.

Skipping those periods, though—how had she missed that? Her periods came like clockwork, every twenty-eight days, almost right from the start. It had been happening every month since she was thirteen years old, so you would think she would notice when they just stopped, but no. She had other things on her mind. Freddy and Cory and that bear—

"I could move to Medford, we could move in with your parents, at least until the baby is born, help out with your dad—"

"No!" She slapped her hands on the dashboard. "How's that going to work, Cory? I already share a room with my little brother. I'm supposed to be helping them out, not making everything ten times harder."

"Move in with me and my mom then," he said. "Just until we come up with a plan. We could get married."

"Married?" She scoffed at this, said the word as if it disgusted her, as if it was the last thing she would ever do. "It's not 1965, Cory. We don't have to get married."

Cory didn't say anything for a while. He kept both hands on the wheel as he drove. By then they had entered back into the park and were winding up a mountain pass. She looked out the window and tried to take it in, the scenery. It always grounded her, that landscape. It protected her. Or it used to.

They drove in silence for a bit. She couldn't stop thinking about how impossible it was. How could she have a baby? She couldn't stay with Cory—she knew that. It seemed so obvious to her, as soon as he laid it all out. Live with his mom? No. Go home to her own parents, not triumphant, with fistfuls of cash that would save them all, but penniless and pregnant? Impossible.

~

I listened to her tell me all this in the back of that darkened dining room, and I didn't move a muscle. I almost forgot to breathe, terrified at whatever it was she was going to tell me this time. Whatever it was, I didn't know if I could believe it. There would be no reason to believe her, to believe this was the right version of the story, the final version.

"I told you I went up there alone," Amy said. "That he never met me up there, that he abandoned us." She shook her head. "That wasn't true. We went up together. I shouldn't have lied about it. I didn't want to tell you."

"Didn't want to tell me what?" I almost whispered.

"The truth. What really happened up there." She looked out into the room, at all the empty tables and chairs, everything dark, the moonlight casting shadows. "Look, Ramona," she said, suddenly brisk and efficient, hostess mode. "I'm not going to be able to get through this with you just sitting there staring at me. I need something to drink—some wine or a few shots of something—anything." She sprang out of her seat. "Can I get you anything? Are you hungry?"

"I'm fine."

"A glass of water?"

"Sure. But Amy—"

Amy was already halfway across the dining room, bumping up against chairs in the dark, feeling her way to the kitchen. "I'll be right back!" she yelled.

A few minutes later she returned with a bottle of wine, a corkscrew, and two glasses. She set one glass in front of me, the other in her place, and then she opened the wine and poured it as if I was one of her guests at her finest hotel and she was the lead server. "Oh!" She slapped her forehead. "I forgot your water."

"Don't worry about it." I took a sip of my wine. I needed it.

"You sure?"

"Sit down, Amy."

She sat back down across from me and took a sip from her own glass. "Okay," she said. "So we were on the way back from the pharmacy, driving through the park, and suddenly Cory jerked the steering wheel and swerved off the main road. I was like, what are you doing, and he said it was a split-second decision. He had pulled off into this little parking lot. Quiet, empty, a lone outhouse, a couple picnic tables. I asked him where we were, and he goes, 'You don't recognize it?'"

It was the end of Shangri-La. Cory was getting excited now. We could leave the car here, he said, at the parking lot. Seth—the guy he borrowed the car from—didn't need it back until the evening. They could hitch up to that mile-marker sign a couple miles up the road, go to Shangri-La, then drive Seth's car back. They had plenty of time.

He wanted to go back there, Amy told me. He insisted. Remember the beginning? he kept saying. Remember how it used to be?

"Four months pregnant and I'm doing that crazy hike. Halfway up and he realizes it—it was a stupid idea, going up there, but you know how it is. Once you're halfway up, you have to keep going. There's no point in going back. And part of me wanted to believe it, believe that going back there would give us the answer somehow, get us out of this mess. Make everything make sense." Amy took an experimental sip of her wine and then swirled it around her glass.

"And then we get up there, and everything is different," she continued. "That first time, a year and however many months earlier, it was the beginning. The beginning of summer. The beginning of us. The way the sun hit the lake—it was the most beautiful thing I'd ever seen. Either of us had ever seen. But now it was September, and the surface of the lake was just murky with these strange, undulating waves that didn't break. Like wrinkles. Wrinkles on fabric.

"We sat on the shore and watched those waves, and I had this terrible feeling, like this is it. Whatever started that day, right here on this lake, is over. Everything got screwed up somehow, I screwed it up. I didn't even know if the baby was his. And I was about to tell him this, I looked over at him, but it was like he could sense it, because he was still trying to make it work—that was why he brought me up there, to remind me, to remind us, and so he looks at me and he says, 'Let's get in the boat.'"

"So there was a boat," I said.

"There was a boat, a rowboat. Stuart and this guy Jake had told us about it the summer before. No one knew how it got there, but it was there, protected under this ledge, this sort of shallow cave along the shore. You and I walked by it on our way out the other day."

I nodded at this, dimly picturing a spot along the edge of the lake where a boat might have once been stored.

"I didn't want to get in the boat," Amy said. "I mean, it wasn't a good day for it. I told him no but he kept insisting. He thought it would be fun, he said. I could tell he was just—desperate, you know? Casting around for something to fix this. First the hike up to Shangri-La, now the boat. I told him it wasn't a good idea. The water was choppy, and he didn't know how to swim."

"That's what she told me," I said. "Cory's mom."

"That's why I freaked out earlier. You and Gabe, at the lake. For months after, just the sound of water—anyway. Anyway, I agreed. I shouldn't have agreed to it, but I did. If I had just insisted—no, Cory, let's stay on shore! Let's go back down, this isn't working, let's go—everything would have turned out differently, wouldn't it?"

"So you went out in the boat?"

"We dragged the boat out from under that rock and tested it. It was in pretty good shape. I don't know how it survived the winters up there, maybe that rock protected it from the elements or maybe some of the guys—Stuart and Jake and those guys—made sure it stayed in good condition. It floated just fine and so we got in. Cory rowed us out. And as he rowed, the water seemed to calm. The sun shone out through the clouds a bit, and I began to relax. It was a sign."

"Like the bear."

"Yeah. Like a sign that maybe we would get through this after all. Cory was right to take us up here. To take us out in the boat. He kept rowing and rowing and the shore was far behind us, but it was magical there, in the middle of the lake, like being at the bottom of this great bowl, surrounded by the edges of the mountains, the sky arching overhead, like we were the only two people in the world, two little dots at the bottom of this great big globe.

"He stopped to rest, and the boat skimmed over the surface of the lake. He was breathing hard, his face flushed. I leaned in toward him, and I placed my hand on his cheek." As Amy spoke, she reached up her hand, as if she was reliving this moment, reaching up to his cheek. "I could feel his pulse," she said. "I could feel it beating beneath my fingertips. And then we kissed. Soft at first, tentative, like we weren't sure, but then harder. The oars almost slipped out from his hands, out of the oarlocks, but he caught them just in time.

"We broke apart and he looked at me. He looked at me in such a strange way, and I wondered what he saw—like it was this new version of me, the pregnant version, and he was adjusting his vision to understand it. 'I want to look at you,' he said, and he pulled my shirt up over my head. 'Take that off,' he said, and I reached behind myself to unclasp my bra. He was lifting his camera up to his face, and he said he wanted to remember me just like this. The shutter clicked.

"And then a breeze came up and I shivered but he was looking at me over his camera—and the way he was looking at me, I didn't feel embarrassed at all. I believed him, believed him when he said I looked beautiful. It was like I believed in us, believed this could work, and I smiled for him, for the camera.

"He wanted me to lie back, lie down in the boat, and I did, and he stood up over me to get the shot, me lying back half naked in the boat. He stood up on the bench, and I was laughing and telling him he was crazy, to get down from there. I remember looking up at him, and the sun shone through his hair like a halo, the camera obscuring his face, and he kept saying how he wanted to remember me just like that and the shutter was clicking, but then I felt it—I felt the boat teetering. He was in those boots, those heavy boots he always wore, the Doc Martens with the duct tape, and he had tripped over himself somehow, and then he fell over, into the water. One minute, he's taking pictures and then—" Amy took in a sharp breath. She reached for her glass of wine, but it was empty.

I reached over and filled her glass.

Amy nodded and curled her fingers around the glass, but she didn't lift it to her mouth. "The boat was already drifting away, away from him, and I grabbed the oars. I was calling his name and his arms were flapping up and down. I got the boat right next to him and yelled for him to hang on to the oar so I could pull him back in, but he was panicking. It was like he couldn't hear me, and I was terrified, terrified he was going to wear himself out, splashing around like that, gasping for air."

Amy looked at me then, and I wondered what she saw. Me, sitting across from her. That fetus that was growing inside her all those years ago, those two lines on the pregnancy test. Here I was. I didn't move a muscle. I didn't even blink.

"I could have jumped in." Her voice was trembling. "I could have tried to save him, but I didn't. He would drown us both—that's what I was thinking. And the baby—for the first time, it seemed real to me. I was pregnant. This was happening whether I had wanted it to or not, I was going to have a baby. I mean, the thought came to me in a flash, all at once, while I was sitting on that boat, panicking, watching it happen, and that's why I didn't jump in. Couldn't jump in. He would drown us, I thought. He would drown us all."

CHAPTER 18

AMY

Ramona put her hand to her mouth.

"I should have jumped in!" The wine was hitting me, finally. My head felt strange, lighter now. The story was coming out faster. I was getting worked up. "I just sat there—I just sat there, watching, watching him struggle, and then—"

Ramona was watching me, her hand still on her mouth, her eyes wide open, terrified.

"Then the lake was silent and I was alone. Alone in the middle of the lake. I didn't know what to do. I don't know how long I just sat there, in shock. I couldn't believe it. It didn't seem believable, that one minute my hand would be on his neck, feeling his pulse, and the next . . ."

"It was an accident," Ramona said. "You could have gone to the police."

"I know. I know. And I should have."

"You can go now, tell them the story."

I shook my head. "I can't," I said. "It's too late."

"It's *not* too late. Cory's mom—all those years, not knowing what happened to him. And then when his body was found, it made no sense. Think about that, Amy, she could get some closure."

"I know." My voice caught on the words. I put my hand to my face and was surprised to find tears there. I don't know how long I had been crying, but both of my cheeks were wet. "But I can't do that. I can't do that to Jonathan, to Gabe. He's eight years old. I can't go to prison."

"You won't go to prison!" Ramona said, and she reached across the table toward me. I put my hands, my wet hands, into hers. They were soft and warm. She squeezed them. "It was an accident. They won't put you in prison for that."

"But there's more to it than that," I said. I could see Ramona steeling herself. Her mouth a hard, determined line. "There's what I did next."

~

I didn't know how long I sat in that boat, in that silence, in the middle of the lake, in the middle of the world. It all happened so fast, only minutes between here and there, together and alone, life and death. The crash into the water, the splashing and yelling, and then—nothing. It was so quiet out there, so quiet I became attuned to the sound of the water, like it was breathing, tapping against the side of the boat. The boards of the boat, too, creaked. I couldn't stand it, couldn't stand the sound of it. I covered my ears with my hands and closed my eyes and prayed that when I opened them again, Cory would be sitting across from me, snapping another picture, and we would row back to shore and everything would go back to the way it was. We could do it—move in with his mom, move in with my parents and brother, have a baby. Why not? Why had that all seemed like such a problem? We could have made it work. We could have.

When I opened my eyes, though, he was still gone, and the water was still tapping the edges of the boat. I found my bra and shirt, both soaking wet, and I got dressed. I rowed myself back to shore. It was awkward at first. It took me a while to get the hang of it, but I did it. Rowed myself all the way back and pulled the boat up the shore, gathered our things—Cory's backpack, mine—and put the boat back where we had found it, under the rock.

Somehow I made it back to the car. The keys were in Cory's bag. I didn't run into one person on the trail back down. If I had, I might have told them, I might have begged them for help. We might have called a ranger, summoned the police—but I didn't. I don't remember planning what I did next. I just did it, as if on autopilot. I drove back to McArthur Lodge and left the keys in the car, tucked behind the sun visor. Up in Cory's room, everything was just as we left it. One half, empty. His plaid blanket askew on his bed, some of our things strewn on the floor. We had left in a hurry to get to the pharmacy. It seemed like a lifetime ago, driving to St. Anne, buying the pregnancy tests.

Light shone in through the windows, filtered through the trees, all those layers of green, like a stained glass window. It was late afternoon. I needed to clear it out. I moved quickly and efficiently, as if someone was chasing me, as if I was taking part in some essential military operation and time was of the essence.

I emptied the contents of the built-in dresser into Cory's duffel bag. Top drawer, underwear and socks. Second drawer, stacks of neatly folded T-shirts, third drawer, pants. He didn't have much. Every single thing he had brought with him fit in that bag, including his sheets, the fleece blanket with the satin edge. I don't know what I was thinking—or rather, I wasn't thinking anything. It didn't pain me to go through his things, not while I was doing it. What happened earlier, at Shangri-La, and there in his room, shoving everything into the duffel bag, felt disconnected somehow. I didn't even know why I was doing it. I didn't think about it, not until later.

Bottom drawer, personal effects. Not that I would have used that term when I opened it, when I saw what was in there. A couple paperback books: *Siddhartha* and *The Hitchhiker's Guide to the Galaxy*. All the letters I had written him during our months apart. We had emailed mostly, so there weren't too many, maybe a dozen letters and cards, all fastened together with a rubber band. A black folder with a zipper—a portfolio. It wasn't large, not even as big as a ream of paper. I knelt down on the floor in front of that bottom drawer, holding it in my hands. I didn't open it. I didn't want to look at what was inside. I couldn't do it. Not then. I added it to the duffel bag, along with the books and letters. That was everything. I zipped it shut.

I made it back to Seven Glacier by dinnertime. My roommate, Brooke, had already left, back to college. I was starving, shaking with hunger. I hadn't eaten since that morning, since the diner, but I couldn't go to the dining room, not in this state. I hadn't talked to anyone on the shuttle—a few tourists, older, who kept to themselves at the front while I hunkered in the back, watching the scenery flash by. I hadn't talked to anyone since Cory. Since I was yelling out to him, begging him to grab the oar so I could pull him back in.

My stomach lurched and I felt dizzy, the way I had felt some mornings these past months, like I was carsick. Morning sickness. That was what that was. The white plastic bag from the pharmacy was still in Cory's daypack, which I had stuffed into the duffel bag with everything else. Two pregnancy tests with the two pink lines. Candy bars and a Clif Bar—that was what I needed, what I was looking for. I tore the wrapper off the first candy bar and stuffed it into my face, barely chewing, just to get something into me, to stop this nausea. The sugar hit me all at once. I didn't feel sated, but I did feel better somehow, more alert.

I tore through the next one, too, eating it in just a few bites. Then the Clif Bar, the kind with almonds and dried cherries, my preferred flavor. I looked at the candy bar wrappers next to me. Twix and Snickers. My favorites. These weren't just grabbed randomly from the shelves and thrown into the basket to cover up our real purchase, the pregnancy test. He had chosen these for me. My favorite candy, my favorite energy bar.

Here I was, in my room, surrounded by Cory's things, shoving food into my face, food he bought me with his own money. It hit me, all at once. God, what was I doing? I looked around, dumbfounded, as if I had just reentered my body after a long absence and didn't know where I was or where I had been, like a time traveler or victim of an alien abduction. I was shaking.

He was gone; this was all that was left of him. Just a daypack and some grubby old T-shirts and an old fleece blanket. And right then, I felt it. Something moving inside me, an unmistakable sensation. Something stirring, moving. Yesterday I hadn't even known I was pregnant and now—I lifted up my shirt and stared at my abdomen. My stomach, which used to be flat, protruded, but only slightly, my skin still taut. It happened again. The baby—and suddenly, that was what it was to me, a baby—stirred again, and this time I saw it. A foot or a hand reaching out, out through the womb, visible from the outside. I laughed and poked at it with my hand, and it went back inside. When I was pregnant the second time, with Gabe, I read that this couldn't have possibly happened so early in the pregnancy, but it did. I could have sworn it happened right then, at that moment.

There was no explaining it now. If I had encountered someone on the trail, if I had gone straight to the front desk at McArthur Lodge—I could have reported it. I could have explained it. My boyfriend drowned in an accident, I could have said to someone. To anyone. But I didn't. I had cleared out his room. I had taken the shuttle back to Seven Glacier. It was too late to go back.

It was too late for Cory. He was gone. But I was still here. I needed to think about what would come next for me—for me and this baby. And then I knew. I knew what I was doing, why I hadn't told anyone, why I needed Cory to disappear. I owed it to myself, to this baby. Because I *was* having a baby. Cory and I couldn't do it together, it never would have worked, even if he was still here, still alive, but he wasn't. Cory couldn't do that with me, but someone else could.

Freddy—and he could actually be the father, I thought, he could very well be the father—Freddy and I could make a life for this child, the life I had always wanted. We could be like his parents, a power couple, roaming the halls of hotels. He could perform in the cabarets while I ruled on the board. We could do it all. We could have everything!

Cory's daypack was covered in patches. He must have had it since high school or earlier, judging by the patches. Bart Simpson, bands I was sure he didn't like anymore—the Rolling Stones, Led Zeppelin. He was into indie stuff now, ambient music, the kind of thing they played in small venues in Portland and Seattle or Manchester or something, places he had never been to but wanted to visit someday. Places he would never go to, bands he would never see.

I picked at the edge of the cherry-red Rolling Stones lips patch until I could grasp it between my fingers and ripped it off. It made a satisfying sound as it released from the fabric. I tried another and another until the backpack was stripped, denuded. I needed to get rid of everything, everything that could tie back to Cory. The backpack with the patches, the Slowdive T-shirt.

By the time I left my room, the sun had dipped behind the mountains and the sky glowed electric blue. I ran from the dorms to the front of the lodge. The lake was dark, a blank space, and I tried not to look at it as I shoved one of the plastic bags filled with Cory's things in a garbage can. I burst inside, through the doors of the kitchen, where I shoved the second bag under crumpled napkins and old food, just like I had planned. I was panting, breathing hard, keyed up. Now I needed to find Freddy. I needed to tell him.

I rushed into the employee dining room, hoping to find him there, but it was empty. It was late; dinner was almost over. The kitchen crew was already cleaning up. I heard someone calling my name. "Amy!"

I turned to find Stuart, Stuart Swiftcurrent, staring at me. He had said my name so sharply that I had the impression he had been calling my name for some time. "What are you doing here?" he asked, and I realized then I had wandered back into the kitchen, the kitchen where I used to work with Cory, back when everything was simpler.

"Oh, hey," I said, and the way he was looking at me—a concerned, almost scared expression on his face—made me raise my hand to my hair. It was a mess, tangled. Had I looked like this on the shuttle? How many people had seen me like this, my hair a rat's nest filled with shriveled leaves and dried-up blades of grass?

He put a plate of food in front of me and sat me down at the prep counter. Once again, the baby inside me moved, kicked those little legs, and I looked up at Stuart, alarmed, sure he could see it, see what was happening to me, but he was busy shuffling around, adding things to my plate: a biscuit, a spoonful of penne in some sort of zucchini and eggplant sauce, a square slice of chocolate cake. I ate it, all of it, stabbing my fork into it and shoveling it into my mouth.

Stuart was asking me what happened to me, what was wrong with me, but I pointed to my mouth, still chewing, my cheeks filled with food. Only after he had fetched me a glass of water and I washed it all down did I attempt to answer him. I laughed a little, trying to appear normal. I told him I was fine. Hungry, but fine.

It didn't seem like he believed me. His hand reached out and plucked something from my hair. A leaf. He studied it for a moment and then turned his gaze to me, inspecting me, and self-consciously, I covered my abdomen with my hands. "Have you seen Freddy by any chance?" I asked him.

~

I'd never watched Freddy on the stage before. I was never around. I spent every weekend with Cory, taking the shuttle back first thing Sunday morning to start my workweek. All the seats were taken, so I stood at the back and leaned against the wall. He was magnetic up there, snapping his fingers, accompanying the words of the songs with funny little dance moves, showing he didn't take himself too seriously. I wasn't enjoying the show so much as observing him, the effect he had on the audience.

The day had been almost impossibly long, and I struggled to pay attention, to keep my eyes open, and when my eyes did close, I slipped straight into a jumble of dreams. Cory standing over me, the sun shining through his hair, Cory's face underwater, sinking down, the water tapping against the edge of the boat, tap tap tap taptaptaptaptap—

I gasped and my eyes sprang open, as if I was the one underwater, coming up for air, and I was in the basement at the cabaret. Everyone was clapping, and the singers were taking their bows. It was over.

And then I went to Freddy, brought him up to my room. His hands traveled over my skin, my bruised skin, crosshatched with scratches. I had gone on a hike, I told him. Bushwhacking through brambles. I was a disaster, my tangled hair, dirt under my fingernails. He wanted me anyway. I had held off all summer. He wanted me and I wanted him. I needed him.

When we were together, I knew I had made the right choice. Everything would work out after all.

～

"I can't believe this," Ramona said. Outside the dining room windows, the moon had risen higher into the sky, a gleaming disk. Its mirror image reflected in the surface of the lake, picture perfect. We had both been watching it as I told my story, mesmerized by it, but now I could feel her eyes on me. I pretended not to notice. "You threw everything away, like you were covering up a crime," she was saying. "Made it look like he disappeared. All so you could go around pretending Freddy was the father, so he wouldn't know Cory existed? So no one would ever know what happened to him, so he would just disappear from the face of the earth?"

"No—god, Ramona, is that what you think?" When I did turn to her, I could barely stand it, that look on her face. As if I had broken her heart. "I wasn't just thinking of myself. I was trying to make the best of a terrible situation. If Freddy knew—knew about Cory, that he was the father, or that he even might be the father—he might not have agreed to it. If he didn't"—I held up my hands in a "who knows?" gesture—"if he didn't, he would step up, he would take care of me, of us. I knew he would, and I was right. He wanted to be with me. He asked me to move to New York with him, and I did. Days later, there we were. It wasn't a perfect plan—it wasn't even a plan, it's just what I did in the heat of the moment."

"You loved him. You said you loved him, and then you just threw everything away, all his things, until there was nothing left of him."

"That wasn't the only thing left of him! That was the point—remember?" I put my hand to my abdomen, as if to demonstrate. "I felt you kick. Right in that moment, going through his things, right over there." I pointed in the direction of the employee dorms, one building over from this very hotel where we sat. "*You* were left of him. I had you."

"You didn't even know I was his."

"I'm just saying—"

Ramona sat up straighter in her chair. "What about the photographs?"

"What photographs?" I asked, although I knew exactly what she meant.

"The backpack, the T-shirts with the bands on them. You threw them away, right? Anything that could be traced back to him, to Cory. But you never said what you did with the letters you sent, or the photographs. That portfolio you found in his bottom drawer."

"Ramona." I didn't know what to say. She had been so angry at me, and now she looked hopeful, her eyebrows raised, pleading.

"I shredded the letters at the front desk. They were from me anyway. They weren't really his. I mean, they wouldn't mean anything to anybody but us, the two of us."

"And the pictures?"

I hesitated a beat before answering. "I still have them," I said. "Not here," I added. "But no, I didn't throw them away. I couldn't."

Ramona smiled a little bit and then stood up. "Sure, Amy," she said. "Look, it's late. I'm going to head up."

I stood up also, too hastily, almost toppling my chair over in the process. "Wait, Ramona—" It took me a second to replay the last few lines of our conversation over again to understand what had happened. Then it hit me. "You don't believe me," I said.

"You're just telling me what I want to hear."

"But it's true," I said. "I kept them. I have them. I can get them for you. You can come visit me again, in Seattle, I'll show them to you. You can have them; they belong to you now. They were your father's—"

Before I could even finish my thought, Ramona was striding out of the dining room, making her way through the maze of tables and chairs, out into the main lobby, which was empty and mostly dark, all the lamps set on their dimmest setting. "You know what, Amy, just stop. Okay? I have heard enough. I'm going to bed. I'm checking out first thing tomorrow."

I trotted after her, through the lobby. "Ramona, please." She was walking at full speed now; I almost had to jog to keep up. "I named you!" I blurted out.

She had reached the base of the staircase by then, had already climbed a few steps, and she stopped short. She turned around to appraise me. "What?" She said the word with impatience. One hand rested on the railing.

She looked so beautiful like that, from my vantage point at the base of the stairs. Her nostrils flaring, her eyes hard and intense. I smiled a little. I had missed this, missed this version of her, that angry little child, the surly teen, all those versions of her over the years. "Ramona," I said. "As soon as I knew you were a girl, that was the name I picked out for you. I named you after the character in the books, the Ramona books. I loved those when I was a kid. She was so—so impish and impetuous, you know? Always getting into trouble. But she had a great imagination. And she was from Oregon, too, just like me."

The anger had drained from Ramona's face. She was watching me, blinking.

"When you contacted me, when you first reached out to me, I couldn't believe it. I couldn't believe they had kept your name, the one

I'd given you. I thought they would have changed it. They kept it—I gave that to you. Your name."

I started toward her, reaching my hand up, but Ramona stopped me. "It's true!" I added. She didn't believe me. Or she wanted to believe me but didn't know if she could. "The name on your birth certificate, the original one, the one you weren't supposed to see—what was it?"

"Ramona Bennison," she admitted.

"Yes! See, it's true. I'm telling you the truth."

"Thanks, Amy," Ramona said. "That's a great story."

"Don't leave, okay. You can't. Not like this."

"The thing is, I came here to get to know you. My whole life, I've dreamed about that. Finding my birth mother. And meeting you—it was great. It really was. But it's like—what was the point, you know?" Ramona wiped at her face, as if checking for tears. "I'm done."

"Don't say that. Let me explain—"

"What's left to explain? We've talked and talked, and you've told me all sorts of crazy things, but what's the point of any of them if you aren't going to do anything about it? If you aren't going to make anything right?" When she turned around and headed up the stairs, I didn't chase after her. I watched her as she marched up. At the top of the landing, she turned back around and said, "Say goodbye to Gabe for me, okay? He's a cool kid."

CHAPTER 19

AMY

The next morning, I woke up early. Beside me, Jonathan was still asleep, buried completely underneath the sheets, the way he always slept, like a forest animal in a children's book who burrows underground at night, finding comfort beneath blankets of leaves and ferns. I crept out of bed slowly, trying not to wake him. The room was still dark, but light peeked between the gaps in the curtains.

I riffled through the closet, working mainly by touch, in search of the right clothes, clothes that would send the right message. It was summer, summer at Seven Glacier. Most of my clothes were T-shirts, shorts, underlayers of merino wool. I knew I had something—there. My hands landed on a silk blouse, a wool skirt. In the bathroom, I changed into it, and then started up on my hair and makeup. I should have done it in reverse order; it had been a while since I had dressed up, since I had had the occasion to dress up. I was out of practice.

Once I was ready, I checked in on Gabe. He was sprawled face down on his bed, a starfish. I located his cheek and kissed it gently, leaving a pink lipstick stain, which I then tried to rub off with my fingers. He stirred and slapped at his own cheek, but he didn't wake up.

I waited in the kitchen until Jonathan came stumbling in, rubbing his eyes. "You're up early," he said, and after a moment, he took me in, fully dressed in business clothes, waiting patiently at the table, my hands folded in front of me.

"Coffee?" I poured us two mugs and went to the fridge for the half-and-half, which I poured into a little ceramic pitcher. This was for me. Jonathan drank his black.

"What's all this?" he said. "Some investor meeting I don't know about?"

"You'd better sit down," I said, but he was already doing it, pulling out a chair next to me.

He put a hand to my cheek and looked into my eyes the way a doctor might, checking for signs of a concussion. "Is everything okay?"

"Remember 2015?" I asked him.

Jonathan kept his eyes on me as he took his first sip of coffee and grimaced. I had made it too strong. Jonathan usually made the coffee. "What about it?"

"Remember when I came up here?"

Jonathan appeared to be inspecting something on the ceiling of the cabin. Then he looked back at me. "Amy, whatever this is about—"

"They found a body!" I said. "A body at the bottom of a lake, here in the park. I came up here to deal with it."

"Damage control," Jonathan said, remembering.

"Right. Okay, well—" I exhaled loudly and then took a sip of my own coffee, which I had lightened with half-and-half. It wasn't so bad, really. "The body they found. It was Ramona's father."

Jonathan's cup was halfway between the table and his mouth when I said that. He froze. "Wait—what?"

"Yes, and last night, I told Ramona. That's why she came here, part of the reason, anyway—to ask me about her father."

"Slow down, slow down." Jonathan had put his cup on the table by then and was just staring at me, his mouth slightly open.

"We kept it out of the papers. The national papers. It was right in the middle of tourist season, we wanted people to feel safe—"

"Of course." Jonathan nodded, approving.

"But they ran a little thing in some of the local papers around here, you know, it got buried in the back pages, a couple column inches, no pictures, and then Cory's mom—his name was Cory—she saw it. She lives around here and she went to the police and they were able to match his dental records and—it was him."

"And you found out about this four years ago and—why is this the first I'm hearing of this? I mean, where am I in all this, just like sitting at home with Gabe or—"

"I *did* tell you about it. I told you about it as soon as we heard about it, when they called us in Seattle. I said I would go over there myself, I'd take care of it. And I did—I took care of it. I kept it out of the papers, I—"

Jonathan buried his head in his hands and scrunched up his hair with his fingers. When he looked back up at me, I could see he was attempting to breathe steadily, to remain calm. This wasn't like him. Usually he didn't have to *try* to be calm, to make such a concerted effort at it.

"You wanted to deal with it personally," he said, and he was speaking very slowly, very calmly. "I remember this. I remember thinking, Why is Amy handling this? But you insisted. I knew you had a connection to this place—" Jonathan still seemed to be stuck, working this out.

"I knew it was him," I blurted out. "I knew it was Cory. I knew it was him because I was there." I talked in a rush, telling him the whole story, an abridged version. I wanted Jonathan to catch up. I hadn't even gotten to the relevant part, the reason I had gotten up early, put on this outfit, made this too-strong coffee.

"The thing is," I said, wrapping up, "back then, when I talked to the police, I didn't tell them what I knew. I didn't tell them I had thrown out his things, made it look as if he had disappeared. I mean, I knew how it looked. It was an accident, but the way I acted, it was like I was guilty, guilty of something, and it was wrong. I shouldn't have done that, but I wasn't exactly thinking straight. All I was thinking was that I needed to figure something out, a plan, a plan for me and my baby."

"Wait—the police?"

"Yes, the police. I didn't tell them what I knew, but I should have. I need to make it right. I need to go down there, *now*, and set the record straight." When Ramona walked out of the dining room last night, I knew I was losing her. I couldn't lose her, not again. I thought about what she said to me once, how I wanted her to find me, despite everything. She was right. I knew it as soon as she said it. Now she was leaving, and she would probably never talk to me again, unless I did something about it, something to show her how serious I was. A grand gesture.

"The police—you didn't say anything about talking to the *police*."

"Well, yeah, I had to. I cooperated fully."

"But you didn't tell them you were there? That you knew the victim—"

"They didn't ask, did they? I mean, they had no reason to." Back in 2015, when the body was found, I figured the police would catch up to me eventually, and I would deal with it then. Months later, when the identity of the body was verified, I thought, Well, this is it. I waited for the cavalry to arrive. Nothing happened. All those letters Cory and I had written to each other, during our eight months apart—I had destroyed them. We had emailed each other, too, but Cory had gone to the library to do it. His mother probably didn't even know about the emails, so they were never looked into, even back when his mom first reported him missing. Once his body was found, the police probably asked Bennison Hotels for their employment records, but what was the likelihood they had kept them for seventeen years? Not likely at all. The trail went cold.

I stood up. "I need to go now, before Ramona leaves."

"So this is about Ramona."

"Yes, Jonathan!" I was impatient. "If they arrest me, you might need to bring me some things. I don't know what they let you take in with you. There's a possibility I'll have to stay in jail overnight or something but—"

"Amy, what are you *doing*? Slow down, okay? Let's get a lawyer, discuss our options."

Now Jonathan was back, the tormented expression wiped from his face, the we-can-deal-with-anything attitude firmly back in place. He stood up, too. "I'll wake up Gabe, I'll call up Morgan in Seattle for a list of names, we'll—"

"No! You stay here with Gabe. I need to go now." And before Jonathan could say another word, I was out the door and running down to the lodge.

I banged on Ramona's door and yelled her name. It was only eight o'clock, and checkout wasn't until eleven, but I didn't want to take any chances. Already the hall was buzzing with activity. A family of four, all in their hiking clothes, was exiting the room down the hall, giving me curious looks. I stood up straight and smoothed my hair with my hand. "Good morning." I smiled brightly at them. "Enjoy your breakfast."

"Thanks," the wife said, hustling the kids along.

I banged on the door with the palm of my hand, and the door opened midbang. "Ramona!" I was out of breath by then, after running all the way from the cabin and making this big production in the hallway. Ramona stood in the doorway, all dressed and ready to go, one hand on the handle of her rolling suitcase.

"Excuse me," she said impersonally. "I'm checking out now."

"I'm ready," I said. "That's why I'm here. That's why I'm in this outfit." I gestured to my clothes, the silk shirt, the skirt, though I realized as I was doing it that I probably didn't radiate the professionalism and poise I had hoped. The blouse had come untucked from the skirt, and my heels were covered in a layer of dust. "I'm turning myself in."

"What are you talking about?"

"Last night—you said I should go to the police, tell them what I know. I'm going to do it. I'm ready to do that. For Cory. For his mom, to give her closure. That's what you want, right?"

Ramona was watching me skeptically, her eyebrows lowered. "You could actually get in trouble for this, you know," she said. "What you did—it was a crime. You know that, don't you?"

"Of course I know that. Jonathan, he wants me to get a lawyer—"

"That's probably a good idea."

"But what do I need a lawyer for? I'll tell them everything. All these years, there have been all these secrets. I can't even keep them straight anymore, you know? It's exhausting. But the thing is—"

The door next to Ramona's opened and a young couple, both very tall and very tan, with golden blond hair, like two models from a Swedish adventure sport catalog, came out. They were laughing and looking into each other's eyes. Honeymooners. They paid no attention to me standing in the hallway, to Ramona still on the threshold.

"The thing is," I continued once they had passed us by, "everything would have worked out better if I had just come clean in the first place. I see that now. I see that so clearly. Look at Freddy. Even when he found out he wasn't the father, he would have stuck by me, stuck by both of us. And Jonathan and Gabe—I mean, all these years, I never told them about that summer that I got pregnant, that I had a baby, and then you showed up and I finally told them and they loved you. They love you, Ramona! And I should have told them years ago, and I should have told someone about Cory right after it happened, but I didn't, and I should have told them later, when they found him, when they found him at Shangri-La, and I didn't then, either, but I'm going to now, okay? I'm ready."

I exhaled triumphantly and waited for Ramona's reaction. For a moment she just stood in the doorway, studying me. She bit her lower lip for a second, and then, as if she had made a decision somehow, she nodded once. "Okay," she said. "Let's do it."

∼

The policewoman at the station was a Native American woman with a round face and black hair parted straight down the middle and twisted into a neat bun at the nape of her neck. Despite the severe hairstyle, she looked very young, too young to be a cop, and at first I wondered if they had handed us over to some sort of junior park ranger or cadet, maybe an ROTC volunteer from the local high school, but she introduced herself as Detective Lenora Swiftcurrent.

She was seated behind a large desk, which also had the unfortunate effect of highlighting her youth, like she was playing around in her dad's office. Ramona and I sat in the two chairs provided to us and waited as she frowned at her computer screen, presumably going over the case file from 2015. She was really taking her time, and it was unnerving, just sitting there. If I were hosting, I would put on some music, maybe ask if anyone wanted something to drink, set out a tray of pastries. Okay, but she was young, and not everyone had my background in hospitality, in making their guests feel at ease.

"Swiftcurrent," I mused. "Detective Swiftcurrent." I liked the sound of that. Of course they wouldn't let a junior ranger or even some common beat cop interview me. A detective—that was a higher ranking, wasn't it? You had to earn your way up to that position. "Any relation to Stuart Swiftcurrent, by chance?"

The detective looked from the computer screen to me. "Stuart?" She looked back at the screen and clicked something on the mouse. "Yeah, he was my uncle."

"Was?" I couldn't help noticing the past tense.

"He died in 2011," she said. "Car accident."

My hand flew to my mouth. "Oh my god. I'm so sorry to hear that." To Ramona I said, "Stuart was in charge of all of us in the kitchen when I first worked at Seven Glacier."

"I know," she said.

"Right." I had already explained how he figured into all this. He was the one who had told us about Shangri-La in the first place, me and Cory. He drew us a map. Then that second summer, he wanted me to work with him again, he requested me special, and after—after I went up to Shangri-La again, after the accident, he saw me, he picked the leaf from my hair, and when I came back in 2015, I kept thinking I would see him. He could connect the dots. Me, Cory, Freddy, Shangri-La. Once they talked to Stuart, it would be a matter of time before they came to me, asking me about my role in all this, and I'd been prepared for that. I had braced myself for that, what I would say, what I wouldn't say, but that never happened. They never asked and I never told.

"Poor Stuart," I said out loud, to no one in particular. His niece didn't seem to be broken up about it; she was still inspecting the report on the computer screen. Of course, it wasn't news to her. She had had time to process it, to wrap her mind around it. And maybe they weren't even close. I had no way of knowing. I wanted to ask more about it, the circumstances of the accident. Was he married? Did he have kids? Something told me he didn't. A perpetual bachelor. Older than I was—twenty-five, twenty-six when I first met him? I didn't know—but still young at heart, joking around with everyone. I smiled, picturing him with his 1970s shag hairstyle, his mischievous grin.

Finally Lenora Swiftcurrent, Detective Lenora Swiftcurrent, turned her attention to me sitting across from her giant desk. "Your name is Amy Linden," she said, all business.

I agreed. That was my name.

"You are the CEO of the Adventurprise Hotel Group and currently hold the contract with Seven Glacier Park to run the accommodations there?"

"Co-CEO," I said. "With my husband, Jonathan Gladstone. And yes, that is correct."

"You came down in 2015 after hearing the news about the body found at the bottom of Lake Shangri-La by two hotel employees who had gone up there with diving equipment."

"Yes," I said. The detective seemed to be reciting the information she had read in the file.

"And was this something you would normally deal with, Ms. Linden? Flying in from—where were you at the time, Seattle?—to cooperate with the police about an incident in the vicinity of one of your hotels?"

"It wasn't just an incident. I mean, a body was found. We run a business. We have to think of our guests."

"The comfort of your guests—that's the reason you flew in from Seattle in 2015?"

I wasn't sure what she was getting at, but I agreed. That was more or less the reason. I could feel Ramona's gaze on me. I turned to look at her. "Amy," she whispered.

Right. Right. I wasn't here to go over the particulars of 2015 and my possible motivations for coming down and dealing with "the incident" myself. I was here to confess.

"There's more to it," I said. "More to the story."

"And you are?" Lenora Swiftcurrent directed this to Ramona.

"Ramona." I answered for her. "Ramona Crawford. She's my daughter. My biological daughter."

Lenora's facial expression didn't change. She also didn't move at all.

"Mine and Cory's," I added.

Lenora Swiftcurrent may have blinked. I expected more. She couldn't have dealt with many exciting cases in this county. A few Podunk towns and a sprawling park. Maybe someone stole someone else's rusted-out car or a tourist got their car ransacked by a bear or something every once in a while. "Cory Duncan," I said. "The—uh, the victim."

The young detective frowned before pushing her chair back. She spent some time opening and closing the drawers of her desk. After a moment, she produced a yellow legal pad, which she set on her desk. She wrote something down on the pad. I strained to read her writing but couldn't make it out. "Amy Linden + Cory Duncan = Ramona Crawford," I imagined her scrawling. Later, after we left, she could pin our pictures to a large corkboard, connect them with strings. She would stand back and study the board, her arms folded across her chest, trying to work it out.

She looked up from her legal pad. "You're telling me that you knew Cory Duncan, whose body was found at the bottom of the lake. He worked at the park for two seasons, in 1997 and 1998, and is presumed to have drowned at the end of the second season. You're saying that you knew him back then, and when you came back here in 2015—"

I was nodding as she spoke, and at that point I interrupted. "Yes, that's right. I knew it was him."

"And you knew this—how?"

"Because I was there."

"You were there." The detective tapped her fingers on the desk. "You were there. And you didn't tell anyone." She wrote something else down on her pad.

"No," I said quietly.

"And seventeen years later, when they found the body, you came all the way down here, spoke with the police, but you didn't mention anything about knowing the identity of the body. Didn't mention that you were there when he drowned."

"I was afraid, okay? It was an accident but I was with him. I was pregnant. I didn't know what to do."

"What *did* you do?"

I looked over at Ramona, who gave me an encouraging little nod.

"I rowed the boat to shore. I hiked back down—I cleared everything out of his room. I threw away all his stuff, anything that would tie back to him. I made him disappear. That's what I did. And after I did that—I mean I couldn't tell anyone then, could I? He drowned, and I panicked. I—failed to report an accident. Tampered with evidence. Obstructed an investigation. I don't know. I was afraid I'd get in trouble. I mean, what I did was a crime, right?"

Detective Swiftcurrent jotted a few more things down on the pad. She reached the end of the page, flipped the paper over, and continued writing on the next one. Ramona and I exchanged worried glances.

"I mean, I could be in serious trouble over this, right, Detective?"

She spent a few moments looking over her notes before looking back up at me. "I'm going to have you go over the whole story," she said. "From the beginning."

I was sitting very straight in my chair, my hands folded in my lap. I bobbed my head. Yes. I was prepared to do that.

"But yes," she said grimly. "I'd say you could be in quite a bit of trouble."

CHAPTER 20

—

AMY

Five months later

I usually spent visiting hours in the library, where I could sit in peace inside a giant window well behind the stacks. No one else seemed to know about it, so I could gather up an armful of old paperback books and outdated, dog-eared magazines and sit there for hours, reading about the celebrity gossip of yesteryear or crying over some heartrending romance that featured either a plucky Amish woman or a teenager in love with a dangerous yet handsome otherworldly creature. Usually, though, I would drift off halfway through the story and just stare out at the landscape. There was a beauty to it, the snow over the plains, the mountains in the distance, miles away, just out of reach.

The window was so thick, made out of reinforced, bulletproof glass and then, for good measure, sealed in with an acrylic layer that warped my view, that it was hard to see everything clearly. The snow was coming down hard now, not peacefully drifting in gentle clumps but buzzing around angrily, and I had the distinct sense that I was sitting at the bottom of a snow globe a demented child had just grabbed and shaken with all his might.

Since I rarely had a visitor, I sometimes spent this time writing letters. I had so much to say—so much left to say to her, to my daughter.

I hadn't seen Ramona since that day at the police station, when I had turned myself in. I had done it for her, and she knew that. I *thought* she knew it, anyway. I thought it would fix things—they put me in jail for Christ's sake! I had come clean, I had risked everything to show her how sorry I was, and she had thanked me. After I was done telling the story to Detective Swiftcurrent, who set up a video camera and had me tell the entire story, from beginning to end, with Ramona watching on, Ramona had said, "Thank you, Amy." So much happened after that. Jonathan showed up with lawyers, Detective Swiftcurrent brought in some other officers, and Ramona—she just slipped out somewhere in the commotion.

She was with Evan now—I had heard that through Jonathan. She talked to Jonathan, told him all about dropping out of college in Ohio and enrolling in courses in Missoula, a few hours from here, this facility. It had been almost five months. She could have visited me, she could have answered my letters, but nothing. Not a word.

I had pled guilty to two charges and waived my right to a trial. The judge sentenced me to one year for failure to report an accident resulting in a death and five years for falsifying physical evidence. They had also reopened Cory's case, and there was always the possibility the DA would bring more charges against me. I tried not to think about it too much. If you think about it too much, you'll go nuts in a place like this.

"Linden!" Someone was calling my name, and when I looked over, there was Issa, a nineteen-year-old in for stabbing her boyfriend, the father of her two-year-old girl. He didn't die from it, and from the reports she got from her mother, he would eventually make a full recovery. Better luck next time, Wanda had quipped when Issa told us this story as we sat around the lunch table together, picking at our plastic cups of applesauce, and we'd all laughed.

"Make me run all over this place," Issa grumbled. "You have a visitor."

I put my magazine face down on the concrete windowsill where I was sitting, as if I would return to pick up where I had left off. "A visitor? Who?"

"Hell if I know. They called your name in there as I was leaving."

I craned my head around in search of a clock. Most rooms had them hung high up, with a little metal cage around them in case we got any ideas of climbing up there and breaking them with our bare hands, using the glass as a weapon. At least, that was what I assumed when I saw them. No one actually told me that.

There was still an hour left for visitors. "It can't be someone from the hotel," I said. "It's offseason."

"Maybe it's your husband." Issa waggled her eyebrows. She was very short and had to look up at me. When she waggled her eyebrows, she stuck out her tongue, too, and then she doubled over, laughing.

I laughed, too. The thing about Issa was that she was always clowning around, distorting her face into the goofiest expressions. She liked to cheer us up, never in a bad mood. Except for that time she tried to kill her boyfriend, I guess. Anyway, Jonathan and Gabe had visited me a few times, flying in on weekends from Seattle at first, and all the girls—we called ourselves "girls" here—agreed that he was "imminently bangable," as Leela put it.

"It's not him," I said. "I'm not expecting him, and anyway, he was just here yesterday. Wait—unless there's news?" I mused out loud as we walked down a windowless corridor. "Jonathan hired this team of lawyers for me. He's convinced I won't have to serve my full sentence. I turned myself in, after all, and I 'cooperated fully,' so I'm not like a threat to society—" I stopped short, looking over at Issa to see if I had offended her.

She crossed her eyes and pointed at herself, and both of us cracked up. I was really meeting some interesting people in here. It was a good experience, in the end, I decided. No matter what wound up happening, how long I had to stay here.

"Maybe they decided not to press any more charges," I continued. "Or they could be relocating me somewhere—somewhere closer to Seattle, though really, I've settled in here, so—"

"See ya, Linden," Issa said as she headed down the hall, leaving me at the entrance to the visiting room. I checked in and seated myself at an empty table. The room was large, with shiny linoleum floors and a smattering of round tables with built-in benches, like a high school cafeteria. From the windows high up in the walls, all I could see was that blur of snow. The room was warmer than the library, maybe because in the library, I'd insisted on sitting in a concrete-block window well, and I removed the oversize sweatshirt they gave us all. If I had known Jonathan was visiting, I would have dressed up a bit, not that I had much choice in clothing. I could have thrown on some ChapStick, brushed my hair at least. Self-consciously, I combed my hair out with my hands and restyled my ponytail.

And then I heard someone call my name. Not "Linden," as all the girls called me in here, but my first name. "Hi, Amy." It was Ramona.

CHAPTER 21

RAMONA

The letters Amy wrote me from prison were all the same, a variation on a theme. The first one arrived in January, shortly after I moved to Missoula. After leaving Seven Glacier, I didn't go back to college. I went home, to my mother. I figured she would need my help managing her chemo appointments. I could take care of her, try to make sense of my life, figure out my next steps, since going to Seven Glacier certainly hadn't done that for me.

It turned out—to my surprise—my mother had everything under control. She had a group of friends who had rallied around her when she was first diagnosed, and new friends she had met in the various support groups she belonged to. She had lost her hair during the second round of chemo, but that was months ago and it had started to grow back. She was in high spirits, making plans for the future. I was the one floundering.

The first few letters sat in a sad little pile on the entryway table. I didn't throw them away, but I didn't open them, either, not at first. What would be the point? Meeting Amy, going to Seven Glacier, even meeting my biological grandmother—had any of this made any difference at all? I didn't have that sense of peace and contentment I thought I would have. I only had more questions, questions there were no answers to. Or, if there were, they wouldn't be in those letters.

I heard from Jonathan the same day the fourth letter arrived, right around my twenty-first birthday. He and Gabe were moving from their house in Seattle in order to settle somewhere closer to Amy, he told me. The two of them would be visiting Missoula soon, and we arranged a visit.

I opened the letters then, the ones I had left sitting on the table, and the ones that came after that, week after week. Amy talked about life in prison and made it sound as if she was having a grand old time. She invited me to visit her there. She had something to tell me. She *needed* to tell me what really happened out there. I had taught her something, she said. When I showed up in her life again after twenty years, she started letting go of the secrets she had been holding in, one by one. And with every secret that came out, she realized how much lighter she felt. That was why she went to the police, why she confessed, why she self-surrendered. She was ready to tell me *everything*. She underlined "everything." She wanted to come clean.

That there was more to the story didn't rattle me in the least. Of course there was. How many renditions had she already told me? There was always going to be a different iteration. It was the story she would just keep telling and retelling forever.

And whatever Amy wanted to tell me, maybe I didn't need to know. I didn't know myself any better than I did before. Nothing had changed. I told this to Evan one night, in our place in Missoula. Evan and I had become friends—if you could call it that—at Seven Glacier. When I finally checked out of the lodge, after Amy made her confession to the police, Evan offered to drive me the two hours to the airport. We talked the whole way over, as if we had known each other for years. We kept in touch, and she visited me in Saint Louis over Thanksgiving, and—well, that was that.

It seems like everything's changed, Evan said to me that evening.

Well, I supposed that was true. But I didn't need to know where I was from, I didn't need every little puzzle piece from the past to figure out who I was. I could do that on my own. On my own or with Evan, or with my actual mother, the one who raised me. With the people who cared about me, and that included Jonathan and Gabe. I could stitch together my own family. Family wasn't all about heritage or genetics. It was like everyone was always telling me: That didn't matter. It shouldn't matter.

I always had this sense that something was missing, and that the missing piece would arrive in the form of knowledge. If only I knew who my birth parents were, what the whole story was, I'd be complete. But now I wondered if everyone felt that—felt that same emptiness. Maybe it had nothing to do with being adopted at all. This made me feel better, in a way. Maybe I wasn't so different after all. Maybe I was just like everyone else, taking part in this universal experience of not knowing.

Then on the night Jonathan and Gabe said they were going to be in town, Evan and I invited them over for dinner. Jonathan, probably worried about what two twenty-one-year-olds would prepare them for dinner, wisely offered to order us pizzas. Gabe missed me, he said. He missed his mother. I felt guilty about that, too. It was my fault. I confessed as much to Jonathan: if I had just let the past stay in the past, they would all be in Seattle, going on with their lives.

At that point in the evening, I may have had a little too much to drink. Gabe and Evan had gone into the living room to play some sort of video game, and Jonathan and I sat across from each other at our kitchen table. "I don't want you to think I blame you for any of this," Jonathan said. He was just as handsome as ever, but perhaps a bit more tired than before. Little creases around his eyes that hadn't been there a few months earlier, back when I was visiting Seven Glacier. "None of this was your fault," he was saying. "I don't blame you, and Amy doesn't, either."

"Why are you still with her?" I blurted out. I slapped my hand over my mouth. "Sorry." I had been wondering, though. Look at everything she put him through! Look at Gabe, still his same, scrappy self, but different now, in a way that sent a pang through me. As if he had grown a little older, a little wiser to the ways of the world in just a few short months. And what had she done it for? For me? I couldn't understand it.

Jonathan didn't seem offended by my question. He smiled, even, when he answered. "She's not a bad person, you know," he said. "She tries to do the right thing. I believe that."

I thought about that, nodding slightly, taking it in. Yes, she probably did think she did the right thing. It was just for Amy, the right thing meant something different than it did for everyone else.

"And she always keeps things interesting," Jonathan said.

"Yes," I agreed. "I will give her that." And then I added, "She has a very active imagination."

We both kind of laughed then, but when our laughter faded, I felt the chill of its absence. I lifted up my wineglass and looked into it, though it had been empty for some time, just some ruby-red sediment stuck to the bottom. "She says I got that from her," I said. "She said I should be an artist." I looked up at Jonathan.

"That doesn't sound like her."

"Well, she didn't say I should *be* an artist," I amended. "She said I *was* an artist, that I came from a long line of artists." I lowered my voice. "My dad was an artist, too. Or could have been."

I worried sometimes about what I inherited from Amy. I wanted to hate her, but I didn't. She took my father away from me, and that pained me. I got to know him through her, through her distorted lens, so do I even know him at all? Silver eyes and crooked teeth? She had a wild imagination, and look where it got her. What if I went down that same path? What if I couldn't help it? What if that was what I learned about myself—that I had it, too, this imagination that ran away with me, made me do impulsive, irreversible things, made me tell crazy stories, terrible lies?

I had been discussing this with my therapist, actually. She was trying to get me to think of it another way. What if instead of using my imagination to hurt people, I channeled it into something good? I remembered my childhood obsession with those beautiful, hidden worlds in the flowers and leaves of the botanic gardens, how I wished I could shrink down and live in those worlds, a walnut shell for a bed like Thumbelina. What could I do with that? Evan and I would lie in bed and joke about it, throwing out ideas. I could make doll furniture. Bake petit fours. Paint epic scenes on grains of rice.

Jonathan cleared his throat and placed a manila envelope on the table between us. "This is for you," he said. He wasn't sure if he should bring it to me, he said, but Amy had insisted.

"What is it?"

He said he didn't know. "Amy made me promise not to look."

I could feel my heart beating in my throat as I opened the envelope and peeked inside. Then I looked back up at Jonathan, who was watching me expectantly. "I can't believe this," I said. "She kept them."

That was when I decided to visit her, just once. She hadn't lied about everything, and she hadn't tried to erase everything she had done, either. She had brought me into this world; I was here. She met me, she invited me to Seven Glacier. She saved Cory's photographs. She had turned herself in. She was trying to be accountable. So I would go there, to the prison, and I would meet with her. I would thank her. Get some closure.

~

She looked terrible. It was a shock, how terrible she looked. Her hair stringy, with dry ends. Rings under her eyes, as if she hadn't slept for weeks. She seemed smaller somehow, fragile and nervous. Yet when I called over to her, her eyes lit up.

I hadn't seen her since that day she turned herself in at the police station. She didn't have to turn herself in. If I had never come to Seven Glacier, she probably never would have. Everything would have remained the way it had been for twenty years.

I didn't feel glad, the way I thought I might feel, knowing the truth had come out. I wasn't sure it would end up doing much good. At least

Cory's mother—my grandmother, as I tried to think of her—could stop wondering. She confessed, I thanked her, and it was over. Or so I thought.

"Ramona," Amy said to me in the visitors' room, her voice choking on my name.

She made a move to come around to my side of the table, to hug me, and I quickly sat myself down before she could. She settled in across from me. "I'm so glad to see you," she said, and this time, she was crying. "How's your mom?"

I smiled then, a real smile. "She's doing great," I said. "Her last scan was clear. Cancer free."

"Oh, that's incredible news," she said, and she laughed as if in relief, as if she had a personal stake in it, and maybe she did. Amy had picked my mother out from dozens of other prospective mothers, and she had been the right choice. My mother had been a good mother; she had taken care of me, and now, she was going to be all right. *I* was going to be all right.

"I know what it's like," Amy was saying, "taking care of a parent. I'm just so glad."

"Me, too," I said. "We're planning to take a trip together this spring. Hawaii, maybe. Or Europe. Anywhere she wants."

"You're not worried? About this virus that's going around?" It was spreading, Amy informed me. It could be here in a matter of weeks. They had already printed out signs and placed them in the bathrooms about washing their hands an extralong time, and they were going to have a special emergency meeting about new cleaning protocols because "our health is their number one priority." Amy rolled her eyes, as if she didn't believe this. "Jonathan's worried about the hotels," she went on. "They're already predicting travel restrictions."

"I hope it doesn't come to that." I hadn't been paying much attention to the news lately.

"I feel like I should be out there," she said. "Dealing with this." She gazed up at the windows, at the snow coming down.

I looked up, too, imagining the snow piling higher and higher, so high it reached the windows, then passed them, trapping us inside here forever.

We hit a lull in our conversation, and for a few minutes we just sat there, smiling shyly at each other like two teens on a first date.

"I brought something for you," I said. "They let me bring it through security." I had the manila envelope in my hands, the one Jonathan had given me. I slid it across the table.

"What is it?" She didn't touch the envelope.

"Just open it," I said.

She hesitated and then took the envelope in one jerky movement, as if she had just psyched herself up to do it. She lifted out the contents: a stack of photographs in varying sizes, from the standard four-by-six to eight-by-ten. I watched her face as she sorted through them. Close-ups of raindrops on fern leaves, iridescent, reflecting and refracting light. An image of a bee pollinating a stalk of beargrass. Two young deer, their antlers still fuzzy, standing in a clearing, trees arching overhead. Both staring straight into the camera, their eyes docile and unafraid, their young bodies teetering on those long, knobby legs, like they were professional models, fully aware of their youth, their aliveness, their vibrant beauty.

There weren't very many photographs with human subjects. Just a few. The subject was always the same, a young woman with messy dark hair, large dark eyes, a small mouth and pointed chin. When Amy got to those, she leafed through them more quickly, until she landed on one picture in particular. She stared at it a long time, and then she held it up to me. "This was it," she said. "That first time we went to Shangri-La." In it, she was wearing wet clothes. Her hair dripped down in strings on the sides of her face. "I thought I must look so hideous," she said, smiling a little. "Like some sort of sea monster. But he said no. I looked entrancing."

I could see it, too, the way her eyes challenged the camera, the dark hair against pale skin. He had captured her spirit somehow, the feeling she had described to me, the feeling that she was wild and daring, plunging into glacial waters, splashing around laughing, the feeling of being young and alive and ready to fall in love.

Amy shivered then, and she filed that picture beneath the others. Swiftly, she stacked them all back up, placed them in the envelope, closed it, and pushed it across the table to me.

"You've never looked at them before?"

She shook her head. "I couldn't."

"Jonathan gave them to me. They're good, you know? He really had talent." I wanted to believe I inherited that from him. He was an observer, like me. He saw the beauty in small things, in the little details.

"I asked him to send them," Amy said. "As soon as he got to Seattle. I kept hounding him to look for them—I had stashed them under some loose floorboards. Really original, right? I was like, just find it, okay, send it to Ramona, and he kept saying he would—"

"Well, he did. I mean, he found it, the portfolio. He held on to it for a while."

"He didn't tell me."

"Maybe he didn't know if I'd want to see them. Didn't know how I'd react."

Amy nodded. "Makes sense."

"He brought it over to me last week, in person. He and Gabe visited us in Missoula. Gabe's teeth are really growing in."

Amy smiled, but I could see the sadness behind it. Jonathan had told me that when he and Gabe visited Amy, Gabe refused to speak to her. He wasn't ignoring her, not exactly. He just sat there, silently, watching her with a baleful expression. He'll come around eventually, Jonathan had told me.

I knew it must kill her, being apart from him. The idea that he was growing up without her. Despite everything, she did care for him, in her own way. I almost admired the way she raised him, letting him run wild, pursue his own interests. She didn't try to turn him into her mini-me, dressing him up in little suits and making sure his hair was always perfectly combed. He was his own person. I loved that about him, and about Amy, for letting him be Gabe. It made me think that even if I had grown up with her, even if my childhood had been completely different—growing up in hotels, traveling to far-flung destinations—I would still be me.

"To be honest, I was shocked when he gave them to me," I said to her. "The pictures. I assumed you had destroyed them along with everything else."

"I told you I didn't!" she said. "I couldn't."

"You told me a lot of things, though."

"I'd do anything for you," she said. "You can't even imagine."

I sat back and tilted my head, trying to assess Amy. I knew from her letters that she had turned herself in for me, because she thought it was what I wanted, to repent for all the harm she had caused, the damage she had done. And she did seem to be suffering from this choice, by the look of her. Those dark rings under her bloodshot eyes. "How are you holding up in here?" I asked her.

She widened her eyes. "Oh, it's great," she said. "I'm getting a lot of good ideas, actually. Ways they could run this place, little tweaks that could improve our experience here."

"I don't know how interested they are in making your experience more pleasant," I quipped.

This didn't faze her. "Oh, I know, I know. But I'm keeping a list going."

"You look a bit—" I wasn't sure how to put it, so I gestured to my own eyes. "Are you getting enough sleep?"

Amy looked away for a second, running her hand over her hair, which lacked its usual luster. "It's probably these outfits they make us wear," she said. The prison garb at this place reminded me of doctor's scrubs, faded denim colored pants with an elastic waistband and an oversize but not quite matching shirt. "I've never been able to wear blue," she went on. "It washes me out."

I wasn't sure what to say to that.

"I actually had this great idea," she said. "This is a good example of what I'm talking about. What they could do is bring in some of those color experts—you know, where they do your colors, figure out what season you are? It was big in the '80s. I think it's still a thing. Anyway, then they could give us uniforms in our colors. It could really boost our morale, seeing a little more variety around here. Plus it would allow us to reflect our personalities a bit. I actually mentioned this idea to one of the guards here and she loved it, but she said they probably weren't so interested in having us reflect our personalities. It's just not a priority for them. Oh well. I have a lot of other ideas, too."

"I don't think it's the uniform," I said. "Are you sleeping okay?" I asked her again. In her letters, she had mentioned staying up late into the night, presumably haunted by everything that had come up during my visit to Seven Glacier.

"Sure," she said. "I mean, as well as can be expected. It takes forever to get to sleep some nights. I'm just tossing and turning, and then when I do get to sleep, they're already waking me up, hours before dawn. It's messing with my circadian rhythms."

"You look tired." It was rude to talk about how tired someone looked. I knew that. I guess I just wanted her to admit that everything wasn't going great for her in here, that something was wrong.

"Well, yeah," she said, less cheerful now. "I'm tired. I'm locked up in here. I'm on this narrow little cot in this building made out of cinder blocks. I can see the pipes—" Amy raised her eyes to the ceiling, and I followed her gaze. In this room, the visiting room, you could see the ductwork and the plumbing pipes way up there, too high to reach, even if someone stood on a chair. "Obviously they can't have exposed pipes and things in the dormitories," she continued. "That would be dangerous. Some of the girls here—they're self-harming. So you can't see the pipes, but they're there, you know? Behind the walls somehow. In the ceilings."

"I'm not following—"

"You can't see them but you can hear them. All night long. Like if someone flushes the toilet or turns on the sink. Water gushes through the pipes. It makes this big racket. I try to block it out, to bury my head under my pillow, but it just gets louder somehow. It doesn't make any sense."

"Are you having the dreams?"

She widened her eyes. "Dreams?"

"This sounds just like that time in the Hedgewick—you told me about this. When you were pregnant with me?"

"Oh yes." She tried to laugh it off. "I mean, not really. It's just loud, is all. They need to insulate the pipes. I put that on the list, the list of improvements they should make around here."

She wrote about the dreams in her letters. The nightmares returned to her the very first night she slept here, tossing and turning on the bottom bunk in a room with five other women, a tiny dormitory room, like they were orphans in a children's home.

That water gushing through the pipes, the drip, drip, dripping of the sink in the communal bathroom down the hallway, it leaked into her, somehow, into her head. She could barely sleep, and when she did she could feel herself sinking, sinking underwater, face up, eyes open, sinking farther and farther down, the light shining through the warped and wavy water, getting smaller and smaller, eclipsing. At first it was peaceful, almost, sinking down, down, and then she would try to breathe and realize she couldn't, she was underwater, and she would panic, try to kick her way back up, try to break through the surface, but when she got there, when her face was just about to burst up through to the air, something would hold her back, hold her down. Hands pressing down, keeping her under. She could never see a face, she could just feel the pressure from the hands, and then she would sit up in bed, gasping for air, choking almost, coughing, and someone would yell You all right, Linden? or Shut up, Linden, and she would apologize softly, trying to catch her breath, but quietly, so as not to make more of a commotion.

"They're getting worse." She held her hands to her hair and closed her eyes. "Even when I'm awake, I feel as if I'm sinking underwater."

"I mean, it makes sense."

"What?" Her eyes were still closed.

"If you were having the nightmares again. Nightmares of sinking underwater. Drowning."

"Yeah," she said. "I'm talking to my therapist about it, in our sessions. She gives me these breathing exercises to do."

"And? Do they help?"

"I can't do breathing exercises if I think I'm underwater, can I?" she snapped. When she opened her eyes, they were wide open, as open as she could possibly get them. Then her face relaxed—or at least, made an effort to relax. "Sorry," she said. "It's the sleep deprivation."

"Did she have any other ideas then?" I asked. "The therapist?"

"I'm supposed to try meditation. And I'm reading all these books. They're supposed to help me understand—you know, everything."

"Like what kind of books?"

"Books about . . . radical honesty. About being true to yourself, you know. Anna—that's my therapist—says I told all those stories because I have a compulsive need for approval." She shrugged. "I don't know about that."

"Well, I think it's good. It's good you're talking to someone."

"You think so?"

"Of course I do."

"I want to be honest with you from now on," she said.

That was my cue to leave. I had told myself I would come here, show her the pictures. I wasn't going to get sucked in by her, though, for another round of storytelling. I twisted my body, trying to extricate myself from the table. The benches were attached to the tables, and everything was bolted into the floor. I made my way out and looked around for a guard to escort me out. "You know what, I think I'm done hearing these stories."

I could see the panic on Amy's face. "I *want* to tell you," she said, the same thing she had said in all her letters, the same thing she had been saying from the very start. "I want to tell you the truth."

"I'm sure you do," I said. "But it's not my responsibility to give you closure, or to make you feel better about everything." I tried to laugh, but it came out strangely. One of those sad, pathetic kinds of laughs. "I've been going to therapy, too."

"But you wanted to know."

I held my hand up to her, a stop sign. I bit my lip, trying to hold everything I wanted to say back in. It wasn't worth it. I needed to go, to get out of here. I took in a deep breath. But then I sat back down across from her. I couldn't stop myself. "That's what I wanted, but I don't need it anymore." I made an effort to keep my voice calm. Steady. "Not from you. It wasn't helping, it wasn't good for anyone. Look what came of it! Look at Gabe! His mother is locked up. And me, I've dropped out of college, and for what? All for this stupid quest to find out who I am, where I'm from. It didn't matter. Everyone was right! *It didn't matter.*"

"But you're happy now. With Evan, right? And your mom is better and—and everything worked out."

"Everything didn't work out!" I wasn't yelling, to keep the guards' attention from us, but it was *like* I was yelling. I could feel my face blushing a deep shade of red. "How can you say that? Cory is dead. His mother . . ." I trailed off for a moment, trying to gather my thoughts. "Listen, I knew it was a bad idea to come here. I can't keep doing this. I can't get wrapped up in this."

She nodded sadly. "You're right," she said. And then she was looking at me, really looking at me, as if she was trying to memorize my features in case this was it, the last time she would set eyes on me. "I guess I got what I deserved," she said.

CHAPTER 22

—————

RAMONA

It sounded so familiar, the way she said it, and I knew she had said it before, but I couldn't put my finger on it, not at first. I guess I got what I deserved. When she said it before, she had looked different, her hair sleek and smooth, that mischievous little smile on her face—then it came to me. Seattle, our first meeting, in that hotel downtown, Amy in her blue velvet gown, like a figure from a John Singer Sargent painting.

"You said that before," I said.

"What?"

"That you deserved it. That contest—you were going to win that scholarship. You found that bag of peanuts."

"I didn't *open* the bag of peanuts," she said.

I waved my hand, impatient. The whole story came back to me: Jessica Jenkins with her peanut allergy. Amy finding the bag of peanuts. No, she hadn't opened it.

"But you thought about it." I understood then what Amy was trying to tell me. And despite myself, I needed to hear her say it. I needed to know. I couldn't help myself.

Amy nodded.

"You want to tell me what happened out there, on the lake," I said. "So tell me. I'm listening."

Her voice went so quiet I had to lean in to hear her in that room, the room filled with the chatter from the other prisoners and their visitors. Young women and their boyfriends, young women and their children, old women and their husbands, middle-aged women and their grown-up children. "If I tell you," she said, "you have to promise not to go to the police."

"I can't promise you anything," I said, and I told myself I didn't need to know. I could stand up and walk away, right now.

"You were such a beautiful baby," she said, and her eyes filled with tears. She blinked and they spilled down her cheeks. She made no move to wipe them away. "You were so beautiful, but I kept having these dreams. Not dreams—I don't know what they were." Her eyes went glassy, remembering. "It was like you were sinking. Like you were underwater and I—" Amy reached her hands out in front of her, palms facing out. "It was like I was pushing you under."

"It's normal, right?" I said. "Postpartum depression? The hormones can make you crazy. Give you crazy ideas."

"I was afraid," she said. "I was afraid I'd give you a bath and push you under." She let out a sob, but then, as if remembering what she had sent me here for, she straightened up and wiped at her face with the back of her hand.

"It's okay," I said. "You didn't do it. I'm here. I'm here now."

"I gave you away," she said. "And the dreams stopped. For a while."

"But they're back now?"

"I need to tell you. I need to tell you what happened that day. At Shangri-La."

"You've told me before. You told me you found out you were pregnant. And Cory wanted to go there—"

"No!" Amy cut me short. "That's not what happened."

The chatter around us seemed to dim, and all I could hear was the sound of Amy's voice.

"It wasn't his idea," she said. "It was mine."

247

~

"Maybe this isn't such a great idea," Cory said to Amy. They were already through the brambles, halfway up to Shangri-La, at the base of the rocks.

She knew what he meant. Maybe it wasn't a great idea to climb up the side of a cliff, to crawl along a ledge. She was pregnant. Her center of balance might be off. It explained a lot, this pregnancy. All summer, she hadn't been herself. Nothing was the same as before. Maybe it was the hormones. Hormones can make you do peculiar things.

"We're almost there," she said, and she led the way.

She had a lot of time to think on that hike. She loved Cory, but it could never work out with him. She had to end it. She tried to work out what she would say to him, how she would break it to him. When they got up there, though, she couldn't go through with it. They were both sitting on the shore, right where they had sat that first time. But this time it was later in the year and the sky was thick and gray, the surface of the lake dark and choppy. The air nipped at their skin.

"Let's go out on the boat," she said.

He looked out at the lake and frowned. "Now?"

"It's too cold to swim." A strange kind of logic. "Let's look at the boat at least." She stood up to make her way around the edge of the lake to the little outcropping of rocks, and Cory followed her. They pulled the boat out and inspected it for signs of wear, for holes.

"I'm taking it out." She took off her shoes and socks and left them on the rocks. She waded out into the water with the boat, so cold it hurt her legs, as if it had penetrated her bones, frozen the marrow. "I'll hold it steady for you," she said, so Cory could get in straight from the shore, and he did. He tested the boat with both hands and stepped in. She hoisted a leg over the side and climbed in after him.

She started rowing, looking over at Cory, the shore behind him, receding farther and farther in the distance. She got into a rhythm. She put all her energy into it, rowing faster and faster. Cory was calling her name, telling her to stop, to slow down, to give him a turn, but she wasn't listening. She just kept rowing and rowing until her arms gave out and she stopped, spent.

The shore looked impossibly far away, like they were in the middle of a dome, a gigantic dome, the center of the earth.

"Amy," Cory was saying. "It's okay. It's going to be okay."

It took a few minutes for Amy to catch her breath, to hear the words he was saying. She looked over at him, at Cory, her first love. She smiled at him. "I'm glad we came out here," she said.

Right then, the sun broke through the clouds, and the lake glinted back at them and she was glad. It was so beautiful there, in the middle of the lake, the most beautiful place on earth. "Take a picture," she said, and in one swift movement, she pulled her shirt up over her head. She reached behind her back and unclasped her bra, too. "I want to remember this, how it was."

Cory lifted up his camera and looked through the viewfinder. She posed for the camera and smiled. The shutter clicked.

"How do I look?" she asked.

"Beautiful," he said, and she leaned toward him and raised her hand to his face.

The boat teetered as they kissed, but she kept her hand on his cheek. She wanted to remember this, the last time.

"It's good that we came here," she said again as she put her clothes back on. The bra, a little too tight now. The T-shirt. "It's good to end this way. Ending it right where it began, where we first fell in love. We'll always have these memories, you know? Of that summer—last summer. It seems like forever ago now."

Cory blinked back at her, uncomprehending. "We're having a *baby*," he said.

She had known he would resist. She had prepared for that, on the way up. He wouldn't let her go; he wouldn't make it easy. She knew what she had to do, to convince him, convince him that it had to end this way. "I'm going to tell you something," she said then, her voice very calm. "It will hurt you, and I'm sorry about that, but it's for the best—I truly believe that—and what I hope is that after I tell you, we can both move on and you won't hate me for it."

He was confused. Of course he was. He loved her. He loved her and she was about to break his heart. He might have even sensed it. He might have guessed at what she was going to tell him, what she was about to say next.

"The baby," she said. "I don't know if it's yours."

"What are you talking about?" He wasn't even angry—not yet. He was more incredulous.

"I've been seeing someone else. Freddy. I didn't mean for it to happen—it just happened." She couldn't watch Cory's face as she talked, and she let the rest come out in a rush. "I'm sorry about it, I'm sorry it had to be this way, but I was thinking about it on the way up. I really think it's for the best. I figured it out. What I hope is that we—you and I—can both move on and that you won't hate me forever." She did look at him, then, for a split second. He had gone completely white. He wasn't watching her but was gazing out into the distance.

"Listen," she continued. She tried to slow down, to sound sure of herself, calm, as if she had made up her mind and that was that. It had all made sense to her, the way she had imagined it as they had made their way up the side of the mountain, the way she had planned it all out in her head. "He didn't know about you, either. I never told him. Like I said, it just happened, and he's actually a really good guy. If I'm going to go through with this—and it looks like I'm going to have to go through with this"—she put her hand on her abdomen for emphasis—"then it makes the most sense to raise the baby with him. With Freddy. He's a Bennison. They have hotels everywhere! Think about it, Cory. I could work in one of them, create a stable home for this baby."

Cory didn't appear to be listening to a word she said. He was still staring off into the distance. She stopped talking. Maybe he needed time. She wasn't sure what to do, if she should keep explaining it to him, try to make him understand, or if she should just stay quiet for a minute. He could let her go. He could go on to live a normal life. She was the one who had to deal with this. She considered saying all that.

She opened her mouth to speak again, but then he swiveled his head to face her and said, "I can't believe this."

"Cory—"

"First you say you've been cheating on me. All summer—since the beginning? We waited for each other. Eight months without seeing each other and then—and then you tell me the baby isn't mine, but you can't know that. You can't know that." Again, Amy opened her mouth to interject, and again he cut her short. "And now you're telling me this is what's best for all of us? Are you crazy?"

She had never seen him like this before. This was not how the conversation had gone in her imagination. "Think about it, Cory! How could we raise a baby, the two of us? I love you, I do. But it wouldn't work. We'd end up like my parents. Is that what you want? With Freddy—"

"You're in love with him? With Freddy Bennison?"

"It's not about love," she said. "It's about what's best for the baby. For all of us."

"So you just decided this, huh? You've worked it all out." Cory was breathing hard, his nostrils flaring. His hair flopped in front of his eyes, and he reached up and flicked it back with his hand in a jerky, violent gesture. "What happens when Freddy finds out about me? Is he going to stick by you then?"

"He's not going to find out. There's no reason for him to find out." Now Amy was getting angry, but she kept her voice very calm. She was going to talk him into this. There was no other option.

"But you don't even know if it's his. You don't think he deserves to know that?"

"He doesn't need to know!"

"So he doesn't even know you're pregnant?"

"How could he? We just found out this morning. You were there."

"So you came up with this whole plan—" Cory waved a hand around in front of him.

"On our way up," Amy admitted. "Listen—"

"You can't just make all these plans and expect everyone to go along with them, Amy. You can't do that."

"I could if you let me," she said gently. "If you let me go."

"You'd just have a baby and not even tell him he might not be the father."

"There would be no need to."

"What if I told him? What then?"

"You wouldn't."

"If you won't tell him, I will. We'll get a paternity test. If you think I'm going to let you run off and raise my baby with this other guy, well—no," Cory said. And then he sort of laughed, a hollow, strange laugh she had never heard him use before. "That's not going to happen."

"Cory—"

"And as for this fantasy about becoming a part of this hotel family, about them sweeping you up in it, handing you your dream job just because you're having a baby—Amy, are you even listening to yourself? It's just that—a fantasy. It's never going to happen."

"It could happen." Amy knew then that Cory didn't believe in her. He didn't want the same things she wanted. He was okay with an ordinary life. He wanted—he seriously expected!—the two of them, plus the baby, to live in squalor. He talked about getting a job at a gas station. What about his dream to become a wildlife photographer? Dangle from cliffsides to get that shot of an eagle landing in its nest? It was a long shot, he said. Just an idea. Dreams didn't work out, he said. They could still have a good life.

He was so willing to give it all up. His dreams. Hers. So willing to let it all go.

She could picture it now, returning home to her parents eighteen weeks pregnant and with an unemployed boyfriend. They would sleep together on her twin bed opposite her teenage brother. They would diaper the baby in old towels and plastic bags and use a laundry basket as a crib because that was all they could afford. This was what Cory wanted, apparently. It was what he wanted her to agree to.

"I can't raise a baby with you." She tried her best to keep the emotion out of her voice. She clenched the sides of the boat, to steady herself. "As much as I love you—and I do love you, I do!—I just can't. Don't you understand, Cory? I can't do it. We have nowhere to go. And what if one of us gets sick? What if the baby gets sick? Then what? We're screwed." She gave him another pleading look. "You have to let me go. You have to."

For a second it looked as if he was softening a bit. The muscles in his face relaxed, and she thought maybe they had reached an understanding, and she lifted up her hand to touch his face, though she was too far to actually touch him, and her arm just dangled like that, in midair, like Adam touching the hand of God in that Michelangelo fresco, and she thought maybe that would be it. They would look into each other's eyes and maybe she would go to him and they would kiss and they would both have tears in their eyes and Cory would make the ultimate sacrifice and let her go.

He would let her go to Freddy, and she would make Freddy believe the baby was his and they would run off to New York, where she'd get swept into his family and meet his mother, Charlotte Bennison, who would see that Amy had something special. She would offer Amy a job and Amy would climb her way up that ladder, and by the time she announced the pregnancy to her own family, it wouldn't even matter, because she would be with Freddy and they'd have this great life as movers and shakers in the hotel industry. Then she would have plenty of money to hire someone to take care of her father, and once the baby was born Amy could visit and they would be so proud of everything she had managed to accomplish in such a short amount of time—with a baby!—and they would adore the baby, of course. Of course they would. Amy could see it very clearly, this version of her future.

All Cory had to do was agree to it. She touched his face. He let her touch him, just for a moment, and he closed his eyes, but then he seemed to think better of it, and his eyes shot open and he pushed her off him. He stood up, stood right up in the middle of the boat, trying to back away from her.

"You've got to let me go!" she said, but the breeze carried her voice off in the wrong direction. She yelled the words again: "You've got to let me go!"

He was laughing. Laughing at her, one of those sad, mirthless laughs she had previously only seen performed by actors in movies, actors playing characters who have lost it all. "You really think this is going to work out for you, don't you?" he was saying, and she could hear him perfectly, as if the breeze was traveling in just the right direction, his mouth to her ear, a direct line. "You think you're going to marry this rich guy, you're going to raise our baby in a hotel. A hotel?"

"Sit down, okay?" Amy yelled. It was tiring, yelling everything in his direction. No one said anything about marrying anyone, she wanted to say. And no one said anything about living in a hotel, as if that would be the worst fate for a child. It would be better than crawling back to her parents and sharing a room with her little brother again, that was for sure. It would be a good life. Wasn't that what he would want for their child, if it *was* their child? Yes. That was what she needed to express to him.

"The baby!" she yelled. "Don't you want the baby to have a good life?"

Cory shook his head and barked out another laugh. He surveyed the lake and raised his hands to the air, as if to proclaim to the world, I can't believe I'm standing here listening to this. "Amy," he said, his voice so steady, quiet almost, but she could hear it perfectly, each syllable crisp and distinct. "Give it up."

At first she didn't know what he meant. Give it up? It was too late to do anything about the pregnancy. Eighteen weeks along, the pharmacist had said, almost halfway through. And then he said, "You're never going to make it. You're never going to be Charlotte Bennison, you're never going to run a bunch of hotels or have a team of guys in suits following you around with their clipboards, and you know what? That's okay. You don't need to do that, you don't need to prove yourself to anyone, all you need to do is—"

And that was when she did it. She rocked the boat.

CHAPTER 23

RAMONA

It happened so fast but also in slow motion. The decision she made—if it even was a decision at all, not just a split-second reaction, an involuntary reflex—was the quick part. Both hands gripped the side of the boat, and she jerked her body to one side. Then time slowed down to a trickle and she watched, helpless, as Cory stumbled to stay standing. His feet wobbled, he teetered back and forth, his arms springing out to the sides, his face shocked, his mouth a tiny little O. He toppled sideways, careening off the boat and into the water.

One of his boots thudded against the side of the boat on the way down, so at first there was a commotion. Thunking, splashing, water everywhere, yelling. The sound of her own voice, calling his name, begging for him to stop thrashing around in the water, to stop panicking, to grab the oar she was holding out for him.

The boat started to drift, and she didn't jump in after him. She couldn't. If she jumped in, he would pull both of them down. They all would drown, the three of them. The three of us. She could only watch in horror at what was happening, at what she had set in motion.

It was only later, years later, when Gabe was three years old, ready for his first swim lesson, that she read about drowning—how to save someone from drowning. Drowning doesn't look like drowning. That was what she learned. The splashing, the flailing—that wasn't drowning. Not yet. That was what they called aquatic distress. When someone was drowning, they bobbed in and out of the water. It looked like they were standing.

That was what Cory was doing, after the splashing had stopped. She thought he had calmed down. She thought he would take the oar. She kept rowing toward him, kept holding it out to him, kept yelling for him to grab it, to save himself. She did that. She was sure she did that. She must have. She must have tried.

Their eyes met. She thought they did. She thought she remembered that. But then he slipped under the water.

And then, as she sat in the boat in the middle of the lake, everything fell completely silent and still. So quiet she swore she could hear the sound of the water tapping against the edge of the boat, like it had fingers, like the water had fingers and knuckles, too, and they were rapping against the side of that boat like they were knocking at a door, begging to be let in. Tap tap tap. Taptaptaptaptaptap.

~

When Amy finished talking, she exhaled audibly, one large gush of breath. "You can't imagine—all these years," she said, and she gave a shaky little laugh. "All these years, I tried to move past it. What I did, it was wrong. A mistake, a horrible mistake, I *know* that—I don't even know if it was a mistake, just a split-second decision. Or not even a decision, but what did I call it? A reflex. But now, saying it out loud, it's liberating, you know?"

I was horrified, of course, listening to her story. Horrified, though not exactly surprised. I sat still the whole time she talked, my eyes probably wide open in terror, taking it in, but she just kept going and going, as if she were in a trance. Now that it was out, I felt heavy with the weight of it, this secret handed over to me. It was mine now. I could take it to my grave and Amy would serve out her sentence and in a few years, she would be out, back to Gabe and Jonathan. Or I could tell the police, and more charges would be brought against Amy. She would go to trial and she would lose and she would certainly go away for a long, long time, maybe the rest of her life.

I found myself relieved as well, though not in the same jittery way as Amy. Relieved and drained, depleted. I would go home after this, back to Evan, crawl under a quilt, burrow underneath it, the snow falling outside, and I would sleep for days or weeks or even the rest of winter. I had that letdown feeling you get on Christmas morning as a kid, after all the presents are open, and you got everything you wanted, but the excitement leading up to it is gone. The tree just standing there looking lonely and sad with no presents underneath it anymore, just crumpled paper and unfurled ribbons.

I had asked for this, I reminded myself, sitting across from Amy. I had demanded the truth, and I got it. There would be no more versions of this story, no more retellings. Amy gave me what I wanted. What I said I wanted.

And so, when Amy reached her hands across the table, the way she had done when we first met, and again at Seven Glacier, I took them in mine.

She smiled at me and said, "I want you to know, I did it for you. I did it all for you." She said it like she was handing me a gift. Like I'd be happy to hear it.

I wasn't happy to hear it. Not at all.

But I understood that she believed this. That she drowned Cory for me, so she could run off with Freddy. That she gave me away so I could have a better life, this fabulous life she picked out for me like she was ordering it from a catalog. That she came clean for me, told the truth after all those fictions, all those lies. She believed all this, or wanted to believe it, the way she wanted to believe every variation of all those stories she told.

Amy was watching me with her ecstatic, wide-open face, like someone who had just witnessed a miracle. Her hands felt so small and cool in mine. I squeezed them and locked eyes with her, my mother, and I said, "I know."

ACKNOWLEDGMENTS

I'd like to thank Theodore Dreiser, who wrote *An American Tragedy* a hundred years ago, prompting me to reimagine the story set in Glacier National Park—or somewhere quite similar to Glacier National Park—with a female protagonist whose ambitions to succeed in the hotel industry are thwarted by her own disastrous choices.

The members of my writing group—Mara Collins, Art Edwards, Chris Struyk-Bonn, and Michael Zeiss—helped me become a better writer each week with their ideas, critiques, and insightful edits.

Special thanks to Jami Eckert, my friend since fifth grade, who generously shared her knowledge of police procedures and very patiently fielded my convoluted questions about boat-related crimes.

I'm grateful for everyone at Lake Union who stuck with this story, allowing me to fulfill my vision on this project. Over several phone calls, Melissa Valentine and Charlotte Herscher asked me to trust their expertise and convinced me to add Ramona's point of view to give the reader a character to root for. I resisted, but now I will admit the book is much stronger for it. I'm indebted to my agent, Laura Bradford, who advised me on the book proposal and negotiated my contract, and to Carissa Bluestone for guiding me throughout the production process. I also owe a big thanks to the rest of the editing and marketing team at Lake Union, who helped me polish up the manuscript and send it out into the world.

And finally, I'm grateful to Andy and Audrey, my biggest champions.

ABOUT THE AUTHOR

Rebecca Kelley is from Portland, Oregon, and is the author of *No One Knows Us Here* and *Broken Homes & Gardens*. Her novels center on complicated women who make impulsive, reckless decisions. Rebecca herself always makes very well-thought-out, sensible decisions. Almost always. When Rebecca isn't writing, she is conducting elaborate baking experiments and dabbling in hand balancing. Find her at www.rebeccakelleywrites.com.